"Where are you ta[...][...] tone casual.

"To this hangar[...][...]ifics, I think you need t[...][...]l be working with on th[...]

"Resources?" He sent a querying thought Jean's way. *She's hiding something,* his wife responded. *But her mind is very disciplined.*

"Call it a specialized unit of trackers, well equipped for ferreting out and detaining concealed nonhumans. Try to keep in mind that they may be essential to saving our world from the Chlorites."

They arrived at the hangar door, and Cooper paused. "Okay . . . we might as well get this over with." She hit the control, and the doors slid open.

Inside, it was dark. Yet Cyclops could tell it was far from empty. Massive shapes were faintly visible within the gloom, towering, metallic. Faint sounds of metal creaking under its own weight echoed through the hangar, like the warning growls of a herd of predatory beasts. Something moved at the top of each one—some sort of massive turret, turning toward them. On the front of each, two red lights snapped on, piercing him with their gaze. . . .

Rows of lamps in the ceiling clunked on one by one, illuminating the red and purple skins of the man-shaped robotic giants beneath. Filling the hangar, dozens of rows deep, was an army of Sentinels.

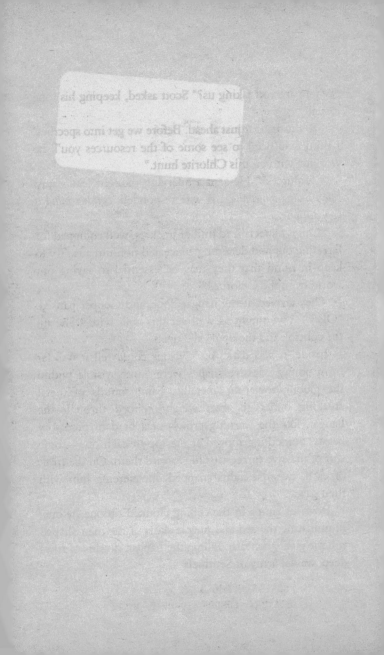

X-MEN®
WATCHERS ON THE WALLS

a novel by
Christopher L. Bennett

based on the
Marvel Comic Book

POCKET STAR BOOKS
NEW YORK   LONDON   TORONTO   SYDNEY

An *Original* Publication of POCKET BOOKS

 A Pocket Star Book published by
POCKET BOOKS, a division of Simon & Schuster, Inc.
1230 Avenue of the Americas, New York, NY 10020

ISBN-13: 978-1-4165-1067-3
ISBN-10: 1-4165-1067-2

This Pocket Star Books paperback edition May 2006

10 9 8 7 6 5 4 3 2 1

Cover art by Arthur Suydam

Manufactured in the United States of America

For information regarding special discounts for bulk purchases, please contact Simon & Schuster Special Sales at 1-800-456-6798 or business@simonandschuster.com.

For Xuân,
who loves Lockheed.

What a troublesome thing a wall is!
I thought it was to defend me, and not I it!
Of course, if they had no wall, they
would not need to have any sentinels."
     —HENRY DAVID THOREAU,
      "A Yankee in Canada"

The work of hunters is another thing:
I have come after them and made repair
Where they have left not one stone on a stone,
But they would have the rabbit out of hiding,
To please the yelping dogs.
     —ROBERT FROST,
      "Mending Wall"

X-MEN®

WATCHERS
ON THE
WALLS

1: Exordium

"So when do we get to meet the X-Men?"

"Forget that. When do we get to *try out* for the X-Men?"

"Hmf. Why do they call them 'X-Men' when half of them are women? What is this, 1963?"

John Chang let the other students' voices wash over him as he followed them inside the stately mansion that housed the Xavier Institute of Higher Learning. He found their prattle to be pointless, just a release of nervous energy. By now they all knew the basics; like him, they had all been sought out by Professor Charles Xavier—or one of his grown former students—who had invited them to enroll in the institute, where they could be schooled in a nurturing environment that would help them learn to accept and master their special gifts, et cetera, et cetera. By now they had also been made aware that the school was the home base for the mutant superhero team known as the X-Men, and that they should therefore not be surprised if occasionally a high-powered jet plane emerged from the swimming pool or a horde of alien bounty hunters descended upon the Westchester campus. (That last had not been in the formal introduction, but rumors abounded.)

But this was the start of the new semester, the first time all these teenaged mutants had come together to drink in the reality of it all and compare notes. John supposed he could forgive them for their excitement. He felt a similar anticipation of his own. But he preferred to keep quiet about his. After a lifetime of standing apart, his difference making him a target of scorn and persecution, it was refreshing to be able to go unnoticed in a crowd.

However, as the students mingled, filing into the large parlor in the north wing to await their instructors, John noticed that the universal tendency toward segregation was playing out even here. The kids who had cool powers were showing off to one another, evoking oohs or laughter as they levitated or wove electricity between their fingers or chameleon-blended with the wallpaper. The rest—those whose mutations only made them look strange or served as handicaps—ended up marginalized, grouping together by default in the corner. John fell into that category himself. He had no gifts beyond the human norm; if anything, his eyesight was rather poorer and his strength below average. He was simply small and pale with four-fingered hands, beady eyes, no nose, and four pairs of canine teeth.

The only noteworthy ability he had was a natural immunity to telepathy. According to Professor Xavier, John's presence had come as a surprise. Cerebro, his mutant-detecting computer, which worked by telepathy somehow, had detected only one mutant in their Canton, Ohio, neighborhood: Harry Mills. But Harry had befriended John when the latter had arrived in Canton the previous month. (Or rather, Harold had, John reminded himself. Harold had stopped answering to the nickname "Harry" when his mutant power had manifested, causing fast-growing blond hair to emerge all over his body, leaving him looking something like an angora gorilla. Everyone else had still called him that when he hadn't been around, though.) When Xavier had come for Harr—for Harold—Harold had introduced him to John. And once the professor had learned how John's foster parents had mistreated him and called him a freak, he had done all he could to expedite the boy's admission to the institute.

So here John was, in the place where freaks were welcome, yet he was already getting shoved into the corner. Well, that was fine with him. He'd be content to go unnoticed.

Harold, however, had other plans. He was a gregarious youth, and he was wasting little time in introducing himself and his friend John to the others in the corner—mainly the girls, John noticed. One was a dainty, round-faced girl with rich brown skin and glossy black hair. She introduced herself diffidently as Meena Banerjee. "So what are you in for?" Harold asked.

"Oh, I'm glad to be here," Meena answered, seeming surprised at his attitude. "The professor saved me. They thought I was schizophrenic. I was in hospital;

they had me on drugs that weren't working. They didn't have a clue what to do with me. Then the professor came and told them I was a mutant. I wasn't having delusions after all. He said I was perceiving alternate realities."

"Whoa!" Harry said. "That sounds like a great power! Why aren't you with the others, showing it off?"

"Nothing to see." She shrugged. "Just me telling about them. And it isn't any use to me. I can't control it, I can't do anything with it. They . . . they come and go at random, and I still have trouble telling . . . what's real and what isn't." She fidgeted in the embarrassed silence that followed.

To break the tension, Harry turned to the other girl, a slim honey blonde with neck-length hair. "So how about you, um? . . ."

"Kristin," she said in a quiet voice. "Kristin Koenig. And . . . it's embarrassing."

Harry smiled. "Come on, look at me. I shed like crazy. You should see what it did to the plumbing in my house. My mom burned out a vacuum cleaner per month trying to pick up after me. And I smell like a wet cat when I take a bath. Okay, your turn."

Kristin still looked embarrassed, but she spoke up anyway. "I . . . uh, the things I touch, they turn invisible."

"Well, how's that bad?" He gestured at the larger group. "Sounds like just the thing that would impress those guys."

Her blush deepened. "I can't turn it off." She tentatively extended her hand. "Here. Touch it."

Harry threw a triumphant grin at John, but it faded when he took her hand. "What—are you wearing a glove?"

"Everything I touch directly turns invisible. Everything except me. I—I've got two layers of clothes on. You just . . . can't see the inner one."

Harry laughed. "So . . . whoa. So what would happen if, like, your chin touched your outer clothes by accident? Would they? . . ."

She glared at him. "I knew I shouldn't have told you!"

"Hey, I was just curious."

Kristin turned away, crossing her arms in pique. Meena still tried to engage her, though. "What about makeup, or jewelry?"

Kris shook her head but kept it lowered. "It just disappears. I can't pretty myself up or anything."

"Oh, you look fine!"

"Yeah, right. It's hard even to groom myself when I can't see my hairbrush and toothbrush and stuff."

"Hey," Harry said, "that makes me wonder, how do those vampire characters on TV manage to keep so perfectly coiffed?" But the girls ignored him, continuing to commiserate.

So Harry turned instead to the remaining member of their group, a boy who sat in a wheelchair and was covered in heavy, dark brown armor scales. He introduced himself as Todd Watkins. "Sure, I'm bulletproof," he explained, leading John to wonder how he knew that for a fact. "But what good is it when I can't stand up under the weight of this dang stuff? The

Thing has it easy—at least he's got the superstrength he needs to lug that rock hide of his around."

"So what about you?" Meena asked John. "You have anything to tell us about besides, well, the obvious?"

He shook his head. "No powers. I'm just me."

"Hey, don't be modest," Harry said, putting an arm around his shoulders. "John forgot to mention he's immune to mind reading!"

John shrugged. "Nothing impressive about that."

"Sure there is," Meena said. "The kinds of people I hear the X-Men tangle with . . . I bet sometimes they could use someone whose mind can't be messed with."

"Yeah," Todd said, "but try tellin' them that." He gestured—as well as he could—at the other students. "It's nothin' you can show off with. Even if any of them can read minds. Even if any of them *got* minds."

"So . . . anything else?" Meena was still curious about John, though he couldn't fathom why and it made him somewhat uncomfortable. "Do you . . . I don't know . . . do you swim a lot?"

"Um, no. Why—"

"Good afternoon." The soft-spoken, cultured voice cut through the students' clamor with uncanny ease. All eyes promptly went to the entrance, where a familiar figure was rolling into the room on a sleek, motorized wheelchair. Charles Xavier's famous, hairless head turned to take them all in. "Welcome, all of you, to the Xavier Institute. I apologize for keeping you waiting, but it was unavoidable. Given the . . . other responsibilities of myself and most of the school's faculty, I'm afraid you'll all have to get used to some rather unpredictable scheduling." A nervous chuckle ran through the parlor.

"Well." Xavier took a moment, looking over the different clusters of students that had formed. His gaze seemed to linger on John's group in the corner. "All of us are here because we are different from most other people. Different in ways that the majority often has trouble accepting or understanding. Most of us know what it feels like to be judged, excluded, even mistreated for being who we are." He gave a self-deprecating smile. "I lost all my hair by the age of sixteen, well before I lost the use of my legs. Don't ask me to tell you which loss felt more traumatic at the time." The students laughed.

"But that goes to show that there are many ways in which people can be different—many grounds on which they can find themselves excluded or devalued by those around them." His angular brows drew together. "I don't mean to blame anyone for that, however. It is part of our nature, part of the instinct of the human animal, to be wary of that which is different, and to create hierarchies based on degrees of similarity. People do this all the time, without meaning any harm by it, without even realizing that they're doing it. We can see it occurring right here, in this very room." The larger group of students looked around, taking note of John's group set apart in the corner. Some of them exchanged abashed glances, though others didn't seem to get it or to care much.

"But as we all know, it can do harm. Sometimes the greatest harm is inflicted not by deliberate malice but by simple thoughtlessness. That is what makes the struggle for justice and equality such an enduring challenge. Inclusion is something that must be learned. It requires ongoing attention and effort, and those who fail to keep it in mind tend to fall short of it, even without meaning to.

"That is the goal to which I have dedicated my life and the resources of this institute: to keep the principles of fairness and equality in the minds of all people. To strive to make them aware of how they treat their neighbors, and to consider whether they would wish to be treated in the same way.

"But that lesson must begin here, in the school itself. Yes, here you will learn how to master your mutant powers and perhaps, in time, to use them for the protection and betterment of human and mutantkind alike. Here you will learn to endure the whips and scorns of bigotry, which are a tragic fact of mutant life, and to maintain your self-esteem in the face of them. But here you must also learn to *understand* those who exclude and judge others—to understand that the same instincts and habits exist in all of us. And with that understanding, we must lead by example, and show others how to overcome those instincts and reach out to those who would otherwise be outcasts."

He fell silent for a moment, letting his words sink in. "I hope I've made my point clear," he said. "Now, if you'll all please follow me into the dining room, I'll introduce you to some of the staff, and we can all enjoy a brunch together."

John kept his eyes on the professor as the students followed Xavier out of the parlor. The speech hadn't been what John had expected. All at the same time, he had called out the more popular clique of students for their behavior, subtly shamed them for it, forgiven them for it, and encouraged them to be forgiving of their own persecutors. It had been deft and diplomatic, and surprisingly effective. As the students came into the dining room, John, Harry, Meena, and the rest found the other students suddenly interested in talking to them, sitting with them, and generally including them in the group. Not all the students were suddenly so friendly but enough were. It was remarkable to John what Xavier had been able to accomplish with mere words. Could he have been using his telepathic powers to alter their behavior? No—John doubted that the man who'd given that speech would want to impose his will on others like that. Yet he also doubted that the kind of people who'd persecuted him all his life, people who'd never been on the receiving end themselves as these students had, would be so easily convinced.

"I have a good feeling about this," Meena said to him as they sat down to eat. Even though they were now incorporated into the group, she'd still ended up next to him. "This is a special place. I haven't felt like this in a long time."

"Like what?"

"Like—I'm accepted for who I really am. Like we all are. No matter what our powers or our problems, we'll all have a home here. Maybe even a family."

"Maybe."

Meena seemed annoyed at his closemouthed stoicism. Muttering something about him being a grump, she turned her attention to her meal. But John couldn't share in her enthusiasm.

Because he knew he couldn't let himself get attached to these people. And because there were things about who he really was that nobody here could accept. Not even Charles Xavier.

2: Ex Silentio

Jean Grey flew on the edge of space, straddling the teeming mass of life that was Earth and the infinite death that was the void, and contemplated the balance.

Oh, all right, she confessed, deflating her own poetic moment, *the* Blackbird's *doing the flying, and Charles is piloting. I'm just along for the ride.* Specifically, she sat in the copilot's seat of the X-Men's RS-150 jet aircraft—or, rather, their heavily modified descendant of that Lockheed Aircraft prototype, upgraded with technology the Skunk Works engineers could never have contemplated. Technology, courtesy of the Shi'ar Empire, that allowed the *Blackbird* to take the concept of a high-altitude reconnaissance craft quite literally to new heights and permit this little jaunt to the fringes of the mesosphere.

Still, the contemplation was real enough. The view up here was a striking reminder of the events that had given Jean her special perspective on life, death, and rebirth. Sacrificing herself to pilot a damaged shuttle through a deadly radiation belt, she had been joined with the all-powerful cosmic Phoenix Force. The entity had cocooned her away to heal, in exchange for borrowing her identity, a piece of her soul, and living as Jean Grey for some time—only to die as Jean Grey, sacrificing itself to atone for the evils it had unleashed when the temptations of human passion had driven it mad. Jean had later been revived with no knowledge of these events, but her borrowed essence and memory had finally returned to her by a roundabout route, making her whole again—so in a sense, she had been reborn twice. Her powers now were far less than her doppelganger's had been, though greater than they had been before. Hence her ongoing lessons with Charles Xavier to test and refine her evolving powers.

How ironic, she thought. *I was Charles's first student, all those years ago. And yet despite everything I've been through, here I am still taking classes.*

Learning should *be a lifelong process,* came Xavier's mental "voice" into her mind. It was not his way to intrude on others' private thoughts, but Jean had made no particular effort to shield hers. After all these years of telepathic rapport, there was little between her and Charles that was truly private anymore. In many ways (and she did keep this thought more to herself), this man knew her more intimately than Scott Summers, her husband, ever would.

But even so, sometimes Xavier could still surprise her. "So what did you have to teach me that required flying us all the way up here?" she asked.

Xavier smiled, turning away from the controls. "Are you familiar with the avant-garde composer John Cage?"

Jean resisted the impulse to rummage around in his surface thoughts for the answer; that would be cheating. "I can't say I am."

"One of his most famous works is a solo piece, usually for piano, entitled *Four Minutes and Thirty-three Seconds*. It has three movements, adding up to that total duration, and each one consists of the instruction 'Tacet'—be quiet. And so, for four minutes and thirty-three seconds, the artist performs silence."

Jean's fiery-hued brows angled upward. "Sounds like a very lazy composer."

"The point," Xavier went on patiently, "is to encourage the audience to listen to the silence. Rather, to discover that there is no such thing as silence. Even when the performer doesn't play, there's still an abundance of sounds to be heard. The sounds of your own breathing, the rustling of the audience's clothes, the creaking of the floorboards."

"The yawns of the audience. The trilling of cell phones they rudely forgot to turn off."

"Even those. The audience, the environment, it's all part of the performance. It's the source of the music. And it's a unique performance every time."

Jean was starting to see where he was leading. "So we're here . . . to contemplate silence?"

"Exactly. In a somewhat different way, of course, since we're not in the midst of an audience. The goal is to get away from the psychic background noise that humans generate all the time, the mental voices against which we have to close our perceptions if we wish to have our thoughts to ourselves. With no one around, it should be possible for you to open up your senses and still be essentially alone in your mind—well, present company excluded, of course, though I can shield my thoughts from you. The goal is to contemplate that quiet and see what you can discover within it."

It was an intriguing prospect, and Jean let the professor sense that in her. "But I don't know if we're far enough. Even this high up, there's still going to be a background buzz from the Earth."

"I know. What I want is for you to focus your attention away from that. To extend your senses out into space, into the void." He paused as a thought struck him. "Essentially I'm asking you to try to read the mind of nothingness."

She took that in. "And what do you think I'll find there?"

He shrugged. "That's for you to discover."

"Okay, then." Jean leaned back in the seat, directing her eyes toward the black of space as a focus for her mind. She hesitated to open up to it, though. She'd been in space enough times to know that emptiness. She had memories of the Phoenix Force soaring through it unassisted. She could grasp, as few humans could, just how staggeringly huge and empty it was. She couldn't avoid a fear of becoming lost in it. *Couldn't I just read a politician's mind instead? Or one of those people who leave their phones on in the theater?*

Maybe, she had to admit, there was another basis for her unease. What if, when she opened her mind to the void, some other cosmic force were to sense her and try to join with her? It was an irrational thought; given the immensity of space, the odds against such a freak occurrence happening twice were literally astronomical. But it was hard for her to shake off. Maybe she hadn't come to terms with her past as fully as she'd believed. *Hm. I haven't even started listening to the silence, and already I'm learning about myself. Maybe Charles is really on to something.*

So Jean took a deep breath, calmed herself, and tentatively opened up her telepathic senses. It was the same method she used to reach out to someone's mind and know their thoughts, except this time she directed it outward, going against her reflexes and reaching toward the *absence* of a target, the ground instead of the figure. Her awareness strove forward, pushing on through the void, searching for something to connect with, a flaming arrow racing toward an unseen target. *No,* she told herself, instinctively sensing that this was not the way to proceed. *Not so directional. Outward, not forward.* The arrow dissipated, spreading out into a cloud of consciousness . . . and yet that was a poor metaphor, for the cloud was made of nothingness, nothing except pure perception. She let go of the image, let go of any concept of localization. There was no fire, no cloud, no Jean. There simply . . . *was.*

Yet still there were presences to be felt, vague impressions, shadows in the black. Charles's mind; even with his thought processes screened, the more elemental functioning of that supercharged mind still created a strong aura about him. But she could filter that out through long familiarity. Beyond it, there was more. Tiny voices, not even minds, little more than bundles of sensation and reflex. The millions of microscopic insects that inhabited the *Blackbird,* that resided on their own bodies. An audience of dust mites, ruffling their programs and stifling their coughs.

And still there was more. A pervasive sense of mind, of awareness—not so much of thought or will. Just . . . *something,* at the cosmic level. The telepathic carrier waves of the universe's superbeings? Was she sensing the gaze of a Watcher or an Eternal sweeping across the cosmos? Or could it be something purer, more primal, endemic to the universe itself?

But those were questions for later. Now was not the time to analyze; now was the time to perceive, to absorb, and simply—

Suddenly a psychic noise blasted through her mind, a devastating burst of terror, aggression, and pain. She screamed.

"Jean! Jean, are you all right?" It was the professor, calling her back to awareness. She shook her head, pulling herself together.

"Something . . . out there, something powerful. . . ." No. Not as powerful as it had seemed at first. She'd had her psychic gain turned up to maximum to listen to the silence, and suddenly someone had screamed into the mike. These were normal minds, but they were in terror. They were in battle. It was all too familiar a psychic stench.

Charles nodded, acknowledging her wordless observations as he brought the *Blackbird*'s sensors to bear. "Several thousand kilometers above us, but closing fast. Two ships in pitched battle. No . . . one attacking, the other trying to flee. It can barely defend itself." Jean knew he was getting this as much from his telepathic scans as from the sensors.

"I can't tell who the attackers are. I can't sense them. A robot ship?" Jean asked.

"I don't think so. I can feel . . . someone inside, but I can't make them out. Something about their technology, their shielding, must interfere. As for the others . . ."

Jean nodded. Multiple species, none she'd ever sensed before. They were displaced, deprived— refugees. Their minds were too full of battle, too fixated on raw survival, to let her read much of anything else yet.

"They're heading for Earth," Xavier said, somewhat unnecessarily; they wouldn't be this close to the planet by sheer chance. "Allowing for evasive maneuvers, their course seems to be taking them toward the northeast U.S. They shouldn't land too far from New York."

Give me your tired, your poor, your huddled masses yearning to breathe free, Jean thought. "If their attackers let them get that far," she said. "Charles, I think you should—"

"Yes, Jean. Try to hail the attackers on the radio. I'll see if I can project my thoughts through their shielding." It was a sensible division of labor, given how much stronger his mind was.

But what to say? "Attention, attacking ship. Please break off your attack. There are defenseless refugees aboard that vessel, parents and children." Something they probably knew and didn't care about, but worth pointing out anyway. "Um . . . on behalf of the X-Men, representing the people of Earth, we ask that you discontinue any acts of aggression within our airspace. Please acknowledge." Big talk, considering the fact that the X-Men had no formal authority to speak for anyone and that, indeed, their existence was barely tolerated.

Now the ships were close enough that Jean could see them as points of light in the distance, tumbling Earthward with beams of energy flickering between them. One beam struck the smaller, fleeing point of light, causing it to flare up, and for a moment she feared the worst. But it remained intact, and she could still sense its minds. However, as it passed in front of the Earth's bright clouds, she could see it trailing vapors behind it. The instruments showed that it was no longer under power, falling on a ballistic course that would bring it down in eastern Pennsylvania. The larger ship continued its pursuit, but its bolts were being diffracted by the atmosphere, and friction was forcing it to slow, letting the refugee ship pull ahead. She could sense the refugees struggling to bring their vessel to a safe landing, and there was just enough hope in the pilots' minds to tell her there was still a chance. She was already putting the *Blackbird* on an intercept course. "Charles, it's close enough that we can get a team there soon after it lands."

"Right." She could sense his mind reaching out, checking the current status of the active and reserve team members, seeing who was available at the moment. Then the familiar call went out. *To me, my X-Men!*

3: Exigency

Scott Summers studied the vista of Times Square spreading out beneath him. Not for the first time, he wondered what colors its garish lights and animated signs really displayed. To him, it was always red on red. He could distinguish the shades through long experience, identify them with the colors others saw, but with rare exceptions, he hadn't experienced those colors as they truly were since his early teens. The ruby quartz visor he wore as Cyclops saw to that, as did the sunglasses of the same material he wore the rest of the time. It was the only way he could look at anything—anyone—without smashing it to pieces with an optical force beam more powerful than an artillery shell. Seeing the world in monochrome was a small trade-off for that, he knew—but sometimes he got so sick of red. (Though he would never say so to his redheaded wife.)

Right now, though, it was a particular hue of red he was looking for, on a particular cape and helmet. "There," he said, pointing, as he spotted the familiar armored figure levitating above the traffic. "Take us down."

"You got it, sugah." Rogue tightened her grip on him to make sure he didn't slip as she flew downward. Luckily, she was gentle; the Southern belle had a grip that could crush a tank, and Scott didn't have the benefit of her near-invulnerability. "We'll teach Magneto a new meanin' to 'the lullaby o' Broadway.' "

"Don't take this so lightly, Rogue. We're facing the master of magnetism in the heart of Manhattan, surrounded by metal skyscrapers and intense electromagnetic fields. He's more powerful here than anywhere."

"Okay, Cyke, I get it! Enough with the lecturin'."

Now they were close enough to see Magneto's quarry, a Hummer trying to race away from him at top speed. In New York traffic, it didn't have a prayer. Conversely, Magneto had no trouble closing in on it, slamming the cars aside with casual gestures. The driver of the Hummer made a desperate break, the vehicle's weight enough to bulldoze the cars in front of it out of the way. But a bike messenger was swerving into its path, seconds from being hit. "Dang it!" Rogue cried. They were still too high for her to drop Scott safely, and he couldn't blast the Hummer without doing Magneto's work for him.

To her credit, Rogue didn't hesitate. Unfortunately, her plan entailed tossing Scott upward as hard as he could stand while she dashed ahead to yank the messenger out of harm's way. For a stomach-churning moment, Scott was in free fall, but in the nick of time Rogue returned to snag him and lower him safely. "Sorry 'bout that, sugah. No time to warn ya."

"Good reflexes," he told her. "Now watch out, here he comes!"

The Hummer had swerved when Rogue had flown in front of it, and had gotten wedged between the back of a gridlocked cab and a Times vending machine on the sidewalk next to the Viacom Building. Now Magneto was closing in for the kill. Cyclops squeezed the contacts in his gloves, opening the visor, and a bright red force beam (as red to everyone else as to himself, he was told) shot out toward the magnetically charged supervillain. Unfortunately, Magneto had time to throw up a force shield and block it. Rogue tried charging him, but Magneto ripped the bed out of a pickup truck and flung it into the path of Scott's force beam, deflecting it like a mirror so that it knocked Rogue backward into a Mary Jane Watson billboard across the street.

Angered, Magneto began flinging cars at the two X-Men, unconcerned with the people inside them. Rogue was kept busy catching the cars and lowering their occupants to safety while Scott continued trying to pierce Magneto's defenses. "Dang it!" Rogue cried over the comlink. "Ain't never a friendly neighborhood Spider-Man around when ya need one!"

"Focus, Rogue! I'll keep him occupied, you try to circle behind him!" Scott turned his gaze toward the marquee signs over Magneto's head, slicing them free and keeping Magneto occupied trying to deflect them. No sooner had he done so than he turned his beams back on the villain himself. Meanwhile, Rogue worked her way around to Magneto's blind spot and managed to get in a good hit. He instinctively raised enough of a shield to protect himself—the human body had enough iron in the blood for him to manipulate—but he went flying forward into an electrified sign.

They only fed him, though. He whirled to confront his attacker. "What are you doing, Rogue? Would you protect those madmen? They are masterminds of a conspiracy to develop an anti-mutant plague! They must be stopped!"

Rogue froze, nonplussed. "Say what?"

"Don't listen to him!" Scott called. "Press your attack!" He did the same, but Magneto's shields were back to full strength.

"We have no time for this, Rogue!" Magneto urged, drawing closer to her. "They cannot be allowed to get away! Countless mutant lives are at stake!"

"He's giving you an opening! Take it!" If she could just get her glove off and reach his face before he could react . . .

But Rogue turned to Scott instead. "But what if he's—"

It was all Magneto needed. An SUV slammed into her, crushing her into the front of the Marquis Theater. A cab was hurled toward Scott, forcing him to leap and roll aside, unable to do anything for the driver. By the time he regained his feet, Magneto had the Hummer in the grip of his fields, lifting it into the air, crushing it like a paper cup. He laughed at the screams within.

"End simulation," announced a voice, and Times Square faded around them. Rogue fell to the floor of the Danger Room as the voice declared, *"Mission failed."*

The computer was calmer about it than Scott. "You had an opening," he told her as she clambered to her feet, running a hand through her mane of brown hair with its wide streak of white on top. "One touch, and you could've saved those people." True, she couldn't have absorbed the powers of a simulated Magneto, but her touch would have rendered him unconscious and powerless, ending the threat and the exercise. "Instead your hesitation got them and several other people killed."

"You heard what Magneto said!"

"Like he's never lied before?"

"He's told the truth sometimes too. Sometimes he's even been on our side!"

"That's beside the point. Even if those people were what he said, he was out to murder them, and he was willing to murder countless others to get to them. And that means we stop him, no matter what his motives."

"And what if that meant lettin' a bunch o' mutant-haters go free?"

"How many more mutant-haters would Magneto create by killing so many people in cold blood? How many would we create if we let him?" He took a breath. "Look. You can't be faulted for feeling doubt or sympathy for his cause. We all have, at one time or another. But it's about self-control, Rogue. You have to keep those impulses under control and focus on the immediate mission. Sort out the ethical tangles afterward. If someone's putting lives in danger, that makes them the bad guy. Period. No matter what good they might've done in the past."

Rogue glared at him. "So they do one wrong thing and all the good they did before don't matter none? You just write 'em off? So what about me?" she challenged before he could answer. "I was a bad guy once. What if I had a relapse? Would y'all just try to kill me?"

He met her gaze unflinchingly; the visor helped. "I'd do what I had to do to stop you." He relaxed a fraction, smiled ever so faintly. "So . . . don't do that."

She tossed her hair back, unmollified. "Then don't tempt me."

He sighed. "Don't take it personally, Rogue. Like I said, I can sympathize. It's just about learning to control your impulses. That's something you could stand a little more work on."

"Yeah, well maybe you need to work on not bein' such a control freak all the time! And the lesson's over. I don't have to listen to you no more." She flew over to the exit, punched the control hard enough to dent it, and swooped out the moment the opening was wide enough.

Scott sighed in frustration. Why couldn't she understand? Like him, she knew what it was like to be cursed with a power she couldn't control, couldn't turn off. Scott had learned from painful experience that he couldn't afford to let his guard down, to be careless even for a moment. He couldn't risk forgetting what would happen if he lost his visor or glasses. He couldn't risk losing control of his emotions and giving in to the temptation to hurt someone. It had to be the same for her, always having to avoid contact between her skin and anyone else's. So why was she still so impetuous, so carefree? Why couldn't she understand the need for control?

Or was it possible, he asked himself, that she understood something he didn't? Could that be what really frustrated him?

That line of thought was pushed from his mind, though, as Charles Xavier's face appeared before his eyes. As a telepathic projection, it was the one thing he was able to see in true color. But what mattered was what it had to say: summoning the X-Men on a mission, in defense of a crashing starship. "Got it, Professor. We're on our way." Before Xavier's projection faded, Scott was hitting his comlink. "Cyclops to Rogue. Listen—"

"Yeah, I got the Big Giant Head-o-gram. Meet y'all in the hangar." Her words were all business, but there was still some resentment in her voice. But that would have to wait. A lot more was at stake than hurt feelings.

Stillness.

Silence.

The deer was just a few feet away now, almost close enough to touch, but still it had not sensed Wolverine's presence. His approach through the trees left their branches unshaken; his footfalls made nary a sound. His breathing was slow, controlled, soundless. His battlesuit and cowl masked his scent. The black stripes against its gold broke up his silhouette, kept him hidden in the shadows—but only as long as he avoided the patches of sunlight and made no sound or sudden move to call attention to the spot where he crouched. So it was with measured, patient steps that he drew closer to the deer, moving barely faster than the shadows themselves as the sun crept higher in the sky. Soon enough he had to break the cover of the trees, making it more essential that he make no move or sound to draw the deer's attention. But he had done this hundreds of times. He had mastered it. Stillness. Silence.

But never peace.

Logan was a fighter, a killer. He'd had too many lifetimes' worth of practice for that to ever change. He was as instinctively vicious a scrapper as the wolverine whose name he'd taken. So peace was not an option. Most forms of meditation did him little good at bringing serenity. So instead he'd chosen to be true to his nature and hunt for it. Stalking deer, schooling himself to stillness, drawing close enough to see them at peace, hear their relaxed heartbeats, smell the serenity and innocence in their spoor . . . this was as close as he ever came. Close enough to peace that he could reach out and touch it, for the briefest of moments.

Now he was close enough. The deer was in arm's reach, still unaware of his presence. He could reach out and snap its neck right now if he wanted. But he never would. He might have been a killer, but at least he only killed those who'd earned it. That didn't make him a good man, but he hoped it counted for something. He hoped it earned him the right to do what he did now, reaching out to place a gentle hand against the deer's flank. Maybe someday he would be able to do so without scaring it away. Maybe this time . . .

BAMF!

The deer bolted from the miniature thunderclap and the brimstone stench that accompanied it. Logan whirled, enraged. "Haha!" cackled Kurt Wagner from where he dangled upside down, his demonic tail wrapped around a branch. "Tag, you're it!"

Logan roared, his claws erupting reflexively from his hands. "Rrrahhh! I'll tag you, 'Crawler!" He lunged, but got only a faceful of sulfur for his trouble. But the *bamf* of displaced air when Nightcrawler reappeared was easy to home in on. "Hold still, you blasted elf!"

"Hey, lighten up, *mein freund!*" Kurt scampered easily among the branches as Logan leaped up into them, chasing him. The elf's blue-black fur swallowed up the light, making him hard to see in the shadows, but Logan could still track him by his lingering sulfuric odor. "No need to be a sore loser. I caught you fair and square!"

"You did it on purpose! No way your timing was that good by accident!" Adamantium blades chopped through a branch as thick as his waist, severing it like a twig and forcing Kurt to leap away as it crashed down to the forest floor.

"I wanted to be sure you were distracted! I learned from the best, after all." He teleported again, emerging right on Logan's back. The sudden weight, in addition to the noise and pressure of the air his body pushed aside, knocked Logan forward, and he fell to the ground. The fall would have snapped a normal person's bones, but the adamantium alloy infused into Logan's rendered them virtually unbreakable. It still hurt, but he was used to that, and the bruises started healing before he even leaped back to his feet. Kurt had pushed off his back before impact, and he came down lightly on his elongated, two-toed feet. "Why are you so upset? All's fair, et cetera, et cetera."

"You don't get it! This was . . ." He broke off. With an effort, he pushed his fury down. It wasn't Kurt's fault he couldn't understand. It wasn't like Logan had ever been all that talkative about his inner feelings. That was Charley's bag, and Jean's, not his. "It's just . . . you scared the damn deer."

"Like you weren't about to?"

"I was—" He sighed and made himself retract his claws. They slid back into their sockets with a *snikt*. "It's just a personal thing for me, okay? I don't like people intrudin' on it."

Yellow eyes widened in that furry face. "Ohh. I'm sorry, Logan. I didn't realize."

"Yeah, well . . . you can repay me with a six-pack. Or twelve." Not that his healing factor would let him get drunk; alcohol was a poison, after all. He just liked doing things that were theoretically bad for him, on general principle.

"No, really!" Kurt jogged after him as he strode away. Even though the elf had a good six inches on Logan, he still had to hustle to catch up. "I'm genuinely sorry. You were in communion with nature, I should've known better than to intrude. It's like barging in on someone in prayer."

"Don't go there, elf."

"Sorry."

For about the millionth time, Logan had to wonder how he and Nightcrawler had ended up as such good friends. They could hardly be more different. Kurt was a gentle jokester, an upbeat and idealistic man with a deep religious conviction. He'd suffered a lifetime of persecution for his demonic appearance yet still maintained his faith in human nature. He only looked like a demon on the outside; Logan carried his on the inside.

Maybe Logan could understand why someone like that would reach out to him, trying to help him, redeem him or something. What amazed him was that he could return that friendship. But then, there was a time when he'd been friends with nobody, a committed loner, pushing people away because he was too dangerous to be around. Then Charles Xavier had come along, recruiting him to join the X-Men. At first he'd seen it as just an excuse to resign from the Canadian agency that had used him as a hired gun (or hired claw), while still being able to get in some quality scrapping. He'd never imagined that he could actually become a team player, or grow so close to so many others in the X-Men. Sure, he'd formed bonds with fellow warriors before, but these people had become his friends, people he could hang out with socially and enjoy being around. If it weren't terminally sappy, he might even throw in something about family. And it was all because of—

To me, my X-Men!

Speak of the devil. There was ol' Charley, projecting himself into Logan's mind through the illusion of

a big floating head in midair. Logan sometimes figured
that *The Wizard of Oz* must have left a big impression
on him as a kid.

Xavier swiftly filled them in on the crisis situation.

"Right, Charley," Logan said. "We're on our way. Elf!
Bamf us to the X-Jet hangar. Pronto!"

Kurt extended a hand. "Right. All aboard for the
Brimstone Express!"

Kitty Pryde was in Central Park, playing Frisbee with
Lockheed on the Great Lawn, when she got Xavier's
message. She sensed a touch of disapproval in the professor's mind at her choice of activities; after all, playing around in public with a batwinged, purple alien
dragon, even a merely cat-sized one, was not the best
way to stay inconspicuous. But Lockheed was built for
flying free, and staying cooped up in Kitty's apartment
all the time didn't agree with him—or her furniture
or her houseplants or—if he wasn't allowed out to sate
his considerable appetite—the contents of her cup-
boards. Generally he achieved that by keeping the
neighborhood pigeon population in check, but there
were times when he got in a mischievous mood and
started terrorizing Mrs. Stanek's Pomeranian across
the street. So every so often, Kitty brought him out
here to direct his playful urges in a healthier direction.
He enjoyed playing Frisbee, although he preferred to
treat it more like skeet-shooting than a game of fetch.
She'd talked to him about her limited budget for buy-
ing new Frisbees, but he could never resist incinerat-
ing at least one per session, and she always brought a

few spares. He seemed to like the shapes that the melted plastic ended up in. So far, though, her attempts to sell them as abstract art had proven fruitless.

Despite all that, Kitty felt the professor was too sensitive to the prospect of Lockheed drawing excessive attention. This was Manhattan, after all. People saw far stranger on a daily basis. Just a bit south of the Great Lawn sat the embassy of the Avengers, a superhero team whose roster over the years had included a defrosted World War Two hero, an android, and a Norse deity. Not much farther south was the Baxter Building, which half the time was being visited by aliens, and the other half was emanating strange rays and phenomena, courtesy of Reed Richards's endless experiments. And it had become a matter of routine to find long strands of spiderlike webbing hanging from buildings and lampposts all over town, often with purse snatchers, jewel thieves, or costumed maniacs wrapped up in them. Next to all that, what was one little dragon?

Still, Kitty and Lockheed usually cut these sessions short when they drew the attention of the police. She preferred to avoid having to explain the little guy to the authorities. How much paperwork would be involved in getting a pet license for a creature of unknown species that wasn't even native to the planet? Besides which, Lockheed would take umbrage at being called her pet; if anything, he saw their relationship the other way around, and she often strongly suspected he was right. He might not speak, but there was no question of the little guy's intelligence. Kitty had sometimes considered trying to get him diplomatic immunity in lieu of a pet license, but the United States had no diplomatic relations with Broodworld, thanks partly to its total existence failure some years back. And Lockheed might be many things, but diplomatic was rarely one of them.

So far, no cops had shown today, but Xavier's summons meant their session had to be cut short early. *Sure, Professor, I'm free to help out.*

Time is of the essence, Kitty.

Gotcha. Have the X-Jet swing by, and I'll meet them halfway. "C'mon, Lockheed!" she shouted to the dragonet, who, during her telepathic conference, had begun entertaining himself by chasing the dragonflies that congregated above Turtle Pond. "Duty calls."

First off, Kitty needed to find somewhere inconspicuous to change into her X-Men uniform. Looking around to make sure no one was watching for the moment, she jogged across the surface of the pond, her feet hovering just over the water, and then phased through the wall into Belvedere Castle, walking through it as though it were air. Her vision blacked out as her eyes passed through the solid stone, but she'd walked through enough walls to sense when the edge was coming. She stopped and peered out carefully to make sure the chamber was unoccupied before she emerged and solidified again.

Well, *solidified* wasn't really the word, she knew. The short explanation she usually gave for her powers was that she was able to pass her molecules between the molecules of a solid body, and thus move through it. But the reason solid objects didn't normally penetrate each other was the repulsion between their surface electrons. It wasn't the molecules that made solids solid; it was the energy fields between them. What Kitty did was to alter the way her body's field interacted with other objects' fields, to align its quantum phase with them as though it were a part of them, able to pass through them with no effect. She could also amplify the interaction selectively so that she could gain a solid footing even on the weak connective fields of air molecules. Which was fortunate, or else she would've plunged through to the Earth's core the first time her powers had manifested, back when she'd been a gawky thirteen-year-old in Deerfield, Illinois. And that would've been a shame, because she would never have met the X-Men, never experienced the wonders that membership had exposed her to. Oh, and the being-dead part would've sucked too.

Changing was a snap; her costume was made of Reed Richards's patented unstable-molecule fabric, allowing instant transformation from street clothes to her blue-and-yellow Shadowcat suit. After that she airwalked up and through the roof of the diminutive castle, where she found Lockheed perched on its tower, looking quite at home. "Sorry, no damsels for you to distress," she teased, airwalking up to gather him in her arms. "Maybe next time. Let's go."

She proceeded to airwalk higher into the sky, which soon got a little tiring. It took an effort to stay phased, and walking on air was like walking on Jell-O, requiring care and delicacy. So it took more effort than climbing stairs to the same height. Pretty soon, she decided to let Lockheed fly off on his own and keep pace with her. But there was still a long climb ahead.

Or maybe not. There was a glint of light, rapidly approaching. It hadn't taken them long at all to get the X-Jet scrambled and fly over from Salem Center. But its swift approach was beginning to alarm her. It was decelerating, but not by enough. "Uhh, guys?" she called over the comlink. "Shouldn't you be slowing down more?"

"*No time,*" came Cyclops's voice. "*Just grab Lockheed and go solid.*"

Her eyes widened, but she trusted him enough to comply instantly. No sooner did she have the dragon in hand than she heard a loud thunderclap and found herself coughing at the stench of sulfur. A furry body collided with her and pushed her forward at considerable speed. One second and one more *bamf* later, and she was inside the X-Jet, tumbling backward out of Nightcrawler's furry arms. He'd hit her traveling at the jet's speed, but the collision had slowed him down while speeding her up, so they were now slower than the jet. Wolverine caught her before she could hit the aft bulkhead, but Kurt still piled into her from behind. It was a messy way to board an aircraft, and one that would leave her with bruises, but it had worked. She heard Cyclops over her coughs. "All accounted for, Professor. We're en route." The engines whined as the jet picked up velocity again.

"*Excellent. We're sending you the revised landing coordinates.*"

Kitty looked around the group in the cramped jet:

Cyclops, Wolverine, Rogue, Nightcrawler, and herself. "Nobody else could join the party?"

"Beast's in the middle o' some science project, couldn't get away," Logan said. "Said he'd join up later if he had to. But now you're here, 'Cat, we got all the brains we need."

"And all the blue fuzzy people," Kurt added.

"So let's go kick some alien butt!" Rogue drawled. "And, um, save some other alien butt while we're at it."

Lockheed simply stared ahead with a feral grin.

4: Exodus

When the *Blackbird* arrived, the refugee ship had already come down, southwest of Harrisburg near I-81. It had carved a long furrow through a cornfield, but the corn was wet from recent rains and the fires were small. Some distance away was a barn emblazoned with colorful Pennsylvania Dutch hex signs, which apparently had not been wholly successful at warding off evil. Xavier scanned for minds in the vicinity, but he sensed that the owners were away and the hired hand keeping watch on the farm was currently driving away at high speed in a panic. Gingerly, he reached into the farmhand's mind and tweaked his neurotransmitters just enough to calm him somewhat and reduce the risk of an accident. Meanwhile, he sensed that the only other living beings in the vicinity were a few fleeing cows and horses.

The only ones native to Earth, that is. His scan showed that many of the aliens had survived, though only about half of their original number. He squeezed his eyes shut for a moment, acknowledging the grief he had to process, both from the aliens' minds and his own. Then he shunted it aside for later. Right now he couldn't afford the distraction. The attacking ship was still closing in, and its weapons were still hot.

"I'm going to shield the refugees with the *Blackbird*," Xavier told Jean as he activated the vertical thrusters.

"You're taking a lot on faith," his student replied. "How do you know they won't just blast through us?"

"Look at the scans. That ship is armed with missiles that could vaporize the area for miles around. The fact that they haven't used them already is evidence that they don't want to harm noncombatants indiscriminately."

"You always look for the good in people, Charles. Most of the refugees on that ship were in no condition to wage combat on anybody."

"At least it means there's a chance they can be reasoned with."

As if to contradict him, plasma bolts began raining around the *Blackbird*. None of them hit it, though. "Well, you were partly right," Jean said. "They're shooting around us . . . but we're not a big enough shield. And the refugees are running scared. . . . Charles, they don't realize we're trying to protect them, they assume we're attacking too!"

"Yes." He could feel them as they ran away from the *Blackbird*, only to be picked off from above. He winced and reached out to their minds. *Attention, please! We are here to protect you, but you must stay underneath us! Please, get beneath the black aircraft over your ship with all possible haste!*

Many of the fleeing refugees reversed course, but he knew he hadn't reached them all. Some were simply too afraid, and he wasn't familiar enough with their minds to alter their moods, as he had with the farmhand. Others seemed to be more or less deaf to his telepathy—understandable, given how many distinct and unfamiliar species they represented.

Xavier began moving the *Blackbird* around a bit, hoping it would get the aliens to hold their fire, rather than just getting the plane shot down by mistake. But the alien ship rendered his efforts moot; it grabbed the *Blackbird* in a tractor beam and pulled it aside, forcefully enough to make a point without causing real damage. "All right, then," Jean said and moved toward the hatch, letting him sense her intentions. She was going to fly out there and run interference herself.

It was a risky move. Jean's telekinesis had grown considerably stronger since her early years as an X-Man, when she had been unable to levitate anything heavier than her own muscles could lift, and its full potential remained undetermined. But she still had her limits, and those alien plasma bolts packed a lot of kinetic and thermal energy. She'd also have to move quickly and cover a lot of ground. Still, he resisted the impulse to stop her. She was a grown woman now, and she knew her limits. And they both knew what she was willing to sacrifice to protect others.

Jean handled it quite deftly at first, deflecting the plasma bolts with telekinetic pushes, wisely saving energy by knocking them just enough off course to hit empty ground, rather than trying to block them completely. Years of Danger Room training meant that her deflections were flawlessly aimed. But the rate of fire was considerable, and now the attackers' ship was altering position, shifting its angle of fire to throw her off. Jean did her best, but she wasn't able to block all the bolts. And Xavier's efforts to overpower the tractor beam were futile.

But he sensed the other X-Men drawing near. He reached out to them to coordinate their plans. Within moments, they had devised a strategy and shared it with Jean.

The first move was Scott's. Out of the blue, a livid force beam speared into the side of the attacking ship. At this range, Cyclops's eye beam, even amplified by the special windows of the X-Jet, was attenuated in strength, but it still packed enough of a punch to shake up whoever was inside. More eye-blasts followed, homing in more closely on the ship's weapons emitters. Jean and Xavier were both sharing their senses with Scott, helping him narrow in on his targets.

Now a streak of green, gold, and brown came in parallel to the red beams and hit the ship even harder. The craft lurched, and the laws of action and reaction meant that Rogue bounced back a bit from the collision. But she caught herself in midair and made contact with the ship again, pushing on it with all her considerable might. "Knock, knock," Xavier heard her say through her own ears. "Anybody wanna come out an' play?"

"I do," came a rougher voice, but it was Wolverine's. He and Nightcrawler had just teleported together onto the hull of the ship, and Logan wasted no time deploying his claws once he'd stepped free. "Let's find out what's inside this tin can. I'm in the mood for some lunch meat." He drove his claws down into the ship's armored hull.

And they skidded off. He'd left a few significant gouges, but nothing more. "Blast! This is tough stuff."

"You said it, Wolvie," Rogue replied. "Don't seem like metal, though. More like some kinda fabric."

"Probably carbon nanotubes," Xavier told them. "The strongest fibers in the universe."

"Yeah, well, I got the strongest metal in the universe right here." Wolverine resumed his attempts to slash through, but it was slow going.

Meanwhile, Shadowcat was trying to maneuver the X-Jet to shield the refugees, flying from the copilot's seat while Cyclops concentrated on blasting. One force beam managed to knock out the tractor emitter and free the *Blackbird,* allowing Xavier to resume his own shielding efforts. While Rogue and Wolverine continued their attacks, and Jean continued to deflect fire, Nightcrawler used his acrobatic gifts to clamber over the hull of the ship, looking for a viewport. Without being able to see the internal layout, he'd be unable to teleport inside without the risk of materializing fatally inside a bulkhead.

But suddenly something happened that might render the issue moot: A hatch opened on the side of the ship, and a number of humanoids poured out. Xavier scanned their minds and was stunned to discover that he knew them. He felt similar shocks of recognition from the other X-Men, for they were faced by a contingent of the Shi'ar Imperial Guard.

"Shi'ar?" Jean asked. "How can that be? This isn't a Shi'ar ship!"

It was indeed a surprise. The Imperial Guard were the highly trained military elite of the Shi'ar Empire, fiercely loyal to their Majestrix, Lilandra Neramani—who happened to be the love of Xavier's life. But it was a complicated relationship. At times the Guard had fought alongside the X-Men as allies, but at others their duty to their empress had forced them to be foes. Once, they had even been both, as the Guard had been divided into two factions, one supporting Lilandra, the other her usurper sister Deathbird. Could this be another dissident faction, siding with whatever civilization had built this ship? Xavier could not sense Kallark, the Gladiator who commanded the Guard, and whose loyalty to his empire was as unshakeable as his body was invulnerable. His absence made Xavier wonder if this was an unauthorized operation.

But he and the X-Men knew the faces that confronted them now. Vril Rokk the Smasher, in his black-and-white uniform with its red exo-spex goggles. Flashfire, with his white skin and flaming hair. Manta, the ethereal flier, with her capelike black wings. N'rill'iree, the brown-furred giant, with his batwing ears. Blue-skinned, pale-haired Nightside, cloaked in black. Magique the illusion-caster, with her upswept white mane. Blackthorn, the plantlike humanoid, with his thorny carapace. And lithe, brown-haired Astra, whose phasing powers matched Shadowcat's. Xavier knew them all from his time among the Shi'ar, and knew them to be loyal.

"Hear me, X-Men!" Rokk called. "In the name of the Empress Lilandra, and her allies of the Diascar Confederacy, I hereby command you to stand down from your defense of these creatures! They are a mortal threat to all life! Make no further attempt to aid them or go near them! For the sake of your world as well as all others, they must be exterminated!"

Diascar? Presumably the owners of the ship, Xavier thought. He recalled that Lilandra would occasionally detach divisions of the Imperial Guard to assist allied worlds; judging from Rokk's words, that was the case here. However, he had never heard of the Diascar before. He activated the *Blackbird*'s loudspeakers. "Smasher, this is Xavier. I cannot believe that Lilandra would sanction the cold-blooded slaughter of such defenseless people! If you have accusations to make against them, then make them through proper diplomatic channels!" As he spoke, he sensed Kitty landing the X-Jet so that she and Scott could get out and move freely. Yet she had chosen to set it down some distance from the refugees. *Just in case there's any truth to his claims,* Xavier overheard her thinking.

"There is no time! Xavier, know that you have our respect as our empress's erstwhile consort and ally in battle. But there is more at stake here than you know. These creatures are a deadly perversion of nature! So long as they continue to exist, all life of our kind is imperiled! We must strike quickly, for the safety of your Earth!"

"Sounds like the same old trash they say about mutants, if you ask me!" Wolverine snarled. "I didn't think you Guardies were cowardly enough to shoot at sittin' ducks, especially children! But if you're gonna try it, bub, you're gonna have to go through me first!" With a snarl, he leaped off the ship into midair, hurtling toward the Guardsmen. Xavier felt the pain as Wolverine's claws sliced out through his own skin, a pain that Logan embraced and used to feed his rage as he raised the claws, ready to strike.

But before he could make contact, Manta spread her wings, engulfing him in the searing blue-white light they emitted. Xavier felt what Logan felt as the light blinded him, as its powerful ultraviolet component burned his skin. Smasher, who, like the other non-fliers, was no doubt levitating via Imperial flight patch, dodged out of Wolverine's path and allowed him to fall Earthward.

I'll catch him, Jean sent, halting Rogue, who'd been starting to fly down after him. Rogue deftly changed course and shot up toward the Guardsmen, taking them by surprise. She homed in on Smasher, aiming her fist at his exo-spex, thinking that damaging them would eliminate his ability to "download" extra powers. But Rokk was able to turn his head at the last second and take the blow on his temple. Still, the force of it sent him flying. Rogue lashed out at the other Guardsmen around her even as Cyclops began blasting at them from the ground, forcing them to scatter. "Keep them from reaching the enemy," a recovering Smasher called out to his troops, "for their own sake!"

Stay between them and the refugees, Xavier called to his X-Men, *before they do the same to us!*

Now it became a matter of jockeying for position. The refugees—the ones still alive after the bombardment from the Diascar ship—were now huddled around the ruins of their crashed vessel, above which Xavier hovered in the *Blackbird*. Jean levitated nearby, between them and the Diascar. Cyclops and Shadowcat were on the ground off to the right, on the wrong side of the Guardsmen. Wolverine had smashed down into the cornfield—Jean had only been able to spare so much energy to slow his fall—but was healing with his usual speed and was now running to take up position before the refugees. Rogue and Lockheed were in flight, chasing after the Guardsmen. And Kurt remained perched on the Diascar ship. "I'll keep looking for a way in," he said; the hatch that had disgorged the Guardsmen had closed. "So I can bring my disarming personality to bear, *ja?*"

Have you tried teleporting a piece of the hull away, Kurt? Xavier sent.

"*Ja, Herr Professor,* but I only got a little and it drained me. The molecular bonds must be incredibly strong."

Cyclops was still blasting away at the Guardsmen, trying to hold them at bay. Smasher, N'rill'iree, and Manta were the most durable, so he struck at them directly; with the others, he tried to stick to warning shots, forcing them to dodge. But Astra was phased, allowing her to fly through the force beams with no effect.

Flashfire was moving fast enough to keep clear of

Scott's beams and was unleashing bioelectric lightning toward the refugees. Rogue chased after him, pulling off a glove and trying to make contact to drain his powers. If she succeeded, not only would she take him out of the game but she could also wield his powers against his fellow Guardsmen—assuming she had no trouble mastering them. Right now, though, the hothead was giving her enough trouble reaching him.

Blackthorn managed to reach the ground, digging his feet in. "Good soil," the plantlike creature said. "Very nourishing. I feel the connection strongly." Even as he spoke, the cornstalks began moving, growing with unnatural speed under his command, reaching to entangle the X-Men on the ground and the refugees. It had little effect on the X-Men; Cyclops narrowed his beam to needle thinness and sliced through the stalks and tendrils, Wolverine hacked through them with his claws, and Shadowcat simply walked through them unaffected. "This is the corniest strategy I've ever seen!" Kitty exclaimed.

Wolverine groaned. "You just had to say it, didn't-cha? Leave the puns to the 'Crawler, kid."

"Now that you mention it," Kurt replied over the comlink, "I was just thinking we should've brought Husk!"

Suddenly Astra rose up out of the ground and grabbed Shadowcat. Kitty tried to phase away, but Astra kept up with her phase and retained her grip, forcing them both back into normal phase. "Now, Blackthorn!" she called, and the cornstalks wrapped themselves around Kitty's torso and neck, tightening around them.

Lockheed didn't approve of that. He had been chasing Manta around the way he did with pigeons back in the city, but now he tucked in his wings and dive-bombed Blackthorn, opening his beak and letting forth a torrent of flame. Blackthorn screamed as his woody body caught fire, and Astra was left with no choice but to release Kitty and phase her comrade into the ground, smothering the flames. Shadowcat was instantly out of her tightening bonds, even before they began to relax on their own. But Xavier was concerned when the Guardsmen failed to emerge from underground. *Kitty, try to retrieve them,* he sent. But before she reached the spot, Astra rose out of the soil, pulling a charred and unconscious Blackthorn behind her. She looked somewhat singed herself and was gasping for air. "Sorry," Kitty said as she took Astra out with a karate kick. "Hate to hit you while you're down, but you did it first."

Distracted by this, Xavier was slow to realize that something was wrong. A crackling of psionic energy pervaded the air, and Xavier quickly homed in on its source. What appeared to be Smasher, N'rill'iree, and Manta were in fact psionic constructs! *Cyclops, Magique has replaced your targets with illusions! Look out!*

But it was too late. Scott was already being struck by an energy blast not unlike his own, emitted from Smasher's exo-spex. He fell unconscious, out of the fight. *Scott!* Jean cried out in shared anguish, launching a telekinetic burst that knocked Smasher down, but had little other effect.

N'rill'iree erupted from the cornfield and lunged at

Shadowcat, but she phased and vanished into the corn. A moment later, she was plunged into darkness. Nightside had projected her Darkforce shroud over a wide expanse of the cornfield, engulfing Shadowcat and Wolverine. Xavier heard Kitty cry out over the comlink, but it was hard to read her thoughts while she was phased. "Shadowcat, what is it?"

"I lost my footing—I can't tell where I am! Can't risk unphasing inside the corn or the ground. I don't even know which way is up!" Normally her other senses could guide her, but Nightside's void was disorienting, an interface with a frighteningly alien, extradimensional realm. It would be hard for Kitty to tell what was real. And Xavier couldn't guide her mentally as long as she was phased.

But Wolverine was not so disoriented. His preternaturally keen senses were affected by the Darkforce too, but he was still able to feel the reality beneath them. Xavier felt him shutting down his thoughts, reducing himself to pure animal instinct and homing in on the scent of his quarry, unaffected by any other input. In moments he was upon his prey, tackling Nightside to the ground, slashing with his claws. Xavier was relieved that he had reawakened his higher faculties enough to pull his blow, to wound instead of kill. The Guardswoman had been an ally of his in the past, and though Logan would do what he felt he had to against an enemy, he also valued the camaraderie of warriors, and that had stayed his hand, though just barely. This combat would have to be resolved fairly soon if she was to get the medical attention she would need.

Nightside's dark shroud faded, and Kitty was able to pull herself into the clearing plowed by the crashing ship. Tired from staying out of phase so long, she risked solidifying to catch her breath, and the mental static cleared. Smasher caught sight of her and flew toward her. *Jean!* Xavier called. She whirled and knocked Smasher aside with a telekinetic burst, but he touched a hand to his exo-spex and a burst of energy shot out, engulfing Shadowcat. She convulsed as though shocked and fell senseless.

"Kitty!" Kurt called, sensing her pain through the telepathic link. "That does it!" Abandoning his efforts to find a porthole, he teleported off the Diascar ship and materialized on Smasher's back. "No fair giving yourself new powers at will!" He grabbed the exo-spex in his three-fingered hands and *bamf*ed away with them, reappearing on the ground nearby. " 'And immediately there fell from his eyes as it had been scales, and he received sight forthwith!' " Kurt tried them on. "Now, how do these things work? Be honest, do they make me look cool?"

"All the folks here, fuzzy," Rogue called, "you're the last'un who'd be needin' rose-colored glasses."

"Ahh, but—yow!" That last was because he saw Smasher barreling toward him, his now-visible eyes burning with the intention to live up to his codename. Kurt teleported away just in time, materializing atop the X-Jet. Smasher changed course toward him but found himself with a faceful of dragon breath. Lockheed had seen him knock out Kitty, and he wasn't happy about it. Rokk shielded his eyes just in time and came out of the flame relatively unscathed. His body's ability to absorb quantum energy to augment the strength of its molecular bonds made him extremely resistant to injury, even with his technological advantage removed. But Lockheed continued to harry him, drawing on his seemingly unlimited reserves of flame.

Meanwhile, Rogue and Flashfire were still chasing each other around. N'rill'iree had engaged Wolverine, keeping him busy. Manta was now closing in on Jean, spreading her wings to deliver a blast of light. Jean saw her in time and sent a telekinetic burst to knock her away, but not before she was able to discharge. The periphery of the blast hit Jean, searing her. Her concentration broken, she fell from the sky, the cornstalks breaking her fall.

That left Magique. Xavier scanned for her psionic signature and found her sending illusory Guardsmen at Nightcrawler, keeping him jumping. *Kurt, ignore them! They aren't real! Follow my lead.* He told Kurt where to find the source of the phantasms that harried him. The dark-furred X-Man teleported in above Magique, poised to piledrive her to the ground. But she whirled, caught him, and tossed him aside, then struck with a well-placed blow. Illusions or not, she had the same hand-to-hand training as any Imperial Guardsman. Kurt barely *bamf*ed away in time. He rematerialized and struck again, but she had cloaked herself in an illusory form, giving herself multiple pairs of arms, legs, and heads like a Hindu goddess, all whirling around and making it impossible for Kurt to tell which was illusion and which was flesh. Xavier's perceptions could be little help in such close quarters. Kurt had his own ability to attack from concealment, able to quick-teleport and strike from multiple directions within seconds, vanishing before a return strike could connect and before his cloud of smoke could even dissipate. But this ability and Magique's largely canceled each other out.

Now Smasher had managed to connect with Lockheed. Knocking the dragon for a loop, he broke free to help Flashfire against Rogue. Xavier sent her a warning, concerned; Vril Rokk was the only being here who was stronger than Rogue. But he was also faster and dazed her with a blow to the jaw before she could block it, his gauntlets protecting him from her absorption power. "Yes! My turn!" Flashfire crowed and struck Rogue with a bioelectric bolt, blasting her toward the ground. She landed in the midst of the refugees, who scattered.

"Fool!" Smasher cried. "You were told to keep them away from the Chlorites!"

Chlorites? Xavier wondered what it meant. It sounded more like a laundry product than a species name, and there was clearly more than one species represented among them.

Xavier's attention had been occupied with the combat, but now he listened in on the surface thoughts of the refugees surrounding Rogue. They were frightened of the battle going on above them, yet many of them recognized that the X-Men were trying to protect them and felt a gratitude deeper than Xavier could plumb. They came forward and tried to help Rogue to her feet. But one of them, a yellowish bipedal male with a pebbly hide and spines down his back, made the mistake of reaching for her ungloved hand. "No," she called, but they did not understand the language, and she was too dazed to move away in time.

With the flesh-to-flesh contact, Rogue's body and nervous system psionically linked to the alien, thirstily drinking in his life energy, his genetic code, his memory. Her skin became yellowish and pebbly, and spines grew from her back, tearing through the fabric of her jumpsuit and jacket. As the alien fell comatose to the ground, his fellow refugees backing away in alarm, Xavier felt Rogue's disorientation as a lifetime of traumatic memories poured into her. She had years of experience at handling such an influx, but this was so alien, so intense, so full of pain that it was difficult for her to process. And something about his biology was making her sick to her stomach.

Rogue! he called. *Focus on who you are. We need you.* There had been attrition on both sides, but if Rogue couldn't pull it together, Smasher's strength would be an insurmountable advantage. Jean was recovering from her fall, but was weakened. Cyclops and Shadowcat were down. Lockheed was punch-drunk and wolfing down whole ears of corn to try to replenish his strength. Nightcrawler and Wolverine were still active but stalemated. And Rokk, Flashfire, and Manta were still at liberty, along with the Diascar ship and its plethora of weapons. Xavier didn't like to do it, but he tried to shock Scott and Kitty back to wakefulness, to tweak their brains to send more adrenaline through their systems. He would need all of his X-Men, to fight to the end if necessary.

But now another sound was impinging on the scene. After a moment, Xavier recognized the beat of helicopter rotors. There were many of them, and they had a military sound to them. As the choppers hove into view, confirming that they were U.S. military, a radio transmission came in on the X-Men's frequency. *"Attention X-Men. This is Dr. Valerie Cooper of the National Security Council. Please cease and desist your combat immediately!"*

Val Cooper—it was a familiar name. The NSC operative had first become known to the X-Men as an adversary, a representative of the forces in government acting to curb mutant freedoms, or at least the activities of mutant crimefighters. Over the years, though, her stance had softened and she had at times been an ally, a sympathetic voice in government. Her agendas were still her own, though, and it was unclear where she might stand in this instance. "Dr. Cooper," Xavier replied, "this is Charles Xavier. The X-Men are acting to protect a shipful of refugees—"

"The Diascar have informed us of the situation and reached a diplomatic agreement with the United States and the UN. You and your people need to know, Professor, that those aliens pose a grave and immediate biohazard threat. My team is here to take them into quarantine."

"Quarantine, nothing!" Wolverine snarled over his comlink. "These hosers are tryin' to quarantine 'em from breathin'!"

"Even now," Cooper replied, *"the Diascar commander*

is instructing her forces to stand down. This is American soil, and they've agreed to respect our sovereignty." Indeed, the Guardsmen had halted their assault and were regrouping. Xavier signaled mentally that the X-Men should do the same and allow the Guardsmen to retrieve their wounded—while still staying between them and the refugees. *"But you need to step aside,"* Cooper went on, *"and let us contain the aliens. And you'll need to come with us for decontamination procedures."*

By now, Cyclops had recovered enough to speak for the team. "Cooper, you can't trust what these Diascar are claiming! They're slaughtering these defenseless people. How can you just swallow the excuses they're making?"

"I'm doing nothing of the kind, Summers," Cooper replied coldly. *"You better believe I'm gonna be demanding some solid proof of this from our own scientists. But if there's even the chance that what they're telling us is true, then we can't afford not to listen. It's that serious, people. I'm talking fate-of-the-world serious. So either you stand down and follow my lead, or we can put the latest anti-mutant ordnance to the test. How about it?"*

Xavier reached out to skim her surface thoughts. Her mind was very disciplined, giving away little, as one would expect from a national security agent. And he wasn't about to intrude deeper. But from what he could sense of her emotions, she was sincerely convinced of her words—all of her words. And if Lilandra had really sent a Guard contingent on this mission, then she must have felt it was for a good cause. *Scott, I think we should do as she says . . . for now.*

After a moment, Scott nodded, though it was with reluctance. "All right, Cooper. But if you allow any of these refugees to be harmed—"

"Come along as observers if you want. In fact, I insist—you still need that decon."

"Blast," Wolverine said. "And I already had my bath this week."

5: Extinction Agenda

The government forces had come prepared. Once the helicopters touched down, soldiers deployed in full biohazard gear, a yellow, faceless horde. The alien refugees reacted to the sight with alarm, huddling together as the soldiers drew near. A few of the more robust-looking specimens stood before the rest in a defensive posture. But as Cyclops looked them over, he doubted they'd be able to do much. They appeared as desperate and malnourished as those they sheltered, dressed in tattered rags and the odd piece of worn-down plastic or ceramic that seemed to be comlinks or other electronic gear. The group exuded a strong, foul chemical smell, alien yet in some ways familiar, the stink of squalor, blood, disease, and death. They represented more than a dozen different species, with no obvious commonality Scott could see; yet they stood united here, made one by a common peril. Scott moved to stand between them and the soldiers, and the rest of the X-Men moved to follow.

A smaller figure stepped forward out of the mass of yellow, and Val Cooper's voice emerged from behind the faceplate. "Please listen to me," she said, addressing the aliens. "We don't mean you any harm. We're here to take you to a place where you can have shelter, food, and medical care."

Scott noticed Jean closing her eyes, concentrating. He realized she was acting as a telepathic translator, relaying Cooper's words to the refugees. A few mutters came from the group, and Jean interpreted. "They don't trust you," she told Cooper.

"I guess I can't blame them," the other woman replied. "We must look pretty intimidating. But they seem to trust you. Can you convince them to come along with us quietly? There's been more than enough force used here today," Cooper said, looking around at the bodies littering the ground, "but we can't afford to delay and risk further contamination of the environment."

Her implicit threat came through clearly. "I understand," Jean said coldly. "I'll do what I can to persuade them."

It appeared to take some doing, but within a few minutes, Jean managed to convince the refugees to go peacefully. Some were reluctant to go, weeping or keening over the bodies of their loved ones, but they put up little resistance when their fellows pulled them away. Scott got the sense that these beings were used to losing people and moving on.

But when he started to lead the team forward after the refugees, Cooper stopped him. "Sorry, Summers.

The Diascar want to handle the decontamination with their own equipment, aboard their ship. You'll be going with them."

Rogue, who had by now recovered her normal appearance save for the holes in her clothing, stepped forward angrily. "Nothin' doin', Blondie! You said we could go with 'em, watch out for 'em!"

"And Professor Xavier is welcome to do so. He wasn't exposed like you were. But from what they tell me, our decon procedures may not be good enough. Especially with you, Rogue, after your, uh, close encounter."

Now it was Wolverine's turn. "And you expect us to just walk blindly into that ship and let 'em do what they please to us?"

Kitty backed him up. "They do seem to be the shoot-first kind of people." Lockheed, perched on her shoulder, turned up his beak at the proposal.

But Cooper addressed her reply to Cyclops. "Isn't Xavier the one who's always saying you shouldn't judge by first impressions? Go meet the Diascar. Listen to what they have to say. They might not be the monsters you're assuming. Maybe they even have good reason to shoot first."

"Why don't you explain it to us?" he replied.

"No time. We have to get a move on. The wind is picking up. We have to clear the area and decontaminate it ASAP."

Scott studied her eyes, as best he could through his visor and hers. "All right," he said after a moment. "We'll go with them—for now." If the Diascar tried anything, he was confident in his team's ability to escape. "But I'm holding you personally responsible for those refugees."

Xavier telepathically expressed agreement with Scott's decision and said that he would remote-pilot the X-Jet to the government facility for decontamination. As Cooper's people led the surviving refugees away, Smasher and Flashfire came over to escort the X-Men. The Diascar ship had sent down a capsule, which, Rokk explained, would deliver them to the decontamination center without contacting the interior environment of the ship.

They were given little chance to ask questions, though. As soon as they were inside the capsule, they were bathed with an initial dose of sterilizing rays. "Great, like my kids won't be mutated enough," Kitty muttered. "Assuming I can still have kids."

That proved not to be the last of her worries, though. Once the capsule reached the ship and disgorged them into the decon area (shunting the X-Men and Guardsmen into two separate, parallel decon corridors), a computerized voice gave them instructions in what the Diascar presumably considered a soothing tone. Unfortunately, the first instruction was to remove all their clothes. "Don't we get any privacy?" Jean demanded.

"Individual facilities are not available," the voice replied. "For your own safety, please proceed with alacrity."

"There's another problem," Scott told the disembodied voice. "I can't take off this visor without damaging your ship."

"Please proceed with alacrity."

"I mean it, you don't want me taking this visor off!"

After a moment, the computer seemed to make a decision and advised him that it was contacting an officer for assistance. A new, live voice came on the line, gruff but feminine-sounding, and Scott explained the situation. After a little discussion, the Diascar consented to let him put in his emergency ruby-quartz contact lenses. Since he kept them inside a pocket, the Diascar granted that they were probably uncontaminated. "Also the energy emissions from your eyes would presumably kill any Chlorite microbes on their surface. You may proceed." Scott declined to point out that his beams were kinetic force rather than heat or radiation, but he reflected that the effect would be much the same on any microbes that got in the way. Hit something hard enough, and much of the kinetic energy would be converted to heat anyway.

Not that Scott was all too happy about the Diascar's concession. Not only were the contacts large and uncomfortable but there was still the group disrobing to contend with as well. He, Logan, and Kurt graciously took the lead as they filed into the decon area, taking care to keep their eyes facing front.

The decon process was a thorough and uncomfortable series of high-pressure sprays, chemical baths, room-temperature plasma immersions, and energy-ray exposures. It left Scott feeling rubbed raw and irritated rather than cleansed, though Logan claimed to find it bracing. The one small mercy was that they weren't required to shave off their hair; that would've left Kurt looking rather silly, though for Logan it might have been an improvement.

At the end of the process, they emerged one at a time into a changing room containing jumpsuits laid out for them, along with their returned equipment, which had no doubt been subjected to a sterilization regimen as thorough as their own. Scott busied himself with dressing and removing the contacts while the others emerged. The removal, like the insertion before it, was a tricky operation; inside a spaceship, with no safe direction to look, he had to hold his visor in front of his eyes while he removed the lenses. Once he was finally dressed and visored, Jean emerged, her skin on one side sunburned from Manta's attack—though after the decon process, they were all somewhat reddened all over. Soon thereafter, he looked away as Kitty came through the door, accompanied by a rather surly and bedraggled-looking Lockheed, who was coughing up smoke. However, the heavy door then closed behind Kitty, with Rogue still inside. "Hey!" came Rogue's voice from the other side when the door failed to open. "What's the big idea?"

Scott heard the muffled reply of the Diascar as she addressed Rogue. "Please proceed through the door on your left. Due to your closer contact with the Chlorites, we need to place you in medical isolation for observation. Do not be alarmed."

Scott expected Rogue to protest, but it was a moment before she spoke. "Cyke? Can you hear me?"

"Yes, Rogue!"

"I don't know how far I wanna trust these guys . . .

but the way I felt after touchin' that alien, maybe a medical check ain't a bad idea." He could hear how shaken she was. For someone who was normally just short of invulnerable, feeling ill had to be an alarming experience.

"All right," he told her. "But we'll make sure to check up on you as soon as possible."

"You better!"

Don't worry, he "heard" Jean think to her. *I'll keep in touch.*

Finally a heavy set of doors slid open and the X-Men were invited to enter the ship proper. As they stepped through it, Kitty paused to examine the seam between the sections of the ship. "It looks like this whole section is designed to be jettisoned if necessary. These folks are really careful about contamination."

"And with good reason," came a gruff voice. Scott turned and finally got his first look at a Diascar. Three of them, actually, and they were armed. Yet they didn't look as fearsome as Scott had imagined—nothing like the Brood, Badoon, or other predatory aliens the X-Men had faced in the past. They were centaurlike in build, two arms and four legs, with thick, stout tails. Their faces were equine, with ramlike horns curling back behind foxlike ears. They were covered in short fur, cream-colored on the snout, chest, and underbelly, brown or greenish-brown along the scalp, back, and flanks. Their four-fingered hands and four-toed feet had thick, hooflike nails—more pronounced on the feet, producing a clopping sound as they shifted their weight. They had the flat teeth of herbivores.

They didn't look like cold-blooded killers. But there was a wariness in their eyes, a look Scott had seen in many veteran warriors, determined to defend their causes at any cost.

The largest, biggest-horned male stepped forward. "I am Taforne, Defense Leader of the *Endless Plain.* Allow us to escort you to meet our fleet leader."

Scott took a step forward, meeting Taforne's gaze. The centauroid's eyes were just above the level of his own. "We expect nothing less. Lead on."

As they moved through the ship, they saw other Diascar, who eyed them with expressions ranging from curiosity to hostility, though it was hard to read their horselike faces for sure. Many of the Diascar were apparently female, with no horns and what appeared to be udders on their underbellies.

The commander, whom Taforne introduced as Fleet Leader Poratine, turned out to be female too, tall and elegant with a rich green coat. She strode across the spacious control center with a commanding gait, taking in the X-Men's arrival without letting it break her stride. She was occupied with other matters. "Status of the Earth personnel?" she asked.

A male crewmember responded. "They are finishing their specimen retrieval now, returning to their aircraft. The craft containing the enemy captives are away."

"Very well. Let us pray their assurances about their containment methods are justified. Emitter charge?"

"Two points from full, Leader," a female told her. "One point."

"All Earth aircraft are free of the hazard zone," the male reported.

"Full charge."

Poratine nodded. "Discharge."

The monitors told the tale. One moment, they showed the crash site from overhead—the cornfield, the crashed ship and the gouge it had left in the earth, and the alien bodies scattered around it. The next, it was all lost in a flare of white, blinding even through Scott's visor. By the time his vision cleared, the entire vista had been replaced by a rising, roiling cloud of flame, smoke, and ash. The ship bucked briefly as the shock wave rumbled past. Scott and the others watched speechlessly as the pillar of debris rose to darken the area, slowly blowing away in the breeze to reveal a smoking crater where a farm had once been.

Kurt was the first to find a voice. "It's not enough to kill them in cold blood? You have to desecrate their dead as well?"

Poratine's head whirled around to stare at them fiercely, her ears folding back. "You know nothing of this." She trotted toward them, a haughty sneer on her face. "You are lucky I did not have you arrested for recklessly endangering your own world. At least you have ignorance as an excuse. Perhaps once you understand the situation you will not be so impetuous."

"What we understand," Scott told her, "is that you were firing on defenseless refugees. And you refused to answer our hails. What were we supposed to think?"

"And who are you, that we were required to answer your hails in the first place? According to Dr. Cooper, you have no authority to speak for this world or even this territory of it."

"Call us concerned citizens, then. We made a judgment call. And you still haven't said or done anything to prove that we were wrong."

"Then listen, and you will hear it. You say you wished to protect refugees. Well, we are refugees as well. Because of the Chlorites." Poratine tossed her head back. "The Diascar were once a peaceful people. We galloped across the plains of our world, grazing them, cultivating them, making them into a paradise. The beauty and peace of Diasca drew beings from across the galaxy. We learned from them, migrated to other, uninhabited worlds and cultivated them as well, building a rich, democratic community of worlds. We fought off those who sought to take what we had by force—Skrull, Badoon, and others—but mostly we lived at peace with ourselves and our neighbors.

"But then the Chlorites came. Just one ship, a small crew of explorers. They told us they were venturing out of their system for the first time, drawn in by the signals we beamed out to other worlds, messages offering to share our knowledge and trade peacefully with other cultures. They came to one of our outlying worlds, and they were welcomed there. They stayed a few weeks, then returned home to share what they had learned.

"And then that world began to die.

"You see, although the Chlorites breathe oxygen as we do, their bodies, and the symbiotic microbes within them, produce chlorine gas as a waste product of their metabolism. When they departed our colony world, they left some of those microbes behind. The microbes thrived on our world, for there were so many unused chlorides in our environment and no competition, because no life of our kind makes much use of them. And the chlorine they emitted made them toxic, so nothing could feed on them."

"My God." That was Kitty, looking very alarmed. "They'd multiply out of control, wouldn't they? And pumping all that chlorine into the atmosphere . . ."

"That wouldn't be very pleasant to breathe," Kurt said.

"No way. Chlorine gas is very deadly. And if it got into the water . . ." She shuddered.

"What's so awful 'bout that?" Logan asked. "We put chlorine in swimmin' pools all the time."

"But we have to put in soda ash too, to cancel the acidity," Kitty explained. Chemistry wasn't really her specialty—that was computer science—but she was a well-rounded genius, partly just to keep her active mind stimulated, and partly to keep up with Hank McCoy. "Chlorine reacting with water turns into hydrogen chloride and . . . well, to make a long story short, you'd end up with a solution of hydrochloric acid and bleach! You think the acid rain we get on Earth is bad . . ."

"Yes," Poratine said. "The environment became extremely corrosive, even as the air became toxic to breathe. Metals, soils, limestone, chalk, almost everything but clays and silicates eroded away. Not only did every living thing remaining on the planet die—aside from the thriving chlorite microbes, that is—but most of our cultural centers, our works of art and architecture, our museums and libraries and hippodromes, all of them crumbled to nothingness. Only the gold and platinum, the quartz and ceramics survived. But no one could safely retrieve them.

"Of course we abandoned the world once it became clear that the Chlorite microbes were breeding too quickly for us to defeat them. But by then, our people's migrations had spread the infection to other worlds. Quarantines were imposed, and our people had to stand by and watch whole populations of their cousins and friends suffocate and die." She lowered her head. "But the Diascar were too gregarious, too mobile. It was hard for us to respond in the proper way, to think in terms of restricting free movement. So our defenses were too little and too late. Whenever we thought we had closed off one vector, another got through, and another world was infected.

"Ultimately, those of us who managed to avoid infection had no choice but to abandon the entire Diascar Consortium. We had always been migratory, but it was a very different thing to be rendered homeless, left with nowhere to migrate to."

Poratine paused before continuing. "But we were forgiving. We saw it as a tragic accident, and when the Chlorites requested permission to settle our worlds, we gave it to them. After all, they were the only ones who could safely live there.

"But they came in greater numbers than we had ever expected. And they came prepared, bringing their own plant and animal species to repopulate our worlds, their own equipment to build new cities out of clay, glass, ceramic, and gold. And as they remade our worlds in their image, we slowly came to realize that they had conquered us without firing a shot."

"And you retaliated?" Scott asked.

"No. That was not our way. We resolved to blockade our—*their*—worlds, to prevent them from traveling to others. But we were willing to live with the situation, to try to coexist through mutual avoidance."

"Good fences make good neighbors," Jean said.

"So we thought. But we were not the only . . . 'neighbors' involved. Eventually, our former worlds were assaulted again, more overtly this time, by another race that had lost its world to Chlorite infiltration. They destroyed the worlds that had once been ours and tried their best to destroy every ship that sought to flee.

"At first, we were horrified at their brutality. But over time, we came to realize they had no other choice. The Chlorites would not have stayed on those worlds indefinitely. We could not isolate whole planets for eternity, and there were other Chlorite worlds elsewhere in the galaxy. After the war, we warned all our neighbors of the threat, but the Chlorites found ways to infiltrate their worlds as well. Even when worlds were warned not to allow Chlorite immigrants, the devious creatures would bombard them with asteroids carrying Chlorite microbes. They would fall unnoticed into the oceans or the empty plains, and the microbes they carried would emerge and thrive and devastate more worlds.

"Once it became clear that these microbes could even travel through space unprotected, the true magnitude of the threat was revealed to us. What if a sizeable asteroid impact on a Chlorite world blasted chunks of it into space? They could drift to oxygen-bearing worlds and contaminate them by sheer accident. The very *existence* of Chlorite life is an intolerable menace to ours. As long as they live, we are in danger.

"It is a terrible thing to admit, I know. It goes against everything that a moral people is supposed to believe. But the inescapable reality, the truth the Diascar resisted but were eventually forced to accept . . . is that if we wish for life as we know it to survive, then all Chlorite life must be eradicated, down to the last single cell."

The refugees were flown to a government isolation facility in a remote part of the Allegheny Mountains. The Diascar ship made good time, arriving slightly ahead of the helicopters and the *Blackbird.* Xavier had already listened in on Poratine's speech courtesy of Jean, so as soon as the Imperial Guardsmen disembarked, he approached Vril Rokk and insisted that he be put in touch with Majestrix Lilandra. "The Majestrix expected as much," Rokk told him. "Matters of state occupy her at the moment, but you will be notified when she is free."

In the meantime, Val Cooper had overseen the removal of the Chlorite refugees to quarantine facilities and was consulting with a team of Diascar techs. "Follow their lead," she announced to the crew responsible for decontaminating their aircraft, equipment, and suits. "Our standard techniques won't be good enough. Any chlorine-based disinfectants we use will feed these bugs, not kill them." Despite her words, many of the government personnel showed wariness at taking instructions from a group of alien centaurs.

Xavier was allowed to observe the refugees in quarantine to ensure that they were being treated well. Indeed, it appeared that standard prisoner-of-war conventions were being followed as far as possible, given the language barrier and other circumstances. Xavier tried to deal with the former, mentally addressing the aliens and offering them his patented high-speed telepathic "language lessons"—really more of a direct upload of functional knowledge from his brain to theirs. There were relatively few takers, and those who did accept the language upload had little to say in return. Xavier sensed the Chlorites' wariness. Although they were surprised and relieved to find themselves alive in oxy-life custody, their reactions were more suspicious than grateful. They had seen the humans cooperating with the Diascar. Although they would share few specifics with him, Xavier could tell that they had suffered much in their lives.

Soon, Rokk came to him and handed him a Shi'ar holocommunicator, leading him to a small conference room so he could take the call in private. A moment later, the face of his beloved Lilandra appeared before Xavier's eyes—that lovely, aquiline face with its proud crest of glossy black feathers, its bright eyes limned by intricate tattoos. His heart lifted; it had been far too long since he had seen her last. It was one of fate's great cruelties that his soul mate had to be the ruler of an empire millions of light-years away, kept from him as much by responsibility as by distance.

Sadly, though, Lilandra had little time for pleasantries. "I wish we could speak longer, Charles, but I am currently endeavoring to avert two civil wars and manage disaster relief for a recent supernova. In brief, yes, Smasher's phalanx of the Guard is there on my orders. And they have acted in accordance with Shi'ar policy."

Xavier was stunned. "Lilandra . . . I understand that the task of ruling a vast empire does at times require a certain ruthlessness. But I cannot accept that you would condone the wholesale *extermination* of an entire order of life, down to its most innocent members."

Lilandra saddened. "Your human sayings can be dreadfully glib, but in this case it truly is either us or them. Everything Poratine told your X-Men is the truth. We have faced the Chlorite threat in our galaxy in the past. The rise of Chlorite life is a rare occurrence, but a galaxy is a very large place. And the Shi'ar Empire is ancient. Many times in the past, my predecessors have faced outbreaks of Chlorite life. At times they have attempted policies of coexistence, of isolation. But it never lasts. Chlorites, as a breed, are never content with the worlds they have. They always find ways to strike out and infest more."

"Given how aggressively their destruction is pursued by others," Xavier countered, "can we really blame them?"

"Perhaps not. But who started the conflict is irrelevant. It is as it is. Our forms of life are fundamentally inimical to each other." She reacted to the look in his eyes. "I know what you must think, Charles. That you have heard that same rhetoric spoken about mutants and normal humans. But this is different. The divide is far more profound. In thousands of years, no one has ever found a way for our kind of life and theirs to coexist.

"And the advantage is theirs, Charles. Our biology is harmless to them, but theirs is intractably lethal to us. Leave nature to take its course, and they would kill us all, whether they wished to or not." She lowered her head, and he knew her pain was genuine. "Which is why we have no choice but to kill them all, even when we do not wish it."

She steeled herself again. "That is why Shi'ar policy is what it is. The rule has been handed down since ages past, and I respect its wisdom. The Shi'ar Empire shall take whatever action necessary to neutralize Chlorite life wherever it is found. We shall assist any other state in its efforts to do the same . . . and we shall show zero tolerance toward any who would impede those efforts. Am I clear, Charles?"

He let out a world-weary sigh. "As ever, Lilandra. I understand what your responsibilities compel you to do. But I am subject to other responsibilities, and I am not prepared to give up. Perhaps there is another option, a way that their life and ours can coexist. I know," he said, in response to her look of disbelief. "No one has found one in thousands of years. But I will not simply accept it until I have explored all the possibilities for myself."

Lilandra smiled. "I should expect no less from you, Charles. I find your eternal optimism sadly naïve at times, yet it moves me nonetheless. There are times when it motivates me to keep trying even when a cause seems hopeless." They communed in silence for a moment. "If anyone can find a new solution to this, Charles, it is you."

She sighed. "But I fear it would be harder for you. Here in our galaxy, the standing order has been in place so long that most Chlorite worlds are discovered and eradicated before intelligent forms evolve. From what the Diascar tell us, in your . . . less-regulated galaxy, numerous such species have been allowed to arise. That makes the threat far greater and more immediate for you."

"No doubt," Xavier said. "But perhaps it also creates greater opportunities for finding new solutions."

Lilandra shook her feather-crested head. "I pray to Sharra and Ky'thri that you are right. But understand that your world is at great risk every moment that those refugees are allowed to breathe its air. And understand that my Guard will use all necessary force to prevent a single Chlorite germ from escaping into your environment . . . even if it means vaporizing the facility where you now sit, with you and all your X-Men in it." Her voice was steel, but there was an agony in it that only he could discern. "Because the alternative, if your biosphere were infested, would be to quarantine your entire planet and abandon it to a slow, agonizing, inevitable death."

6: Examinations

Hank McCoy had been irritated at first when Charles Xavier had contacted him in the middle of a delicate experiment in viral mutation. He had agreed to make himself available if the need arose, but had hoped that the rest of the X-Men could handle the job without him, as they so ably had during his many absences from the team over the years. So he had heaved a sigh of regret when the National Security Council had called him in to serve as a medical consultant in the case of the alien refugees, on the recommendation of Charles Xavier.

To be honest, Hank often found himself torn between his roles, his identities. Was he the noted scientist Dr. Henry McCoy or the superhero known as the Beast? Was he an X-Man, an Avenger, a Defender, or a civilian? Was he a cultured intellectual and bon vivant or a life-of-the-party jock? He'd tried embracing all those roles over the years, transforming himself often enough to give the metamorphess Mystique a run for her money. He'd even deliberately taken the mutagenic compound that had turned him from a mostly normal-looking mutant with oversized hands and feet into the blue-furred, apelike form he had today. He had justified it to himself at the time as a temporary transformation, one he could correct if he took the antidote in a timely fashion (which he had failed to do). But had it really been necessary to take the risk at all? Had it been the act of a man unsure of who he was, seeking to try on another identity for size? And had his occasional back-and-forth changes in appearance over the years been a reflection of the uncertainty of the man within?

At any rate, Hank liked to think he'd found more stability now. Rather than trying to reinvent himself all the time, he'd learned to integrate the various aspects of his identity, to balance them with one another. Even his form had remained unchanged for quite some time now, and he was hopeful it would stay that way. Yet the balance wasn't always easy to maintain— perhaps it wasn't for anyone, he reflected. He felt he had his priorities straight now, or at least comfortably timeshared, but sometimes circumstances upset his careful balance. He had really hated leaving his work at this critical stage. He hated leaving any puzzle unsolved, especially one that could save many lives if he succeeded.

But now he was grateful that Xavier and Val Cooper had called him in. The Chlorites were a fascinating order of life, unlike anything he'd encountered before. Examining the refugees, and the remains that the NSC personnel had managed to gather before the immolation of the farm, had been immensely exciting.

He barely even noticed the discomfort of encasing his massive, thick-furred frame inside an ill-fitting biohazard suit for hours.

"Truly remarkable," he said to his fellow X-Men once he emerged from quarantine. "I've read theoretical discussions of chlorine-producing life, but until now they were firmly in the realm of science fiction. I'll have to write to Stephen Gillett, he'll be thrilled at how close he came! Did you know, their bones and teeth are essentially made of PVC plastic? And some of them give off DDT as a natural pheromone!"

"So this Diascar story makes sense to ya, Hank?" Logan asked, now attired in his Wolverine livery once again. Hank had brought new uniforms for the team when he'd arrived in the spare X-Jet. "About these Chlorite germs bein' able to frag whole planets?"

"Don't you believe Lilandra?" Kitty asked.

"Lil's a classy dame, and I don't mind havin' her at my side in a scrape. But the gal's a politician. And that means I don't buy anything she hands me until I give it a good smellin'."

"Trust but verify," Hank said.

"Well . . . verify, anyway."

"It does seem unlikely," Cyclops said. "A few alien germs turning a whole planet toxic? Wouldn't a biosphere have some kind of defense mechanisms against something like that?"

"As a matter of fact, Scottie," Hank replied, "we know for a fact that such a thing is possible. It has happened at least once to our knowledge, probably many more times."

"Where?" Kurt asked.

"Here. The Earth." Ever the showman, Beast took a moment to enjoy their bewildered reactions. "Once upon a time—in fact, for several billion years' worth of onces—the Earth was populated by anaerobic microbes, obtaining energy through chemosynthesis. The air consisted mainly of carbon dioxide. These life forms had no use for oxygen gas; indeed, it was so chemically reactive as to be a deadly poison to them. When photosynthesis evolved and algae began pumping massive amounts of free oxygen into the atmosphere, it was an ecological catastrophe. Anaerobic life died out, except in isolated conditions like deep-sea thermal vents, or unless it was able to evolve ways to shield itself against the lethal effects of oxygen.

"In fact, the nuclei of our own cells cannot survive exposure to oxygen and are surrounded by many defensive layers to isolate them from the stuff. The same is true of most alien cells I've studied or read about, suggesting that this same cataclysm occurred on many other worlds.

"And apparently, sometimes, it can happen more than once."

Most of the X-Men were subdued, perhaps unnerved at the discovery that they'd been breathing a deadly poison all their lives. Kitty was more curious, though. "What would it be like on a Chlorite world?" she mused. "Corrosive seas . . . a greenish haze in the air . . ."

"Indeed. With only green light getting through, the plants would have to be some other color, in order to *absorb* green. Gillett thinks they'd be black, like rotted garbage bags.

"They also wouldn't do more than smolder. Fires can't burn in a chlorinated environment. Also they'd have no strong metals to build with. I can't imagine how they ever got out of the Stone Age, let alone to other worlds!"

"Most likely," came a gruff new voice, "they obtained technology from hapless starfarers who came to their worlds." Beast turned to find himself facing two Diascar, a male and a female, accompanied by Xavier and Cooper. *I heard the beat of centaur's hoofs over the hard turf,* he thought after Eliot, *As his dry and passionate talk devoured the afternoon.* The speaker, though, had not been Mr. Apollinax but the Diascar female, no doubt Fleet Leader Poratine. "Dry and passionate" described her tone well, though. The surly, ram-horned male with her, Xavier informed him telepathically, was Defense Leader Taforne. *No wise and gentle Cheiron he, I think.*

"We cannot know for sure," Poratine went on. "The first Chlorites to enter space are probably long since driven extinct. But they have shared their technology with others of their kind, and it has spread the plague ever since.

"I am gratified, Dr. McCoy, that you are able to find intellectual pleasure in the Chlorite menace. But my people have long since lost that luxury. We have mourned the deaths of too many worlds. And right now we need your help to ensure that Earth does not become one of them."

Hank gave her a courtly bow. "Rest assured, madam,

that when it comes to saving the Earth, we X-Men have more than our share of experience."

"Really?" Taforne cantered forward to confront him. "Then what intelligence have you gained from the Chlorites, other than what their bones and trees are made from? Did you extract any useful information about their plans, their purpose here on Earth?"

"If you will forgive me paraphrasing my namesake, sir, I am a doctor, not an inquisitor."

"What could they possibly tell you that you don't already know?" Jean asked. "And what threat could they possibly pose now? They're completely at our mercy. They're weak and starving."

"Do not make the mistake of feeling sorry for them," Taforne said. "This is what makes them so insidious. They are a mortal threat simply by existing, never forget that. You are fools even to let them live at all. But if you let your guard down because they seem helpless and pitiful, then you deserve the extinction you bring upon yourself."

"It is a lesson the Diascar learned the hard way," Poratine added. "Our forebears would have been horrified at our ruthlessness. But their mercy and morality brought their downfall."

"You see them as helpless victims," Taforne went on, "but their very presence here is an attack. They know full well that setting foot on any oxy-life planet will mean death to all its inhabitants and a new world transformed for their habitation. The very fact that they set course for your world means that they intended your complete annihilation."

"Desperate people can do desperate things," Jean countered. "Maybe they felt they had no choice if they hoped to survive."

Scott came to his wife's support. "For that matter, how do we know they even intended to land here? They crashed because *you* shot them down. For all we know, they would've requested supplies from orbit and moved on."

"You do *not* know!" Taforne moved to confront Scott, his head angled forward. Hank noted with interest how his body language conformed to the instincts of a horned species, accustomed to quite literally butting heads with rivals. "You do not know how devious they can be. That is why we must use every means possible to extract whatever they might know. Yes, your mate is correct, they are desperate to survive. And they will do anything it takes to survive—just as we will. For all we know, there could be a fleet of Chlorite ships heading this way. Or an asteroid bombardment. Maybe they have infiltrators among you already."

"If that were true," Hank said, "wouldn't it be too late to save our world already?"

Taforne stared at him. "If so, we still must know it—so that your world may be quarantined before the plague can spread further."

Val Cooper stepped in. "In any case, we need to learn what we can from these people. Defense Leader Taforne, I'll allow you to join us in interrogating the refugees. But we'll do it our way. Here in America, we have rules on the treatment of prisoners."

"Yeah, right," Logan said. "Like that makes a difference."

Cooper looked the X-Men over. "If it makes you more comfortable, I'll allow one of you to attend as an independent observer, to watch out for their civil rights. Just for the record, though," she smirked, "as illegal aliens, they don't *have* that many rights to begin with. I'm doing you a favor by allowing this."

"And we appreciate it, Ms. Cooper," Xavier said. "I recommend Jean Grey as the observer. I would like to learn more about . . . our new allies," he said, looking over the Diascar.

Cooper looked to Taforne, who grudgingly gave consent. "All right, then. I'll arrange it."

"In the meantime," Xavier said to Poratine, "we'd like to see our colleague, Rogue. And to arrange for her release, if possible."

The Diascar commander studied him for a moment. "A visit can be arranged. As for the rest . . . that remains to be seen."

Rogue? How are you doing? Charles Xavier's voice spoke in her head. Some of her fellow X-Men said that they never got used to that, no matter how often it happened. But Rogue was used to having other voices in her head. If anything, Xavier's was comforting in comparison, because at least she could be sure it belonged to someone else.

I'm feelin' fine, Professor, she sent back. *'Cept for a bit of a draft.*

She sensed Xavier's surprise and embarrassment at

what he read from her. *Oh. Well, we were just coming in to visit you, but maybe I'd better tell everyone but Jean and Kitty to wait outside.*

Thanks, Professor. I appreciate it somethin' awful. Reflexively, Rogue wrapped her arms around her bare frame. Under normal circumstances, spending so much time in the nude would have been a luxury she would savor. Her absorption powers required her to stay completely covered up most of the time, even in hot and humid weather, lest a stray touch send some innocent passerby into a temporary coma and fill her head with their stolen memories. When she was safely by herself, Rogue took pleasure in feeling the air against her bare skin. If she ever lost her powers, she often thought, she'd move someplace warm and never wear more than a bikini for the rest of her life if she could help it.

But here, in this quarantine ward—more like a prison cell with a hospital bed in it—being naked was no pleasure. The last time she'd been naked in a cell— on Genosha, stripped of her powers and rights as well as her clothes, used and abused by the guards—well, it was not something she wanted to be reminded of.

Rogue reminded herself that she could smash out of this cell easily if she wanted to. She was here voluntarily, if reluctantly. The thoughts she'd taken in from that alien were still confusing, mixed with strange and ugly sensory memories and hard-to-define emotions. But she knew that he knew his biology could kill someone like her, and she knew how *poisoned* she'd felt when she'd temporarily become like him. Who knew what might have lingered inside her? Even if these Diascar turned out to be the bad guys, at least they had experience with these Chlorite critters and could maybe spot things that Beast or the Prof would miss. Or hopefully, not spot them and give her a clean bill of health. She just hoped it would be *soon*.

The outer door opened, and true to Xavier's word, only Jean and Kitty came into the observation room outside her cell. The X-*Men* called in greetings from the compartment beyond while staying out of her line of sight. "Hey, y'all," she called back. "Please tell me y'all're here to get me outta this dump!"

Jean gave her a commiserating look through the transparent wall. "Sorry, Rogue. The Diascar doctors aren't ready to release you yet. They've never seen a case like yours, someone temporarily absorbing Chlorite traits. Uh, have they told you about the Chlorites?"

"I got the Cliff Notes version. Plus what I, uh, remember rememberin' from when I touched the guy."

"Well, they want to make especially sure there are no lasting effects."

"Yeah, I bet. Y'all ask me, it's just another case o' mutie cooties."

"What do you mean?" Kitty asked.

"You know—touch a mutant, and people think you'll get infected or sumpin'?"

"Of course I know what it means," Kitty replied with a bit of heat. "I heard it often enough in school. I meant about the Diascar."

"Oh, sorry. I mean the way they look at me. They think I'm contaminated, and no matter what their tests tell 'em, that ain't gonna change. Hell, they barely even treat me like I'm a person. Won't give me clothes or nothin'. I mean, I can get them not understandin' modesty, with their fur coats an' all, but you can bet I let 'em know it mattered to me. If y'all ask me, I think they like seein' me squirm in here.

"Take it from me—these guys *hate* Chlorites and anythin' that reminds 'em of Chlorites. I don't just see it in their eyes . . . the guy I touched, he'd felt it all his life. Same way every one of us has from normal people."

"What else can you tell us about the refugee's memories?" Jean asked. "The Diascar want to interrogate them. They think there might be a plot of some kind to attack the Earth."

Rogue scoffed. "Yeah, right. Jeannie, these folk were down to wonderin' where their next meal was comin' from. They were just tryin' to stay alive, to dodge everyone that wanted to kill 'em. Weren't no conspiracy."

"At least as far as the alien you absorbed knew about," Kitty said.

"What, Pryde, you believe this load o' bull?"

"I'm just saying . . . yes, they're desperate and impoverished, but so's your average suicide bomber. If you've got nothing, then you've got nothing to lose and will do anything if you think it can bring a change."

"Well . . . maybe." To be honest, Rogue had to admit it was likely. She knew what it was like to be angry and bitter toward a world that hated and feared you, to want to strike back against it. That was what drove Mystique, her foster mother. It had driven Rogue herself for some time, after she'd put poor Cody into that coma, after her neighbors and kinfolk had condemned her and driven her out of town. Mystique had given her a new family and a sense of purpose, a focus for her anger and resentment. Eventually it had almost destroyed her, and only Charles Xavier's guidance had saved her. She now knew that Mystique's way was wrong. But she still understood it. She knew how natural it was.

"Who knows," she said, "maybe some of 'em do wanna strike back at life like us. But I ain't convinced they're the ones started it."

"I don't think who started it is really the issue," Jean said. "Not after a war has been going on this long. What's important now is, can we stop it . . . before the Earth gets caught in the middle?"

There was a momentary silence. "Okay," Rogue said. "But in the meantime . . . can y'all get me somethin' to wear? An' maybe a magazine or two?"

Jean laughed. "I'll see what I can do."

"Why did you come to Earth?"

On the other side of the transparent partition, the Chlorite prisoner cowered at Taforne's tone. "Please, I know nothing. Only that my mate and I need food. They said more would be provided?" The orange-skinned humanoid was an emaciated wreck. Jean, who stood behind Taforne monitoring the interrogation, couldn't tell whether his hairlessness, sunken eyes, and long, bony limbs were natural features or the results of starvation. There were others of his species, the Shuki, among the refugees, but they were all similarly undernourished.

Taforne showed no sympathy, however. "You will be fed once you have answered my questions satisfactorily! Now, again, why did your ship come to Earth?"

"I know of no Earth."

"Earth! The planet you befoul now with your presence. Why did you come here?"

"I am Buza, son of Kussa," the prisoner repeated for the third time. "My mate is Cal. We live in the barracks on the ship. That is all I know. I wash the clothes, purge the cyclers, clean the decks to earn my ration. Where the ship goes, I do not decide, and I do not know why."

"He's telling the truth," Jean said to Taforne.

"As far as you can tell," the Diascar countered. "Is that not what you keep saying? That you will only probe their minds so far?" They had been at this for hours; Buza was the sixth one to be interrogated, a different species each time.

"I won't invade their privacy, no. But honesty or deceit can be told apart with a more superficial scan. I've said that too."

Taforne turned back to Buza. "Very well. So you don't control the ship's movements. But surely you hear things? You talk with others on the ship?"

"We share tales, yes. And songs and prayers and *mah-chi.*" The last term had some kind of ritual meaning that Jean couldn't fully interpret. It had something to do with ancient traditions and remembrance of lost ancestors.

"And news? Gossip?"

"Daily tales, nothings."

"Rumors? Of going to a planet, perhaps?"

Buza looked at Taforne sullenly. "There are no planets where we are welcome."

"But you hear talk of it, surely?"

"We sing songs of the planets we came from—"

"Answer me!" Taforne pounded on the partition with his heavy-nailed fist. "Do you hear talk of going to a particular planet?"

"People talk. They blow vapor. Idle dreams of finding a planet to live on."

"Just dreams? How do you know, if you don't control where the ship goes? How do you know they weren't real?"

"How could I know? They are stories, talk, that is all I know."

"You are here now, aren't you?" Buza gave no reply. "So you have heard rumors, people talking about coming to a planet."

"Not on my ship."

"Other ships, then? You meet with other ships sometimes, do you not?"

"Yes. We must." Buza glared at the Diascar. "We cannot go to planets. Only ships can resupply us."

"So do those on other ships talk of going to planets?"

"I have heard such talk."

"Recently?"

"At all times."

"But recently?"

". . . Yes."

"What more did they say?"

"I do not—"

"Tell me. Did they talk of a world where they would be safe from pursuit?"

Buza glared. "We all dream of that."

"Did you know this planet contains many mutants?"

The Shuki was puzzled by the abrupt change of subject. "Mutants?"

"Beings who are genetically different from the norm. This world has many, of all different types. Some look less human than you do. These people who talked, did they talk of a place where they could blend in? Hide among the populace and be unrecognized?"

"They could smell us. We would poison them."

"Not all of you, not right away. Shuki give off few gases they could not tolerate, and only in small quantities. Many Chlorites give off less. They could hide on a normal world—for a while. But you knew that, did you not? When people talked of it?"

"People talk of many things, fantasies and dreams."

"But *did they talk of this?*"

"Yes! Yes, this and other things besides."

"Of a world where they could hide?"

"Yes."

"And maybe remake as their own?"

"We all dream of this. Yes. But when we try to remake a world, you find us and destroy us."

"So do they talk of remaking a world with arms? With weapons and devices to defend you?"

Buza shot forward, pressing himself against the partition. "Yes! Yes, we talk of finding a home we can defend! A home where we can live in peace, free of you monsters! We talk of weapons, we talk of turning the tables and hunting *you* down for a change! We talk of killing you all so you cannot take our worlds from us! Our fathers! Our sons! Our . . . our daughters! But it is talk, nothing more! I wish it were more, ohh, how I wish it could be more!" He shuddered with emotion and sank to the floor, keening to himself. "You killed my daughters. You killed my only son. You took them from us, one by one. We had two left, two that we had saved from starving. I held . . . them in my arms . . . as we fell through the air. . . . I held them to me . . . tried to shelter them . . . but we crashed and . . . and the metal tore, and it cut through them and not me! Why wasn't it me? It should've been me."

Jean strove to remain outwardly detached, but Buza's grief was wrenching. She had to struggle to hold in her tears. Taforne, however, was unmoved. He kicked at the partition with a forefoot. "This one is useless now. Bring on the next."

"It is as we feared," Taforne reported to Val Cooper after a day of interrogations, while Xavier, Jean, and Poratine looked on. "We uncovered evidence that there may be Chlorite infiltrators already among the Earth populace, disguised as mutants."

"I'm not prepared to accept that it's already too late," Cooper said.

"It may not be as yet," Poratine told her. "Our scientists have tested Chlorite microbes in Earthlike conditions. None of the known varieties shows the ability to survive in your biosphere at this time."

Cooper threw her a look. "Okay, then what happened to this horrible menace that no world could survive?"

"I said 'at this time.' This has happened before. Each world has its own unique conditions. Earth is more unusual than most in many ways, perhaps due to the factors that make mutancy so common on your world. An alien microbe first arriving on your world may find its conditions hostile, may starve from lack of nutrients or be killed by the radiation spectrum from your sun. But so long as it remains safely inside the body of a Chlorite host, it can reproduce, and it can mutate. Microbes have much shorter generations than Diascar or humans do, so they can evolve that much faster. Especially on this world, perhaps, given the exceptional turn evolution has taken here. Given enough time, it is inevitable that a strain able to tolerate Earthly conditions will evolve. Once able to survive outside of Chlorite hosts, these microbes will spread, and if not checked in time, will doom your world.

"Fortunately, we may have a grace period. But it could end at any time. We must track down any Chlorite infiltrators that may be hidden among your mutant population, and eliminate . . . the threat they pose by removing them from your world." Even without telepathy, Xavier could sense what Poratine had been about to say.

"Hold on," Jean interposed. "At this point, this is all based on hearsay. We have some testimony, yes, but no hard evidence to back it up."

Taforne turned to her. "You said yourself that they spoke the truth."

"I said that they weren't deliberately lying. There's a difference." She turned to Cooper. "Taforne's interrogation methods would never pass muster in a court of law. His questions were leading, he intimidated the prisoners. He said they wouldn't get to eat until they answered his questions to his satisfaction. These are weak, vulnerable people, Dr. Cooper. Subject them to leading questions like that, give them an incentive for answering the way you want, and they may convince themselves of it, reinterpret their memories to fit. I can tell you that I read these beliefs in their heads, but I can't say whether they were there before Taforne *put* them there."

"I spoke of nothing that I have not *seen* the Chlorites do before, on other worlds," the defense leader said. "They cannot be trusted!"

"Can you afford to take the chance, Dr. Cooper?" Poratine asked. "If there is any possibility that these infiltrators are on your world, they *must* be found and stopped as quickly as possible."

"And how would that be done?" Xavier asked softly. "I assume if you were able to scan for their presence, you would have found them already. By their emissions of chlorine gas and other such compounds, say."

"Some give off more than others," Poratine said. "And there are treatments that infiltrators could take to suppress their chlorine emissions."

"Then you're saying that they could not be distinguished from human mutants."

"Not without medical examination."

"Dr. Cooper," Xavier said, still keeping his tone

reasonable, "I hope you find the direction of this conversation as uncomfortable as I do."

She met his eyes evenly and paused for a moment before speaking. "A whole lot about this situation is uncomfortable, Professor. But things could get a whole lot more uncomfortable if we don't take this threat seriously." Before he could speak again, she stopped him. "Now, I'd like to thank you, Ms. Grey, and your . . . colleagues for your assistance with the refugees, but this has become a matter for discussion on a much higher level. I need to pass this information to my superiors in the government," she went on, taking Poratine in with her gaze. "In the meantime, Professor, your aircraft are fully decontaminated and you're free to leave at any time. I promise you'll be notified of what the president and the Pentagon decide to do about this—within the limits of security access, of course."

"I'd like to offer myself as a consultant in that decision. This may directly impact the mutant community, and they should have an advocate."

"I'll pass that request along, Professor. Thank you."

Xavier traded a look with Jean. *I read her aura the same way you do, Charles,* she sent. *Her mind's made up.*

"Very well," Xavier said aloud. "But this is by no means over."

"I fear," Poratine said, "that it is just beginning."

7: Ex Cathedra

Before leaving the government facility, Xavier was finally able to persuade the Diascar that there was no need to keep Rogue in quarantine any longer. They still expressed reluctance to release her, but had to admit that she no longer exhibited any hints of Chlorite metabolism and had never had any Chlorite symbiotic microbes in her to begin with. So they grudgingly conceded that there was no medical reason to keep her confined. Upon that declaration, Rogue easily smashed her way out of the quarantine cell, just to underline the point that she'd stayed there of her own free will.

Once back in the *Blackbird,* she wasted no time getting into a replacement uniform. With that done, she dug into a ration pack while she compared notes with the other X-Men, getting briefed on the results of the interrogations. ("We figure you've been debriefed enough for one mission," Nightcrawler quipped, earning himself a crumpled sandwich wrapper in the face.)

"I still don't buy it," Rogue said when she'd been filled in. "These ain't terrorists or conspirators. Jus' scared an' desperate folk lookin' for a home. Sure, they wanted to find a planet they could make their own, but not one with people on it already. Far as the guy I absorbed knew, they weren't even goin' to no planet."

"Mmm, I dunno," Wolverine said. "Space is pretty big. Hard to believe it was an accident."

"Well, there is that major hyperspace warp in our system," Kitty said. "Half the ships in the Local Group seem to pass through here on their way to wherever they're going."

"Still, it's a big system with a whole lotta empty. Hard to end up pointed straight at a planet 'less you were aimin' for it."

"They were runnin' from the horse-folk," Rogue shot back. "Maybe they wanted to duck behind the planet, try to lose 'em."

"Maybe," Logan said. "But I don't let my guard down 'cause o' maybes. And neither do you, usually."

"My guard's *way* up, Wolvie. It's up at the guys who wanna kill every last Chlorite and don't care much what kind o' horse-hockey excuses they gotta make up for it!"

The debate fizzled out without any definite facts to go by. All the X-Men could do was watch and wait. Once they returned to the mansion, Xavier put out feelers to whatever contacts in the government he had left. It had been a long time since the government's active, if clandestine, support for the X-Men had dried up in the face of growing anti-mutant sentiments. Few of the people Xavier tried to contact would answer, and those who did would only say that matters were being discussed behind closed doors at the highest levels.

Hank McCoy had connections of his own, both as a renowned research scientist and a former Avenger, but his inquiries were hardly any more productive than Xavier's.

When the news finally broke, it came through an unexpected channel—or, rather, many of them. The X-Men found out about it along with the rest of the world, when Poratine, Val Cooper, the U.S. secretary of defense, and the UN secretary-general staged a joint press conference. To Xavier's surprise and concern, they spelled out the whole situation to the public. He summoned the X-Men to his office so they could all hear it together, and he sensed that the students of the institute were gathering to watch in the parlor and their dormitories.

Poratine spoke of her people's history with the Chlorites and of the menace they posed. Cooper spoke about the incident in Pennsylvania and the subsequent interrogations. "In conclusion," the defense secretary summed up, "we have uncovered evidence of a credible threat of alien infiltration among the mutant population of our world. These aliens pose a potentially cataclysmic danger to all life on Earth, and the urgency of this threat compels us to take extraordinary measures, in concert with our fellow nations of humanity."

Poratine came forward again as a screen beside the podium began displaying graphics; after a moment, the news network switched its image to display that feed nearly full-screen, with Poratine in an inset box and the inevitable crawl along the bottom displaying incongruously trivial entertainment news. "These images depict the eleven known Chlorite species of approximately humanoid configuration, which cannot be immediately detected by the emission of toxic respiratory gases," the Diascar explained. "Chlorites of any of these types could be living among you, disguised as mutants. Keep in mind that they could have altered their appearance in various ways, so the potential number of appearances they could manifest is much greater than the eleven shown here.

"It is imperative that any infiltrators among your mutant population be exposed as soon as possible. We have no idea how long they may already have been on your world, or how soon it might be before a strain of their symbiotic microbes adapts to Earthly conditions and begins to spread. Every possible effort must be taken to identify and contain them before that happens."

"This has an ominous ring to it," Hank muttered.

The defense secretary took over again. "To this end, the United States and numerous other countries will need to locate and test all nonhuman-appearing mutants as soon as possible. We ask that all mutant citizens whose appearance departs from the human norm come forward voluntarily for medical testing to verify your identity. Those who are cleared will receive identification bracelets to confirm your humanity and will be troubled no further." ("Yeah, right," Logan said.) "So long as you do not avoid or try to resist this identification process, the disruption to your life should be minimal. However, this is *not* optional. It is imperative for the sake of our entire planet that we overlook no one. So we will also have to conduct door-to-door searches. . . ." The secretary's exact words were lost in the cries of protest Xavier heard both in this room and mentally from the students beyond.

Once the defense secretary was done, the UN secretary-general took the podium. "All United Nations members are being advised to comply with these procedures, and we hope that nonmembers will follow our lead in this as well. But we must urge everyone who hears this: Please, take no action of your own against any mutants you may encounter. The vast majority of them are *not* alien infiltrators but are simply persons born with unusual appearances and attributes, trying to lead normal lives as best they can. And those few who are infiltrators may be extremely dangerous if challenged. So please, if you have suspicions about any individual, report them to your local authorities. Do not attempt to take matters into your own hands."

"Like that'll make a difference," Logan growled. "You can bet there are people out there armin' up for mutant hunts right this minute."

"Well, there goes my social calendar," Kurt said. "We're going to be very busy now, aren't we?"

"But are we just going to fight the lynch mobs," Kitty asked, "or the government teams too?"

"I ain't convinced there's much difference," Rogue told her.

Soon, the floor was opened up for questions from the press. "Why was the decision made to announce this publicly, thereby tipping off any infiltrators that you're onto them?" a CNN reporter asked. "Won't that simply drive them underground?"

Cooper fielded the question. "They're already underground, essentially, Barbara. All they need to do to destroy us is *exist* among us. To blend into the general population, as much as any exotic-looking mutant can. By revealing their presence to the world, by instituting this regimen of medical tests and ID tags, we remove their ability to do that. Exotic-looking mutants are easy to identify, so if anyone in the general public knows of a mutant who doesn't show up on our testing rolls, that will stand out and make it harder for an infiltrator to blend in. Also, if it does force them to go to ground, that's a good thing. By limiting their mobility, we make it easier to contain the potential threat they pose, minimize the number of people they can come into contact with."

"Ben Urich, *New York Daily Bugle*. What about the civil liberties that are being infringed on here? Is this search even legal? Is it constitutional?"

Poratine came forward. "I wish there were a way to do this with no disruption to your people's values or your way of life. But please try to understand the magnitude of the threat your world faces. I have personally seen entire planets die from Chlorite infestation because they did not act quickly enough to contain the threat.

"The Diascar were originally a peaceful people, democratic by ancient custom. We respect the concept of individual rights. But like you, we understand that in a time of war, certain rights must be compromised in the name of the greatest right: the right to survive as an individual, a people, a nation, a species. It is not something we recommend lightly, but it is the only recourse.

"If you would blame someone for the compromises that must be made to your way of life, then blame those who wish to destroy your way of life, to end your entire existence. Once we are sure your world is safe from them, the Diascar will leave. This I swear to you.

"But if we do not do this . . . if we do not do everything in our power to stop the Chlorites . . . then your way of life will end. This I also swear."

Meena Banerjee couldn't tell if what she'd just heard on TV was real.

In her case, that was more than just a figure of speech. The alternate timelines she perceived had a way of popping into her head unexpectedly, and sometimes she had trouble keeping them separate from her own. At any given time, she could sense multiple alternate realities on the fringe of her awareness, ghostly echoes blurring the edges of her reality. Usually they were faint enough that she could distinguish her own reality from those other possibilities. But sometimes, unpredictably, her "center" would shift into one of those other timelines; it would feel like reality to her, and her home reality would blur into the indistinct mass of possibilities. While she was in them, those alternate worlds felt as real to her as her own timeline, and she accepted them as unquestioningly as in a dream. And when one ended, she sometimes had trouble reorienting herself to this reality. Some of her other worlds were easier to distinguish than others—like the one where World War Three had happened, or the one where Apocalypse had taken over, or the one where Mr. Logan was a foot taller and Rogue was a teenager who couldn't fly. Sometimes she got confused, though. Like the time she'd been shocked to see Mr. Summers alive after spending some time in a reality that was much like this one aside from his having recently died. And sometimes elements of the more distinct realities lingered in her mind, blurred with her memories of this one. Once, on a trip into nearby North Salem, she'd confused a policeman by asking him for directions to Bayside High School.

So Meena was dismayed to see the other students around her reacting to the same press conference she'd just seen. None of her visions ever lasted this long, and the fact that she was able to question what reality she was in pretty much confirmed that she was "awake" to her own world. But this was one reality she didn't think she wanted to be a part of right now. The world in danger? And odd-looking mutants getting singled out because of it? She was no fool; she knew better than to believe people would heed the secretary-general's cautions. It had suddenly become a very dangerous time to be Harry Mills or John Chang or Todd Watkins or any of the other students who couldn't "pass" like she could. Well, like she could when she wasn't blathering about her visions.

"I don't believe a word of it!" Harry (even he had

given up trying to go by "Harold") cried, waving a long-furred arm in the air. "Those centaur-people, it's just a scam to take over the world or something."

"The X-Men were there," said Sarah "Papillon" Allaire, one of the older students, a delicately pretty French blonde with large, iridescent butterfly wings, dainty antennae, and sparkling skin. "I heard them telling Ms. Moonstar about it. These, these Chlorites, they are for real."

"But that doesn't mean they're as dangerous as the Diascar say they are," said eight-foot-tall Mike "Beanpole" Galbraith.

"Can we afford to take the chance, though?" Kris Koenig asked.

"Easy for you to say," Todd shot back from his wheelchair, straining to lift his head against the weight of its armor plates. "You can pass. Nobody's gonna be trying to bag and tag your butt."

Kris glared at him. "Well, don't worry," she answered sarcastically. "When they come for you, I'll just hide you!" As she spoke, Meena saw her making a clandestine movement with her hands; then she shot one out and touched Todd, making his bony-plated skin turn invisible. Meena realized Kris must have pulled off one of her invisible gloves; she sometimes forgot they were there. Kris's powers only worked on one layer at a time, though (otherwise doubling up on clothes wouldn't help to preserve her modesty), so Todd's innards were laid bare like one of those Visible Man statues (except, ironically, his clothes remained visible). The others groaned in disgust and looked away. "There," Kris said. "Now anyone can see you're human on the inside!"

"Hey!" Todd cried. "What did you—hey, put me back!"

"Don't worry, it'll wear off in a minute," Kris said, though her concentration was on getting her glove back on as quickly as possible. No doubt she didn't wish to repeat the incident when that bully James Wheaton had used one of his energy tendrils to yank off one of her gloves and force her hand into contact with her outer shirt, leaving her upper body exposed in front of the whole class. Professor Xavier had interceded, deleting all the male students' sense memory of what they'd glimpsed and scheduling detention/therapy sessions for Wheaton, but Kris was still sensitive to the possibility of a reoccurrence.

Meena didn't think, though, that any of the students would be in the mood to try that right now. They were too preoccupied with what this news might mean. She turned to the one friend of hers who'd said nothing yet. "What about you, John? What do you think?"

"Yeah," Harry said. "This thing's gonna affect you as much as me or Todd or Sarah."

"Me?" Sarah interrupted. "None of those aliens they showed looked like me, did they? I am normal-looking, mostly, and none of them had wings, yes?"

"Okay, maybe not you. But I could be hiding anything under all this fuzz."

"Forgive me," Meena interposed, "but I was asking John. You've been so quiet," she said to the pale-skinned boy. "Are you scared?"

John shrugged. "Got nothing to be scared of. As long as we pass the tests, we're fine."

"Suuure," Harry said. "At least until they use the tracker chips in those ID bracelets to hunt us all down, or take over our minds, or whatever."

"What tracker chips?" Mike asked.

"There are always tracker chips. It's the government."

"I thought you said it was the aliens who wanted to take over."

"Same difference. Don't you remember from history class? First step to conquest is getting in good with the local rulers, bribing them to do the ruling for you so you don't have to worry about the little stuff."

"But they're not after everyone," Meena said. "Just mutants."

"Just *some* mutants," Sarah added.

"And that's their excuse. Gets the rest of humanity off its guard."

Todd had returned to normal by now and was nodding. "Gotta admit, sounds plausible."

Meena grimaced. "Oh, I wish I could control my powers! The Professor and Mrs. Grey-Summers, they say that if I could, it would help in discovering things like this."

"How so?" John asked.

"Well, if I could tell what realities are close to our own, I could tell how likely something is to be true here. If I could, say, scan through a whole bunch of nearby realities, I could see what's happened in most of them. Like maybe in some the Diascar came a bit sooner and already did what they were going to do.

Oh, I don't know, really," she added, frustrated. "Just forget it. As long as I can't control it, I'm useless."

"But you could learn," John told her. "That doesn't sound useless. I'd like to learn more about how your power works. Maybe . . . it could help somehow," he finished with a shrug.

Meena smiled at John, trying not to blush. He was usually so quiet and reserved. He didn't talk much about himself, saying that he didn't like to think about his past. Harry had told her that he believed John's foster parents had abused him for being a mutant, so it was understandable. Still, Meena found his reserve intriguing, wishing she could break through it and discover his secrets, whether by mastering her powers or simply by getting close to him. It meant a lot that he would reach out to her like this. Her heart pounded in her chest.

Then she glanced back at the TV, where the pundits were still dissecting the Diascar's announcement, and her heart sank. John was one of the people the government would be after, along with Harry and Todd, maybe Sarah, maybe even Dr. McCoy or Mr. Wagner. What if Harry was right? What if something did happen to them?

Now more than ever, she hated her powers for not working right.

"I'm most dismayed, Dr. Cooper, at the direction this has taken. I had hoped that we would discuss this matter in the light of mutant interests and rights before you came to this decision."

Val Cooper suppressed a sigh as she studied Charles Xavier's face on her videophone screen. He maintained his usual poise and measured delivery, but there was an edge to it now. This was a man who did not like to lose control of his emotions, but he was reining in some pretty heavy ones now. "The matter was discussed, Professor, on the highest levels. Rest assured we're aware of the probable backlash against mutants and are taking steps to minimize it. You heard the secretary-general's words. And we're making sure to instruct all our medical and military personnel to approach this matter with proper sensitivity."

"Surely you don't believe that will be effective. There are already reports of anti-mutant violence on the news. And what about the mutants living in other countries that do not extend the same legal rights to their citizens? Do you really believe there aren't going to be mass arrests, possibly concentration camps?"

Cooper was tired of his smug moral superiority and let some of her own emotion show. "I know what the consequences are going to be, Xavier. I live in the real world. But *because* I live in the real world, I have to make tough decisions sometimes. Yes, this is going to get bad. But it's better than the alternative. It stinks, but sometimes, in the real world, a few people have to be sacrificed for the greater good."

"So mutants are to be sacrificed for the good of the unmutated majority."

"I didn't say that. And the mutants will die along with everyone else if the Chlorites aren't stopped."

"How do we even know there truly are Chlorite infiltrators? A few inconclusive, coercive interrogations? Where is the hard evidence?"

"The stories synch up too well. They're consistent."

"All from passengers on the same ship, who could have heard the same baseless rumors."

"And we can't afford to take that chance."

"If the Diascar are telling the truth."

"Come on. Your own science guy helped confirm the ecological danger. Besides, why would the Diascar lie about this? What, do you think they want to take over the world or something? If they wanted to do that, why come to us with a story that only requires regulating the weird-looking mutants, nobody else?"

"And how do we know it would end there? How many times, Dr. Cooper, have a people allowed their freedoms to be eroded away a little at a time? Deprive one group of rights in the name of security, and it sets a precedent for going further. For interrogating possible fellow-travelers, demanding that they incriminate friends and family, imprisoning them if they refuse."

"That's frankly a little paranoid, Professor. There's no reason why this should affect anyone who looks human—or who *is* human. And come on. Given what's at stake, do you really expect to talk me, let alone the governments of the world, out of doing this based on half-baked conspiracy theories? And you ask *me* where the evidence is."

Xavier studied her for a moment. "Very well. It seems I'm wasting my time here. Let me simply ask that you be diligent in policing any abuses that inevitably crop up during this . . . mutant hunt."

"This will be as aboveboard as we can make it. And Professor—if you have any thoughts about sending your X-Men out to protect mutant rights . . . just make sure they don't impede our efforts to register and test those mutants. Because that would be a federal crime.

"And when we come to your institute's doors, I expect you not to interfere with us testing your students."

"I will not allow my students to be subjected to this if I can help it. I can vouch for them. If any of them were not what they claimed, I would know it."

"Oh, like that time when a cosmic energy force impersonated Jean Grey for several months before going on a rampage of destruction?"

Val imagined that the emotion Xavier was controlling now was embarrassment. "The situations are hardly analogous. I will do what I must to protect my students' rights, Dr. Cooper."

She considered him for a moment, then sighed. "Okay. As a show of good faith, and in appreciation for your assistance before, I won't send in the troops . . . *yet*. Also because I don't want to set off one of those super-powered brawls that your 'students' seem to get into with extraordinary regularity. We'll let our respective lawyers hash this out for now. But your students will have to be checked eventually. Your institute is one of the largest mutant enclaves in the nation. If it comes to that, we'll simply quarantine your estate."

Xavier's sharply angled brows went up. "Well. If you

will excuse me, Dr. Cooper, it seems I need to speak to my attorneys."

"You do that." She let out a breath, softened her tone. "Look, Professor . . . I'd really prefer it if we could be on the same side here. I'd love it if this threat turned out to be a big hoax . . . but my gut tells me it isn't."

Xavier studied her for a moment. "I also wish we could be in agreement on this. Good day, Dr. Cooper." The screen went blank.

"You were too easy on him." Val looked up with a start to see Henry Peter Gyrich standing in her doorway. Despite his size and burly build, the red-haired, craggy-faced National Security agent had managed to creep up on her without making a sound. That was Gyrich for you, Val reflected—always the spook. Or maybe just the creep. "We should send in the troops now, arrest the whole bunch of them. They'll be trouble if they're given free rein."

"They'll be more trouble if we give them an excuse," Val told him.

"They're dangerous."

"Especially if provoked." She got up from her desk and brushed past Gyrich, forcing him to follow her out into the corridor. She didn't particularly need to go anywhere, but she didn't like being in an inferior, seated position around him, especially with him blocking the only exit. And this was as good a time as any to get some coffee. "Besides . . . we can't totally discount the possibility that Xavier's right."

Gyrich looked at her in surprise over the dark

glasses he habitually wore, even indoors. "You don't trust the Diascar?"

"If I trusted anybody, Pete, I wouldn't be in this job. Everybody's got an angle. It's in our best interests to cooperate with the Diascar for now, but it doesn't hurt to have a skeptic on the case. Particularly an outsider whose efforts can't be linked to us. If Xavier and his bunch are wrong, they'll get nowhere, and if they get in our way, it gives us an excuse to contain them. But if they're right, and they can prove it, then we've gained valuable intelligence without having to expend a single asset of our own."

"But do you really think they're right?" he asked as they arrived at the coffee machine.

"No, I don't. I think Xavier's idealism is blinding him. But it never hurts to hedge your bets."

Gyrich grimaced. "Well, I hope it doesn't go down that way. I'm sick of us having to depend on super-powered freaks to do our jobs for us. Let the Diascar take them all away, I say."

Val tried not to glare at him, focusing on adding cream and sugar instead. The two of them were often on the same side when it came to the regulation of mutants and other superhumans. But Val did it because she believed that superhuman powers were dangerous if unregulated but potentially very valuable if directed to serve the interests of the United States. Gyrich, on the other hand, did it because he felt threatened by mutants and hated them as a breed. He'd probably have preferred it if they could be eliminated altogether, and he might not even have minded taking a direct hand in bringing that about. He could be a useful ally at times, but Val considered their alliance a necessary evil.

"Yeah, well, right now the Diascar aren't taking people away, just helping us look. And we should be getting back to coordinating that," she finished, starting back toward her office.

"Hm. It's not gonna be easy, you know. A lot of muties will fight it or hide out. Not just Chlorites, but the usual criminals and lowlifes. They're not just going to come in meekly for testing and tagging."

"Hence the police searches. And the Diascar have their scanners."

"Maybe. But I think we can do better."

Val stopped walking and turned to face him. "What are you thinking, Pete?"

"I'm thinking, Val, that the government has a whole warehouse full of special equipment specifically designed for ferreting out mutants . . . courtesy of Project Wideawake."

Her eyes widened. "Uh-uh. Bad idea, Pete. Those things have a way of getting out of hand."

"We pull our punches on this, and the Chlorite germs could get a lot more out of hand."

"We're not desperate enough for that yet. Let's try the less-disruptive approach first. Like you say, it'll be hard enough to track down all the mutants as it is—it wouldn't help if we scare them underground with such heavy-handed tactics."

Gyrich shrugged. "Maybe. But there's no harm in briefing the Diascar on the available resources. Like you say—it never hurts to hedge your bets."

He gave her a smug grin and went on his merry way. As Val watched his receding back and thought about what he was proposing to unleash, she found herself wondering if maybe Xavier hadn't been too paranoid after all.

8: Exclosure

In the wake of the announcement, things turned out not to be quite as bad as the X-Men had feared. Certainly the Diascar's claims fed into the agenda of everyone who already had it in for mutants. Hate crimes against mutants more than doubled overnight, and the team was kept busy patrolling the streets each night, as Kurt had predicted. While some politicians urged tolerance and fairness, others took the opportunity to push forward legislation to erode mutants' civil rights. The usual political ideologues on radio and television used the Chlorite threat as an excuse to condemn mutants in general as a threat to society, and the usual religious ideologues used it to condemn them as a sin against God.

That was the part Kurt Wagner had the hardest time understanding. He was all too familiar with man's inhumanity to mutant; it had been something he had been faced with from childhood, since, unlike most mutants, he had been born with his inhuman, even downright demonic, appearance. Luckily he had been adopted into a community of Roma—so-called Gypsies, a people who understood what it was to be outcasts and who were able to accept him as he was. But he had needed to hide himself from others, showing himself in public only as a performer in the Jahrmarkt circus, pretending his true face was a mask, his hands, feet, and tail clever prosthetics. Once in Winzeldorf, Germany, when he had been discovered outside that context, he had been hunted down by the villagers as a monster, blamed for a series of brutal murders simply because he was frightening to look at. Only Charles Xavier's intervention had saved him; just as the torch-bearing mob had been about to deliver the deathblow, Xavier had telepathically paralyzed them, like hitting the pause button on a B-grade horror movie. He had taken Kurt with him, recruited him into the X-Men, and, showing an odd sense of irony, had dubbed him the Nightcrawler. In the years since, Kurt had seen far more of the hate humans were capable of, as much toward themselves as toward the others they blamed for their insecurities.

But what he could not get his mind around to this day was how anyone could have the sheer chutzpah to blame God for their own petty hatreds. God was infinite, embracing every being within His creation, understanding every being's soul more deeply than they could ever understand their own, and loving every one as completely and unconditionally as any parent could ever love His children. How ludicrous, then, to think that the petty walls mere mortals built between one another, the excuses they concocted to defend their own narrow views of the world and condemn anyone who fell outside those boundaries, could possibly represent God's will!

But as usual, it seemed to Kurt that God expressed His will more through the actions of ordinary people than through the pronouncements of those who claimed exclusive and infallible access to divine wisdom. After the initial wave of negative reactions, anti-mutant tensions began to ease. It seemed that the majority of citizens were skeptical of the Diascar's claims or at least not convinced enough to be driven to act on them. All they had was the word of a few aliens, and no hard evidence. Unlike the X-Men, they had had no direct contact with the Chlorites and knew them as nothing more than an abstraction. "If you ask me," Kurt heard one typical man on the street say on the nightly news, "it's just a government plot to regulate the mutants. Not that that's such a bad thing, mind you. I been stuck in traffic eight times the last two years 'cause of one bunch of super-guys fightin' another. A little less of that, I can't complain. But the feds just better not try any tricks like that on folks like me." Perhaps not the most enlightened view, Kurt thought, but it was a start.

Kurt had to wonder what the Diascar believed in. Their hatred of Chlorites bordered on the fanatical, but there didn't seem to be a religious motive behind it. They justified their actions not as divine law but as grim necessity. But Kurt felt there had to be something they clung to. Like the Roma who had raised him, they were a dispossessed people. With no shared homeland, they had only a shared heritage and history to define them. Surely that must include a belief in something higher, some eternal principle that gave their existence meaning. And if they didn't use that principle to justify hating the Chlorites, was it possible it could pave the way toward making peace with them? After all, the Chlorites were Gypsies too.

The people's skepticism continued to grow when new Diascar ships began appearing in orbit a few days later, setting up a blockade around the Earth. As anti-mutant protests faded quickly back to their normal levels, anti-Diascar protests began cropping up all over. "How odd," Kurt observed as he watched the news coverage of one such protest outside the UN. "It's not like we have that much interstellar trade to cut off. Basically Reed Richards is the only one affected by an embargo."

"It's the principle of the thing," Kitty told him. "People don't like being hemmed in, even if they don't have any reason to go elsewhere. They may ignore something when they have it, but take it away and they'll squawk."

"Right," Kurt replied. "Like freedom."

"Yeah, there's that."

Jean spoke from the doorway. "The tide may be shifting in our favor. I just got back from a protest—some mutants were staging a sit-in, refusing to let anyone in to test them or ID them. And the police refused to break in, even though the Diascar officer with them was insisting. I think the local officials are going with public opinion—they don't want to force the issue and seem like Diascar stooges."

Kitty frowned. "What do you want to bet the Diascar *do* try to force the issue?"

Indeed, it was not much longer before Kitty's prediction seemed to come true. Two days later, Xavier summoned the X-Men to action. "I'm informed that two Diascar ships have just descended on the town of Alcala, Brazil."

"Alcala?" Jean said. "I've heard of that town. They have an official policy of tolerance toward mutants, don't they?"

Xavier nodded. "Yes, and in the few years since that policy was declared, it's accumulated a significant mutant population. It's a small community, only a few thousand people, but at last count over four percent of those were mutants. They promote themselves as a model of human-mutant coexistence."

"And the Diascar attacked it?" Logan asked, sounding unsurprised.

"It's unclear whether it can be called an attack. But they have encased the entire community in a force field. It appears to be airtight, with only two or three days' worth of oxygen inside, I'd estimate. But the Diascar are claiming that Alcala is infested with Chlorite microbes and must be contained."

Rogue scoffed. "That's a dandy excuse."

"Come on, X-Men." Scott rose from the table. "Let's go check it out."

Soon, the *Blackbird* was headed south on a hypersonic, suborbital trajectory. The X-Men would reach Brazil faster than any conventional jet could get them there. For the moment, according to the news reports they monitored, the Diascar were taking no action against the Alcalanos, aside from confining them within the force field. However, they had razed the surrounding forest with their disintegrator beams, leaving a scalded, smoking wasteland around the force-field dome that now encased the city. The Brazilian government had declared the action an attack on their sovereign territory and launched an aerial assault on the Diascar ships projecting the field; but the Imperial Guardsmen had handily intercepted the missiles and forced the planes into retreat. Inside the dome, the Alcalanos appeared to be in a state of barely contained panic. If that panic erupted, if rioting or fires were to break out, the oxygen inside the dome could run out that much faster. So the X-Men were wasting no time in getting to the scene.

Although there was little to do en route but wait or talk. "Ahh, Brazil," Hank rhapsodized once the coastline came into view. "Fifth-largest country on Earth and one of the most ethnically diverse. They pride themselves on what they call their 'racial democracy,' a society predicated on equality and inclusion. Of course they often fall short of this in practice, but the ideal remains.

"Intriguingly, northern Brazil was once home to Quitombo dos Palmares, an African-style kingdom built in the Amazon rainforest by escaped plantation slaves and indigenous peoples. Founded in 1600, Palmares thrived as a free state for nearly a century, defended from Portuguese attackers by its highly trained capoeira warriors. At its height, it reached a population of thirty thousand. Alas, it finally fell to Portuguese artillery in 1694."

"And now it looks like history might be repeating itself," Kurt said.

"It usually does, my boy."

"Unless we learn from it," Kitty added, earning a nod of appreciation from Hank.

Logan was more skeptical. "Some folks can learn better," he said. "But there's always gonna be somebody else who won't. Freedom's always gonna be somethin' people gotta fight for."

"At this point," Scott cautioned, "we don't know for sure what we'll be fighting for, if anything. None of us likes the idea that the Diascar's actions might be justified . . . but we can't entirely rule out the possibility. We're going there to assess the situation, not to rush into action."

"Why did I know you were gonna say that?" Logan snarled. "What's to assess, Cyke? This is an attack! Lockin' people away in a bubble to suffocate to death in front of everybody! Well, I ain't gonna stand by and let 'em get away with it! This is *our* planet, and it's high time we reminded these scumbags o' that!" His claws shot out to underscore the point.

Scott swiveled his chair around to confront Logan. "Cool it, Wolverine! I'm tired of getting this garbage from you! You keep saying you don't want to be a team leader, but every time I make a decision, you're in my face insisting we do things your way! Make up your mind!"

"Maybe I just don't want *you* to be the leader!"

"Boys!" Jean's commanding voice silenced both of them. "If you haven't sorted out this argument the past five hundred times you've had it, what makes you think this time will be any different? Now stop fighting this instant, or I swear I'm turning this plane around!"

After a moment, the tension broke down into laughter. "Yeah, okay," Logan said. "Who'm I to argue with a lady? Nobody answer that."

"Right," Scott said. "Sorry." He swiveled back to face forward, then glanced over at his wife. "Kind of an empty threat, though."

She threw him a wicked look. "Don't worry. I have plenty of others on reserve."

Soon the *Blackbird* was descending upon the state of Espírito Santo, soaring over its verdant hills as it closed on Alcala. The dwindling pillar of smoke and ash still rising from the burn site served as a beacon for Jean's approach. Soon she saw the smoldering wastes surrounding the force-domed city, a bull's-eye at the base of a once-idyllic valley. *At least it should be easy to find a landing site,* she thought.

But then several small shapes shot toward them from one of the ships hovering over the town, and Jean realized the approach would not be so easy. "Guardsmen!"

Almost immediately, Scott was firing through the *Blackbird*'s amplifying windows, forcing the Guardsmen to scatter and dodge. Rogue was on her way to the hatch. "Kitty, take over!" Jean said, unstrapping herself so she could follow Rogue out into the air.

But suddenly a black-and-white streak smashed through the hull, knocking Kurt backward in his seat, then punched out the other side. Jean played it back in her mind: It had been Smasher, living up to his nickname. He'd struck Kurt with something, then whirled to launch another projectile at Kitty, who had been moving forward. Kitty had reflexively gone intangible at the noise of his entry, and the projectile had passed through her, embedding in the bulkhead. The other Guardsmen were a distraction; Rokk had been the surgical strike, targeting Nightcrawler and Shadowcat specifically. Why?

That could wait. Right now, she had to stop them. Luckily, the *Blackbird* was low enough that the holes in the hull didn't depressurize it, but it was still very windy inside. Jean needed to use her TK to stabilize herself as she headed back to the hatch.

She paused to check on Kurt, who was slumped in his seat. Logan shook him fruitlessly. " 'Crawler! Kurt! Rrhaa, no use! He's breathin', but pulse is weak."

"Get the medical kit. I'll stop them. Hank, take over piloting. Kitty, you need to focus on self-defense." Normally Jean would defer to Scott, but his attention was focused outward at the moment. Anyway, being a telepath, she literally knew for a fact that he would have ordered the same.

Jean headed to follow Rogue out the hatch. Telepathically, she reached out to see through Rogue's eyes. She was already in the thick of it, battling N'rill'iree, who was unwieldy in the air. "You're grounded, Chewbacca!" Rogue cried, locating his flight patch and ripping it loose, taking a sizeable tuft of fur along with it. Luckily for the bear-faced giant, the treetops were not far below and helped break his fall.

But then Manta shot past with her wings spread, giving off a flash that dazzled Rogue, forcing Jean to retreat from her mind to avoid bedazzlement herself. Jean moved to the hatch to assist her fellow flier, but Flashfire was there waiting for her, firing lightning at the hatch and forcing her to duck back inside.

"Everyone, keep an eye out for Astra!" she heard Scott call. "She's the only one who can touch Kitty when she's phased."

"I can't see yet!" Rogue called from outside. Hank kept watch on the radar, while Logan and Kitty peered out the holes in the hull. Lockheed stayed perched on Kitty's chair back, ready to defend her. Jean reached out with her mind but could sense no sign of the phase-shifter. Maybe, like Kitty, she was hard to read when phased.

I've got to get out there, Jean thought, but Flashfire's lightning still blocked the hatch. *Hold on, I'm an idiot!* She ran forward and levitated herself through the hole Smasher had left on his way out. Before he could react to her unexpected emergence, she hit him with a TK blast that knocked him away into the air.

Suddenly the *Blackbird* shuddered and lurched downward past Jean. She spun to see Smasher atop the hull, forcing the plane down. "I have no control!" Beast cried.

"Hold on!" Jean flew down after it and grasped the *Blackbird* with her mind, struggling to control its landing. It smashed through the treetops and came to a stop suspended precariously on several damaged branches.

"Everyone out!" Scott called. Logan was the first to leap to the ground, with Kurt over his shoulder in a fireman's carry. Then Hank leaped free with an arm around Kitty, swinging down from the branches with apelike grace. Lockheed flew just behind, his eyes scanning for enemies. Scott came last, just as the branches were starting to give way. Facing the jet, he jumped clear and fired a burst with his eyebeams. Normally, his mutant nervous system shunted the recoil energy from his force blasts through his body and out into the ground—fortunately, or else his head would have been blown backward off his neck the first time his power manifested. But in midair, with no ground contact, Scott's body was propelled backward, safely out of the way of the crashing *Blackbird*. Still, it was ten feet to the ground, so Jean reached out with her mind to guide him down safely.

The team quickly regrouped on the ground. "I don't like this," Logan said, sniffing the air. "All these plants."

As if on cue, vines and branches snaked out to grab them, and roots tore up out of the ground to snare their feet. "A wise caution, X-Man!" came Blackthorn's voice from somewhere in the woods. "You are in my element now." Lockheed's head darted around, searching for the source of the voice so he could set it on fire again. But Blackthorn was wisely staying out of sight. The dragonet contented himself with blasting the vegetation that struck out at his pet girl and her friends. Meanwhile, Logan was doing his best weed-whacker impression, slicing through every tendril of vegetation that stretched his way. Hank leaped his way around the vines and branches, and Scott blasted them apart.

Stay alert, Jean sent. *In all this distraction, Astra could strike at Kitty from underground.*

"Then maybe we should keep you off the ground," Hank said, hoisting Kitty onto his shoulders.

"Why are they after me?" Kitty asked.

"Perhaps because you, like Kurt, could pass through their force field."

"Quite right!" came Smasher's voice from overhead. An energy bolt shot out from his exo-spex, passing through Kitty, who barely phased in time, falling down through Hank's body in surprise, though she instinctively stopped her fall before she passed through the ground.

Hank stepped out of her, and she resolidified. "I'm okay," she said. "But I'd like that not to happen again, please."

Jean looked up at the Guardsmen swooping down upon them, wondering how that could be arranged.

Smasher dodged a retaliatory burst from Cyclops, but a now-recovered Rogue shot out of the sky and struck him a powerful blow, driving him nearly to the ground, well away from the battle. He sometimes forgot how powerful the mutated human could be. But he simply opened himself to the quantum fields of the universe and drew forth more energy to augment his own strength further. There was no amount of force any foe could muster that Vril Rokk the Smasher could not exceed. That was his value to the eternal Shi'ar Empire.

The brown-and-white-maned woman pressed her attack despite his refusal to budge any further, and he struck her with the swipe of an arm, flinging her away at great speed. He used some of the reciprocal momentum to move himself back toward the fight, absorbing the rest into his body as potential energy. He returned to see the conscious X-Men huddled around Shadowcat, guarding her from the vegetation Blackthorn was sending against them. Cyclops was blasting the surrounding trees, his kinetic beam narrowed enough to function as a blade rather than a bludgeon, striking the trees at the base and felling them, depriving Blackthorn of weapons. Smasher reached up to his exo-spex, planning to give Cyclops what the humans would call "a taste of his own medicine."

But there was that persistent Rogue woman coming at him again. She punched his kinetic beam aside, then kicked him in the gut. It did not injure him, of course, but sheer action and reaction guaranteed that he fly back a fair distance before he could halt himself. This time she did not follow, did not make the mistake of close-quarter fighting with the Smasher again, instead flying in a holding pattern above her comrades, preventing Smasher, Manta, or any of the others from getting a clear shot. Cyclops's beams had created a clearing around the group, and he now directed them to add to the aerial defense, as did Jean Grey with her telekinesis.

He led the others in a bombardment action, confident that a continued barrage would wear the X-Men down enough to allow him or one of the others to neutralize Shadowcat with the coma-inducing drug. Or, failing that, through more permanent means. That was not an option he found desirable, for he respected the X-Men as occasional allies. Shadowcat herself, in her first encounter with the Shi'ar and their Guard, had proven instrumental in saving his empress from an assassination plot. But if he had to end her life to prolong that of their world, their galaxy, he would do no less, for that was the duty his empress had bestowed on him.

Suddenly Magique flew toward him, a thoughtful look in her white, intricately tattooed eyes. "Wait," she said. "Why does Grey remain grounded? And why does she move so slowly? I sense a trick!"

Rokk realized she was right—Grey was not using her full range of abilities. She would never hold back in the defense of a comrade. And he could not recall her being injured. Curious, he adjusted his exo-spex to tomographic scan to assess Grey's health status for himself. To his surprise, he got a double image, as though . . . *as though a second body were contained inside hers!* And when he turned the scan on the Shadowcat, who appeared to stand within the circle, he got no reading at all. She was an illusion, no doubt projected by Grey's telepathy. Smasher realized the girl had been out of his sight for some moments. And she had found a truly ingenious place to hide. "Shadowcat is inside Grey!" he cried. "Target her!"

• • •

Ninety seconds earlier . . .

Cyclops returned fire at Smasher, and Rogue came out of nowhere and piled into him. *Keep him busy,* Jean told the others, sending instructions to the team for the plan that had just sprung into her head. The men surrounded Kitty, blocking her from view, while Jean levitated over to her. *You ready for this?* Jean sent to her.

I hope so. This'll be weird.

More so for me, I bet. Jean braced herself. Kitty phased and stepped inside Jean's body. Kitty was a bit shorter and slimmer than Jean and so was able to nest almost perfectly inside of her, as if they were a pair of Russian *matryoshka* dolls. It was a tight fit, and Jean would have to move slowly to let Kitty match her movements. But the others needed to be free to move quickly to use their powers. Besides, Logan was too short, Hank too oddly proportioned, and Scott too tall—and there was no way Jean was letting another woman get that intimate with her husband. For a second she'd considered letting Kitty hide inside Kurt's body where it lay on the ground, protected by the others. But she didn't know for sure how the Guardsmen's drug worked. At times, Kitty had been affected by diseases or contaminants within people or objects that she phased through, and Jean didn't want to take any chances.

Jean moved away slowly and sent out a telepathic illusion of Kitty still standing where she had been. She knew the Guardsmen were shielded against mental intrusion, but hopefully that wouldn't extend to a simple sensory signal.

How long can Kitty keep this up? Jean wondered.

A few minutes, maybe, came the response, *if you breathe deeply.* With their lungs occupying pretty much the same space, Jean realized, they could share breath.

I can read you so clearly!

Well, our brains are overlapping, what do you expect?

Ooh, let's stop thinking about this. It's making me nauseous. Jean also tried not to think about what would happen to both of them if Kitty lost concentration and resolidified inside her.

At least it'll make it easier for me to match your movements. Jean realized, or overheard Kitty realizing, that the younger woman's dance training would be an aid there as well.

Jean and the others continued to shield the illusory Kitty from the attacking vegetation. Scott blasted several nearby trees away at the base, killing them and leaving Blackthorn unable to control them. Soon they were in the middle of a small clearing of their own creation. Rogue continued to shield them from the air while Scott shifted his blasts skyward. Jean added her TK to the aerial defense.

"Wait," came Magique's voice from overhead. "Why does Grey remain grounded? And why does she move so slowly? I sense a trick!"

Jean should have known—illusionists always knew how to recognize illusions. Smasher adjusted his exospex. "Shadowcat is inside Grey! Target her!"

Well, it was a good try, came Kitty's thought.

Stay where you are. I can shield us.

But then Astra erupted out of the ground in front of Jean and tackled her—or rather, tackled *through* her, knocking Kitty out behind her. Already weakened by the effort of staying phased, Kitty solidified as she fell to the ground. Suddenly Blackthorn's arm shot out of the dirt and impaled Kitty with one of his namesake thorns. Jean felt Kitty's mind sink into unconsciousness.

"Objective accomplished," Smasher called. "Disengage!" The Guardsmen promptly halted their attack and went into retreat. Smasher lingered behind. "Do not worry, X-Men. Your colleagues will be unconscious for two to three days at most. In the interim, the rest of you may try all you like to bring down the force dome; learn for yourself how futile it is. And by the time your friends awaken," he said grimly, "you will have learned better than to try."

The X-Men raced toward Alcala by various means: Cyclops and Wolverine on foot, Jean, Lockheed, and Rogue in the air (the latter carrying the unconscious Nightcrawler and Shadowcat), and Beast via brachiation through the treetops. Even as they went, though, Hank found himself unsure of what they should do once they got there. The Diascar's data were compelling, and the Guardsmen were usually straight shooters; he had a hard time believing this could be a trick. But what was the alternative? To allow a whole town, particularly such a model of human-mutant coexistence, to slowly suffocate to death, or worse?

By the time they reached the force dome, Logan and Rogue were past caring about the ambiguities of the situation. Hank called to them to take care; the field's blue shimmer and the convection currents rising around it suggested it was generating considerable heat. But, impetuous as ever, they had to learn this the hard way, and they did so soon enough. Fortunately Rogue was unharmed by its heat and Wolverine only touched it with his claws. But among the Alcalanos who congregated on the other side of the barrier, pleading for help, Hank could see burns on several sets of hands.

Rogue and Logan kept pounding at the barrier, while Lockheed unleashed his own considerable heat against it higher up. The only effect was that Rogue's gloves caught fire and she had to shed them.

Meanwhile, the Brazilian air force was directing its energies against the pair of ships generating the field, hovering just outside it at its apex. But the ships themselves were heavily shielded, and nothing got through.

Before long, Scott's own caution gave way, and he added his efforts to the attack. Hank couldn't blame him; the cries of the Alcalanos were difficult to endure, and even if the threat of Chlorite contamination was real, it was hard to accept that this was the only way to deal with it. But even Cyclops's mighty gaze did not make the force dome blink. He even tried lowering his aim, digging a trench in the ground to see if he could burrow under the field, but it extended down as far as he could reach. Hank himself tried to destabilize the field using equipment he'd salvaged from the *Blackbird,* but to no effect.

By the time night fell, even Logan had given up trying. He had persisted long enough that the field, along with the sheer kinetic energy of his blows, had heated his claws to incandescence—though fortunately for him, the melting point of adamantium had yet to be discovered empirically. The X-Men made camp for the night in a tent provided by the Brazilian military, whose members had expressed appreciation for their assistance.

The next day, the dying began.

Hank's instruments confirmed that the levels of free molecular chlorine in the atmosphere within the dome were rising with alarming speed. They only confirmed what was evident, for the Alcalanos were beginning to choke. The most vulnerable citizens were already succumbing: the elderly, the ill . . . and the extremely young. Mothers wailed, cradling motionless, tiny bodies in their arms. Most of their fellow townsfolk were too preoccupied with their own problems, striving to obtain breathing masks from the local hospital or create makeshift ones from bandanas.

One fish-scaled mutant woman, who presumably needed to immerse herself periodically to preserve her skin, was seen diving into the town pond for her morning constitutional, and perhaps to seek an escape from the choking air. Within moments, she was screaming as the increasingly acidic water seared her skin and eyes. She pulled herself to shore but soon collapsed in the grasses near the pond. Observers outside tried to call to the panicked townsfolk to alert them to the medical crisis, but it was lost in the general chaos.

"It's gotta be a trick," Rogue cried at one point. "Them horse-faces, they're pumpin' chlorine in!"

"No," Hank told her, shaking his head gravely. "My gas chromatograph readings show it's coming from all over. From the ground, from the water, from the trees . . . even from the people. The data are consistent with the spread of a chlorogenic microbe of considerable virulence." He took in the other X-Men with his gaze. "We cannot deny it any longer, my friends. The Diascar have been entirely truthful with us."

Poratine strode across the blasted expanse around the dome, gazing at the begging, choking, screaming humans within. It was almost more than she could bear. She had faced worse before, but these people were so new to it, so innocent. And it grieved her that she could not do more. She would have preferred to remain up in her command ship, to learn of this through her crew's reports, a distant set of statistics. But she owed it to these people to witness their deaths.

Even so, it overwhelmed her for a moment, and she had to look away. Her eyes surveyed the idyllic valley, the lushly forested hills with their oddly green tint. It was not as beautiful or useful as the rolling plains of Diasca had been, not the wide, flat expanse her legs instinctively yearned to run on after so much time cooped up in a ship. But the Diascar had always appreciated the beauty of other terrains, had always been sure to preserve enclaves of nature. Somehow, even though these humans took up less space in their compact, sky-reaching cities, not needing the vast tracts of land the Diascar had required for grazing and moving, it seemed harder for them to leave parts of nature untouched.

Vril Rokk flew down from above, breaking her reverie. "Hail, Fleet Leader," he called as he landed beside her. She nodded acknowledgment to her ally. "The local military is making another air strike on the quarantine ships. Should we intercept them?"

"No," Poratine said. "If they still have not learned the futility of it, let them have another lesson." The quarantine ships had been designed specifically to create impenetrable barriers. Nearly all their power went into shield generation rather than speed or weaponry or life support. Their crews were minimal, and they had needed to be towed here through hyperspace by faster ships. And with two of them, redundancy was assured.

Rokk nodded, but his grimace showed he was far from satisfied with this inaction. She followed his gaze back to the dome, to the desperate people inside. "It seems so cruel, to let them suffer so," Rokk told her. "Forgive me, but were it up to me, I would flash-vaporize them all and make a merciful end to it."

"As would I, gladly," she replied. "But the humans need to be convinced of the horror they face. They need to see it, clearly, graphically, before they will truly believe."

He turned to face her, his eyes unreadable behind their red coverings. "So we condemn them to this as an object lesson?"

Poratine kept her own eyes on the humans. "At least it gives their deaths some meaning."

"Does it?" came a new voice. She turned her head to see Cyclops approaching, the other X-Men (save the two who were still comatose) behind him. Rokk took a step forward, but no more; he and Poratine could both see that the mutants were no longer intent on fighting them. They were still angry, however. "Isn't there any way you can help them?" the visored mutant demanded. "Decontaminate them, like you did us?"

"Impossible. Trying to reach them would unleash the microbes into your environment."

"If Nightcrawler were conscious," the orange-haired female, Jean Grey, said, "he could teleport them into your quarantine chambers."

Poratine shook her head, adopting the human gesture of negation for their benefit. "The microbes have penetrated their systems now. Their lungs, their digestive tracts, probably even their blood. We could not be sure of getting them all. And you see how virulently they spread. We cannot take a chance on even a few escaping."

"Besides," Rokk added, "Nightcrawler could only teleport one or two at a time. There are thousands."

"In all your centuries of battling them," said the blue-furred doctor, McCoy, "you have found no way to kill the infection?"

"The microbes thrive on things that would kill their hosts," Poratine answered. "Yet they also thrive on that which sustains their hosts. It is difficult to kill them without killing those they inhabit. And with a newly mutated strain like this, we would have to begin the search for treatments afresh. It could take weeks, which these people do not have. And again, we dare not risk letting the microbes loose into your environment."

"There is another factor," Rokk told them. "If this outbreak began here, it means at least one Chlorite infiltrator lived here, hidden among the mutant population. If we are fortunate, we've been able to contain that infiltrator before he or she could escape."

"That is the one advantage to this," Poratine said. "It is cruel, I know. But at least when this is over, we will know who the Chlorite is. Microbes aside, it will be the only entity left alive inside that dome."

9: Exequies

When Nightcrawler and Shadowcat finally came out of their comas the next morning, they were still eager to try to help the Alcalanos. Logan had to watch his friends go through the denial, anger, and acceptance twice—first Kurt, then Kitty. The kid woke up last, since she was lighter and the dose had hit her harder. She also had the toughest time accepting it. She'd woken up raring to do some good and couldn't understand the looks of surrender on her comrades' faces. Even when they took her out to see the dome, where even the air was taking on a yellow-green haze, where corpses littered the ground and the only survivors were huddling on the top floors where the heavy chlorine gas was thinner, Kitty was still driven to do something. It was her way; even when she'd just been a skinny, thirteen-year-old computer geek, she'd still shown herself to have as much courage, resourcefulness, and determination as any warrior Logan had ever fought alongside, right up to ol' Captain America himself. She never gave up, and she always found some way to get things done. Almost always.

But this time, there was nothing to do. The only reason she couldn't accept it yet was that she hadn't been awake through the long, painful process. "We have to do something!" she insisted as Logan held her back, urging her not to try phasing through the field. "We can't just condemn them to that . . . that gas chamber!"

"Kid, there's nothin' more we can do. We tried it all. Hell, Stretch Richards himself flew in with the rest o' the FF. He an' Hank were up all night tryin' to work up an answer, and they got nothin'." Kitty's eyes widened. If Reed Richards and Hank McCoy together couldn't find an answer, nobody could. "We got no way to cure that bug and we can't risk lettin' it get out. Only thing left to do is put 'em outta their misery— and the Diascar won't even let us do that. They say we need this pain to convince us the danger's real." He shook his head. "I dunno—maybe they're even right."

She gaped at him. "How can you say that?"

Kitty quailed at the look he gave her in return. "You talk about gas chambers. To you they're somethin' outta history. I was there. I smelled 'em."

She just looked into his eyes for a moment more, slowly coming to understand, to accept. To mourn. He hated to see that in her eyes. He would've rather had her stay mad at him, though there was hardly anybody on the planet he'd want mad at him less.

This was another one of those relationships he never would've imagined himself getting into. How had this sweet, brilliant, good-hearted kid ended up looking to a piece of work like him as a mentor? Maybe the worst thing about choosing this hero life, choosing to fight to protect the weak, was that kids like her needed mentors like him, needed to learn to be tough and ruthless when they had to, so that others wouldn't have to.

"*No!!*" The cry came from inside the dome, in a voice roughened by heavy coughing. It went on in Portuguese, which he understood thanks to Jeannie's psychic language class. "*I can't take any more! I have to get out!*" Logan recognized the voice. The big, brown-skinned Alcalano—one of those hard-to-pin-down ethnic mixes that were common in Brazil—had been seen a couple of times trying to reach out and touch the force field, pulling away when it had burned his hands. Beast's gizmos had picked up a tiny power drain when the guy had done it. He had to be one of the local mutants. Maybe the guy had thought he could drain the field if he touched it, but he hadn't been able to touch it for more than a second, and he'd finally retreated in tears.

But now he seemed to have snapped. He'd found a hospital mask somewhere and had come out of whatever upper floor he'd been hiding in, and now he was charging toward the barrier, ranting about how he had to get out. Somehow, Logan had a feeling that this time he wouldn't pull away.

The mutant slammed himself bodily into the force field. The field sizzled, and the guy screamed in pain. But he was hysterical, beyond caring about the agony, and he kept on pushing himself against the burning energy field. *Why do I always gotta be right about everything bad?*

"Oh, no," Beast muttered. "The field intensity readings are dropping alarmingly around his body! He's actually draining the field!"

"How fast?" Cyclops asked.

"Hard to say. It seems to be accelerating!" Now the guy was slumped on the ground, barely conscious, but his weight was pushing against the field. It seemed to be surging through him, into him, like he was becoming part of it. The skin of his hands was blackening now. Only the airtight field kept Logan from smelling it.

He strode forward, pulling Kitty along with him. "You gotta get me in there, kid. He's gotta be stopped. You strong enough yet to phase two people?"

"What? Are you crazy, Logan?"

"Stupid question, kiddo. No time to argue. Can you do it?"

"I think so."

"Don't think, do. You phase me into the ground, take me across. I climb up, you come back. Don't let any part o' you come up into the air!"

"Or even within inches of it!" Beast called. "Microbes can live in the soil!"

"But as soon as I stop touching you, you go solid!"

"Then I'll hafta jump fast."

"Can you even survive in there?"

"We'll find out. In the ground now, Pryde!"

She hated it (and he hated risking her along with himself), but she was a pro. Without arguing further, she took him by the arm and did whatever it was she did, and the ground rose up around him. She took several slow, deep breaths as they descended, and he followed her lead, taking and holding one last breath before the ground engulfed them.

It was strange. Dense soil and rock were passing through him, but he could hardly feel them. All he felt clearly was her hands guiding him. He couldn't see or smell. He could hear some things—sound traveled better through solids—but they were strangely altered, muffled. He had no idea where they were going, didn't know how Kitty did it. She seemed to have a preternatural sense of her location relative to the world around her. She never got lost.

A hand pressed on his chest, stopping him. They were through. But he had nothing to push off of, except her. Understanding that, she took his hands and let him feel as she made a cradle of hers. He could feel them tremble ever so slightly with fear for his safety. He found her cheek and caressed it once before climbing onto her shoulders and launching himself skyward. He just hoped the force of it wouldn't knock her deeper into the ground.

He shot up into the air but was yanked short, agony tearing through his left foot. It had materialized partway into the ground, merging with its molecules. He tore his foot free; it was a swollen, twisted club, made heavier by the dirt that was now part of it, and burning hot thanks to the friction or repulsion or whatever it was that happened when two sets of molecules argued over who was there first.

But he couldn't worry about that now. The drainer guy was still leaning against the field. "Hurry, Logan!" Beast called. "One field layer has already collapsed!

The other is weakening faster! The energy his body absorbs seems to be strengthening the effect!"

Logan was already limping forward as fast as he could, barely listening. Out of the corner of his eye, he saw Kitty climb out safely from the ground and collapse, panting hard. *Good. At least she's okay.*

He reached the mutant, who was now unconscious and horribly burned. The energy he was drawing in was probably the only thing keeping him alive. But Wolverine still had to stop it.

He reached for the man's legs and was shocked by an energy discharge. Growling, he reached out again and grabbed them, ignoring the charge that coursed through his body. With a roar, he pulled the big mutant away from the field and released his grip, rolling away.

But the field distorted to follow the guy. It was joined with him now, and his body wasn't letting go. Even being unconscious wouldn't stop it. "The drain hasn't diminished!" Hank called.

Logan embraced the pain again, dragging the mutant farther away. The field continued to stretch. "Logan, stop! It's weakening further as it distorts!"

Logan let the man go and looked down at his body, which convulsed as the energy poured into it. "Cyke . . . there's only one way to stop it."

Summers might've been too careful, too deliberate most of the time, but when things were hitting the fan, he could make the tough calls. He paused for only a couple of seconds before saying, "Do what you have to do."

It's what I do best, Logan thought as he clenched his fists, making the claws tear out through his skin. *Sucks to be me.*

The man had done nothing wrong. He was just a guy trying to live a normal life. A scared man trying to live. He hadn't meant to hurt anybody. That wasn't the kind of guy Logan usually killed. Not the kind who'd earned it.

But Logan killed him anyway.

And all the energy stored in the guy's body blew up in Logan's face.

Kurt watched in fascination as Wolverine's body healed itself. The blast of energy had blown him dozens of feet through the air and left a smoking crater (although the remaining layer of the force dome had stabilized again). Anyone else would have been killed instantly, and at first Logan had looked as good as dead when his body had landed atop the hood of an old pickup truck, smashing in its windshield. His entire front had been covered in third- and fourth-degree burns. But Logan needed only seconds to heal wounds that others would take weeks to recover from, and minutes to heal injuries that would get anyone else pronounced dead on arrival.

It was fascinating to watch as his burned skin fell away, as new skin and hair grew in to replace it under the tattered remains of his uniform, as his ruined foot rejected the foreign material and regained its former shape and strucure. In its own disgusting way, it was an inspiring sight. Logan thought of himself as an agent of death, but he carried within him such endless power to heal. Imagine if that power could be directed outward! Maybe it could, Kurt often thought, if he could first turn it toward healing his own soul. But he kept such thoughts private. He would be a poor friend if he did not allow Logan the freedom to choose that path for himself . . . or not. Faith was meaningless if it did not come from within, for one's own reasons.

Right now, it was Kitty who needed his support. She felt terrible about being the one who'd gotten him into this. "What if he can't breathe?" she asked as he placed an arm around her shoulders. "And those microbes, they must be inside him now, in his wounds . . . do we even know if his immune system can kill them?"

"There, there, Katschen, don't worry. You know as well as I, old Logan is too stubborn to die." He leaned in and whispered in her ear. "Frankly, I think God doesn't want him smelling up Heaven with those awful cigars of his."

Kitty laughed despite herself. "Logan probably wouldn't agree with you about where he'd end up. But I do." She rested her head on his shoulder. Kurt smiled to himself. When they had first met, Kitty had been frightened by his demonic appearance, which had saddened him deeply. But soon enough she'd come to trust him, to warm to him, and he'd been her "fuzzy-elf" ever since. Well, not so much these days; she was more mature and serious now. But there was still some of that playful *katschen* within her, that core of innocence that gave her strength.

Soon enough, Logan's eyes snapped open . . . but

almost immediately he began to choke. The air was too thick with chlorine; his body could heal the damage, but as long as he remained within the dome, the damage would not stop being inflicted. It was lucky he had even awakened at all; had he not been atop the pickup, above the densest concentration of chlorine, there might not have been enough oxygen to revive him.

"Looks like . . . the dome's back to normal," Logan called between coughs as he clambered down off the hood.

"That's right," Jean told him, her voice rough. "You did it."

"Don't . . . congratulate me yet. There's still work to do. There's a piece o' Chlorite scum in here somewhere, the one that killed this town. I gotta find him and return the favor."

"I sympathize, Logan," Scott said, "but he could have intelligence we need."

"Ohh, don't worry," Logan said with a purring growl. "I'll make sure he tells it all first." Kurt winced at his enthusiasm. But he forgave, as he always did. Right now he could certainly understand Logan's rage. He would not act on it the same way, but he shared it.

But Logan faltered in his stride, choking harder. His movements were stirring up the low-lying chlorine, sending more of it up to his head level and into his lungs. He tried to go on, but it was a struggle. "There's got to be something we can do!" Kitty cried.

An inspiration struck Kurt. "Maybe there is, Katschen. Hold on."

He looked around, orienting himself and locating the nearby army camp. As he recalled, they had brought biohazard suits with them, though they had had no chance to use them. Concentrating on that location, he decided to be there. For an instant, he was in some other place, a void of brimstone clouds. Then his ears popped with the pressure change as the air was shoved aside, dulling the sound of the small thunderclap that resulted, and he was where he had chosen to be, a few wisps of sulfur dissipating around him.

The soldiers were startled by his sudden arrival, but they knew him by now as an ally and quickly lowered their weapons. He jogged over to one he recognized— Captain Wachtel, one of the many German immigrants who lived in Espírito Santo. Kurt had a decent grasp of Portuguese now, thanks to Jean, but he was happier to speak in his native language.

A few moments later, the soldiers were helping him into a biohazard suit with its own oxygen tank. He wrapped his tail around his midriff to keep it out of the way. Once he was sealed in, they handed him a second suit and tank. *"Danke,"* he said and decided to be inside the dome. An ear-popping second later, he was at Wolverine's side.

"Here, *mein freund,"* he said, helping Logan to his feet and proffering the containment suit. "Your old clothes are looking a bit threadbare, *ja?"*

"Stylish," Logan said, "but it ain't my size." He coughed some more.

"I hear baggy is making a comeback. Here, let's get you fitted."

A minute later, Logan was suited up and breathing normally again. "Thanks, elf. I owe ya."

"Ah-ah, I already owe you one for disturbing your deer hunt the other day. We're even now."

"Hunh. Good." Logan looked up at him. "I figure you don't wanna stay and help me with this hunt."

"No," Kurt replied softly. "I suppose not."

"But how you gonna get outta here? Your suit's contaminated now."

"Ahh, ye of little faith. I'll be fine. But . . . there is something I need to do first," he said, gazing up at the old colonial church that stood in the center of town, rising above the colorful roofs of the houses.

Logan fidgeted, as uncomfortable with Kurt's objective as Kurt was with Logan's. "Well, okay then. I'll get huntin'."

Kurt frowned at his mask. "Can you smell through that?"

"Other ways to hunt than smellin'. And I can take a quick whiff if I need to. Can't hurt me any worse."

"All right, then." It was hard to say, but he said it anyway. "Good luck."

"Right. You too." And Logan was off and running.

Kurt made his way more slowly to the church, stopping over each body to say a quick prayer for the departed. He wished he were qualified to give them last rites, but he did what he could. A few feeble voices cried to him from upstairs windows, begging for help in several languages. It pained him that he could do nothing for them.

Well, almost nothing. Finally he made his way into

the church. He knelt before the altar and prayed to God for all these people's souls. He wept for them freely under his Lord's understanding gaze.

And then he teleported out from inside the suit, leaving it behind. Nothing of Alcala came out with him.

Nothing physical.

As hunts went, this wasn't the hardest. Wolverine was looking for a live, healthy person, and there was at most one other of those in this town besides him. From what the Diascar said, Chlorites weren't that common, and the moles would want to spread out as far as possible. No way a two-bit town like this rated more than one.

But a live person could play dead. So Logan made sure to check every body in town. That meant a door-to-door search, breaking into each house or store or office one by one and checking everyone inside, making sure they were really dead. Sometimes he came across ones who were still alive, feebly begging him for help or mercy. He gave them both, the only way he could . . . once he'd sniffed them to make sure they were really human, really dying. The Chlorite mole would get no mercy from him.

It was a grisly task, and Logan was glad that none of the other X-Men had to do it. This was nothing new to him, but the others deserved better than to face this.

Eventually, he made his way through every building in Alcala. "Nobody left movin' in here but me," Logan reported over the suit radio. "You sure he didn't get away?"

Taforne's voice responded. By now the Diascar had learned what he was doing and had come to observe. "There has been no evidence of other chlorine production in the area. Had he left here with viable microbes in his system, they would have contaminated the regions he passed through. The infiltrator must still be inside."

"Then he's holed up somewhere. Got himself a hidey-hole. I'll make another sweep, check out the basements for hidden rooms."

"Not the basements," Beast suggested. "Remember, though they tolerate chlorine, they still breathe oxygen. Even on their own worlds, they'd have to avoid low-lying areas where the chlorine settled and drove out other gases."

"Right," came Cyclops's voice. "Maybe he's holed up in a loft, or that bell tower."

Logan shook his head. "Nope. This guy knows the drill. Let's face it, there's no way the Diascar are gonna take any chances with this place. You're gonna burn it to the ground, ain'tcha, Taforne?"

There was a pause. "That's correct."

"Then if our mole wants to survive it, he's burrowed underground. Maybe got a pipe stickin' up to get fresh air—if it were me, I'd set up a periscope too. I'm checkin' the outsides o' houses for pipes that don't fit."

That made it quicker than another door-to-door. Having an idea what to look for made it easier too. It was less than ten minutes before he spotted a narrow, extra pipe tucked behind one house's drainpipe, extending into the ground. "Found it. I'm goin' in."

"Be careful!"

Logan rolled his eyes. "Sure, Cyke. Might as well start now."

The house had been empty when he'd searched before; he hadn't bothered checking the walls. Once in the cellar, he didn't need long to spot the seam, to see the curved scratches left in the floor by the bottom of the hidden door. He popped out a claw, not caring as it tore through the suit glove, and wedged it into the crack. He yanked the door open, and the rest of his claws came out.

The mole was ready for him, cutting loose with an old Colt revolver. The slugs punched into his chest, a sensation so familiar that it was almost comfortable. It slowed him down. It didn't stop him.

The mole went flying across the room, not under his own power. The Colt fell in three pieces on the floor. The mole fell better, catching himself, coming up in a fighting stance. He was medium-sized but wiry, agile. Gray skin, slit nostrils, yeah, yeah, not human, got that. Slim, backswept tendrils instead of hair—looked like live parts of him, might hurt him if they got cut off or yanked out. He'd try both.

"You are the clawed one," he said in Portuguese. "How are you still alive?"

"Bub, I asked myself that question more times'n I can count. But right now you should be askin'—why are *you* still alive? And how long before you stop wantin' to be?" He lunged. The alien dodged, struck back, but Logan took it and gave better. It was short and unmemorable, and soon he had the guy by the short . . .

tentacles, yanking them tight, with his claws against the mole's throat. From the way he gasped in pain, Logan figured he hadn't been far off about the tentacles. "Tell me what you know and I'll make it quick."

The gray guy scoffed. "You think I fear torture? Or death? My peoples have learned much of suffering, thanks to your kind. We can bear as much as you can inflict. And death?" He laughed. "You may kill me, you may kill all of us you meet, but my kind will triumph in the end. It is as inevitable as evolution! Wait long enough, and Chlorite life will emerge on every world through sheer chance. Or it will come there on a comet or asteroid. Fight it all you want, and maybe you can delay it for a few millennia. But probability alone will defeat you in time. In a billion years, maybe less, *all* life will be Chlorite life! We are the inevitable future of the universe! You are relics, throwbacks doomed to extinction." He sneered. "If we act to hasten the process, to transform your worlds faster, it is only to—'make it quick.' In the end, we will have shown you more mercy than you have shown us."

"You better beg that's not true, bub! Tell me how many o' you are on Earth! Tell me where they are! Then I'll show you mercy," Logan lied.

"You think I would know?" the alien said defiantly. "We are in cells. Small, hidden, untraceable. Take out one and the others still thrive. You cannot stop us! Nothing will ever stop us!" He laughed.

But his laughter faltered at the sound of Logan's own quiet laughter in his ear. "Okay, then. Maybe I'll just have my fun with you."

• • •

"That is enough," Taforne reported from the ground. *"He will tell us nothing. And there is no one left alive now. I think the humans have learned their lesson."*

"Indeed they have," Poratine told him. "Thanks to the news coverage of this event, public opinion has rapidly shifted in our favor. Earth's governments are proving far more cooperative." Until now, the more democratic nations had resisted the all-out search tactics that Poratine had urged them to adopt—even the one that had come from one of their own advisors, that intriguing proposal from Agent Gyrich. But already that resistance was evaporating. Perhaps, with their cooperation and the help of Gyrich's resources, this planet could still be saved.

Not that Poratine was happy with the cost. She closed her eyes briefly before continuing. "Tell the X-Men we are grateful for Wolverine's efforts and his sacrifice. But it is time to give him a peaceful end."

"Are you sure?" Taforne asked. *"His healing powers are extraordinary."*

"The strain is too virulent. We cannot let our guard down out of sympathy, my friend."

"Yes. I understand."

Poratine opened a channel to the quarantine ships. "Begin sterilization."

"Logan! Get out!" Beast called. *"The force dome has grown even hotter and is contracting inward! It is vaporizing everything in its path!"*

The alien laughed. "You see? Your death is inevitable anyway. Even your own people are making it come sooner." A roaring sound was becoming audible, growing louder, closer. "I am ready to die, for I know my kind will live on forever. Are you?"

"I'm always ready to die, bub. But I ain't stupid enough to stand still for it!" Logan tossed the alien aside. He'd wanted to do it himself, but slitting his throat now would be too merciful. Instead, he dove into the mole's hidey-hole and pulled the door shut behind him. The mole had reinforced the walls; he must've thought this place was strong enough to keep him alive. Maybe he wasn't as ready to die as he claimed.

The screams that came from outside, screams of terror rather than agony, proved Logan right. The agony came a few moments later; then the screams stopped, faster than Logan would've liked.

Then it started to get incredibly hot. The reinforced walls glowed and began melting. The plastic of the bio-hazard suit started melting too. *Blast,* Logan thought before the heat seared his consciousness away. *Not twice in one day.*

Taforne's condolences for Wolverine's demise brought Cyclops no comfort, except in his belief that the Dias-car was probably premature. Reports of Wolverine's death had been false numerous times before, though often not particularly exaggerated. If there was anything that crazy Canuck couldn't regenerate from, Scott had yet to witness its like.

This one had to come close, though. The force

field had flash-vaporized everything it had touched and had left only a flat expanse of ash and the occasional pool of molten metal in its wake. And as if that hadn't been enough, the Diascar had followed behind it with another volley of their disintegrator rays to make sure.

The only consolation was that Jean had gotten a mental impression of Logan diving into the mole's underground hiding place before she'd lost contact. The mole must have believed it would protect him, although judging from that last flash of pain Jean had felt, it probably would not have. But Wolverine was made of sterner stuff.

Once the ground had cooled enough for Jean to levitate over it without being barbecued by the heat, she did an aerial survey, scanning for signs of him with her eyes and mind. Before long she called, "I found him!" She telekinetically tore a half-melted slab of metal free of the ground, laying bare the bolthole beneath it. "He's unconscious and badly burned, but he's healing!"

Beside Scott, Taforne was astounded. "How is this possible? Nothing could have survived that!"

"Wolverine gets that a lot," Scott said. Although to be honest, there might be nothing left but a red-hot adamantium skeleton, had it not been for that bolthole.

"Do not touch him, Ms. Grey!" Taforne called and reached for his comlink.

Scott grabbed his arm. "You can't think he's still infected?"

"Standard policy. We cannot take the chance."

"Think about it, Taforne! If his healing power could cope with *that*"—Scott gestured out at the charred wasteland—"don't you think it could handle the Chlorite microbes? What's more, don't you *owe* it to him to give him the chance, after all he's done for you in the past two hours?"

The defense leader studied him for a moment. "You are right. We do."

Instead of another air strike, Taforne ordered a quarantine module sent down, making the same argument to Poratine that Scott had made to him. Over the next couple of hours, Wolverine was put through thorough decontamination and remote medical examination. To the Diascar doctors' amazement, he was completely free of Chlorite microbes. "Perhaps this could be the answer to your problems," Beast suggested to them. "Is there any way Wolverine's immune cells could be adapted to fight Chlorite microbes?"

The chief medical officer, a mahogany-furred female named Bayrane, shook her head. "Naturally we considered that right away. But it could never work. Your friend's immune cells are so aggressive toward any foreign tissues that if we altered them to work outside his body, they could be as great a danger to your world as the Chlorites."

Even so, the Diascar were still impressed by Wolverine's feat. They seemed to see it as a ray of hope in a bleak situation. This time, it was far easier to convince the Diascar to let Wolverine out of quarantine, and not just for medical reasons. It seemed that a new bond of trust had been formed from the tragedy. Many of the

Diascar's tactics still seemed extreme to Scott, but after what he'd witnessed, he could understand the need for them. Like Wolverine—like Scott himself, sometimes— the Diascar did what they had to do for the greater good, even when it wasn't pretty.

The Diascar gave the X-Men a ride back to New York, picking up the *Blackbird* along the way. The next day, though, they received an invitation to come to Washington to meet with Poratine and Val Cooper. With the *Blackbird* under repairs, Cooper sent a military jet to fly them to the airbase where the meeting was to occur. Even so, it was evening by the time they got there.

Once they arrived, Cooper and Poratine met them and led them away from the jet. "Now that we all know we're on the same side," Cooper told them, "I hope we can count on your cooperation in the search for Chlorites."

"As do I," Poratine added. "You are skilled and resourceful and would prove an asset. Wolverine's tracking abilities would be particularly valuable."

"We'll do whatever we can to defend our planet," Cyclops told her.

"I'm glad to hear that," Cooper said a bit hesitantly. "I know that cooperating with the government . . . when the government hasn't always been on your side . . . can't come easily to you."

"Danger makes stranger bedfellows," Jean said. "Especially when the whole world is at stake."

"That's the spirit," Cooper replied. "The bottom line is, on this you won't be working as an independent team. You're part of a greater whole now, and it'll take, let's say, a degree of cooperation you're not accustomed to."

Scott frowned at the tension he sensed beneath her words. "Where are you taking us?" he asked, keeping his tone casual.

"To this hangar just ahead. Before we get into specifics, I think you need to see some of the resources you'll be working with on this Chlorite hunt."

"Resources?" He sent a querying thought Jean's way. *She's hiding something,* his wife responded. *But her mind is very disciplined.*

"Call it a specialized unit of trackers, well equipped for ferreting out and detaining concealed nonhumans. Try to keep in mind that they may be essential to saving our world from the Chlorites."

They arrived at the hangar door, and Cooper paused. "Okay . . . we might as well get this over with." She hit the control, and the doors slid open.

Inside, it was dark. Yet Cyclops could tell it was far from empty. Massive shapes, towering, metallic, were dimly visible within the gloom. Faint sounds of metal creaking under its own weight echoed through the hangar, like the warning growls of a herd of predatory beasts. Something moved at the top of each one— some sort of massive turret, turning toward them. On the front of each, two red lights snapped on, piercing him with their gaze. . . .

"Oh, for Pete's sake," Cooper said, "I told them to leave the lights on! Just a sec—"

Rows of lamps in the ceiling clunked on one by one, illuminating the red and purple skins of the man-shaped robotic giants beneath. Filling the hangar, dozens of rows deep, was an army of Sentinels.

10: Exitus Acta Probat

"It's a trap!"

Wolverine's claws burst out as he spoke, and he shifted into a defensive posture. The other X-Men followed suit, with Grey and Rogue rising into the air and Beast and Nightcrawler falling into animal crouches. Even the dragon flapped his wings and lifted off Shadowcat's shoulder. Cyclops aimed his visor toward the nearest Sentinel, lifting a hand to the contact on its side.

Val Cooper cursed herself. The lights had been a stupid move. This whole thing had been a bad plan, springing it on them like this with so little preparation. But the Diascar's upgrades had been completed far faster than expected, and Poratine was constantly pushing for more haste. And if Val had told the X-Men in advance about what was in this hangar, they probably never would have come at all.

But if she didn't act now, this could be disastrous. "No!" she cried, striding between the mutants and the

Sentinels. "It is *not* a trap! Are you going to throw away the trust we've established so casually?"

"How can you ask us to trust you when *those* are standing there?" Cyclops demanded.

"Because they *are* just standing there," she countered. "Haven't you noticed? They haven't attacked you. They've been programmed to hunt Chlorites, not X-Men. But they *are* still programmed to defend themselves," she added. "So I would strongly advise you not to start anything."

Poratine came forward to stand by Val. "Please, there is no need for this," she told the X-Men. "Dr. Cooper has told me that you have had conflicts with these mechanisms in the past. But have not recent events proven to you that we all share a common enemy here? Also that we must employ every means at our disposal to hunt down and eliminate the infiltrators?"

"You know as well as anyone," Val said, "that there's no technology on Earth better suited to detect and capture nonhumans concealed in the midst of humans. However that resource may have been used in the past—"

"Or in the future?" Shadowcat challenged, her voice rough.

Val didn't let it break her stride. "The fact is, the Sentinels are the best tool we've got for saving our world from the Chlorites."

"She is correct," Poratine went on. "We have been hunting Chlorites for generations, but calibrating our equipment to each new species takes time. And the diversity of mutant genomes on your world is an added complication. Finding such a sophisticated gene-discrimination technology already in place on your world, integrated into such versatile and adaptive armored units, was a great blessing. These Sentinels, enhanced with Diascar technology, are precisely what we need to ferret out the remaining Chlorite terrorists on your world."

"Even if they hafta stomp on a few hundred mutants along the way, is that it?" Rogue shouted from where she hovered overhead. *If she'd stay at a more civilized height,* Val thought, *she wouldn't have to shout.*

"You know we have no quarrel with the mutants of your world," Poratine told them. Val heard impatience in her voice and could hardly blame her.

"Then prove it," Cyclops said. "Don't use the Sentinels."

"We must!"

"They're too dangerous! They can't be trusted!"

Wolverine backed him up. "They're nothin' but killers!"

"And you're not, Mr. Logan?" Val took a step toward him. "Sometimes it takes a killer to get the job done. Didn't you prove that in Alcala?"

"There's a difference. Those tin cans don't care who they squash."

"Dr. Cooper informed me of their past control problems." Val had to admire Poratine's gift for understatement. Bolivar Trask had been a pioneer in robotic ordnance development, but his programming skills had left something to be desired. Given a mandate to protect humanity by forceful means, Trask's first generation of Sentinels had decided that conquering humanity and imposing machine order upon it was the key to its protection. (Perhaps Trask might have avoided the necessity of sacrificing his life to destroy them if he had only read more Jack Williamson beforehand.) Later generations of Sentinels had been similarly difficult to control, and not particularly bright, either, like that one group that Iron Man had defeated by convincing them to attack the original source of all mutagenic radiation, which he had incorrectly claimed to be the Sun.

"But we have implemented new software fixes," Poratine continued. "Their behavior is now strictly regulated. Observe." She turned to the colossi behind her. "Sentinels! Threat assessment!"

The nearest few Sentinels responded, their heads turning to survey the area. Their networked brains had correctly concluded that only the nearest few would be needed to respond to the command. Using the same program logic, only one spoke, its booming, synthesized voice emanating from the loudspeaker in its anthropomorphized mouth. In this enclosed space, it echoed loudly, making Val wince. "NINE NONHUMAN LIFE FORMS DETECTED. SEVEN MUTANTS, IDENTITIES ON FILE AS X-MEN. CONFIRMED NONHOSTILE. ONE DIASCAR, CONFIRMED AS FLEET LEADER PORATINE NIHENNA. ONE REPTILIAN EXTRATERRESTRIAL, SPECIES UNKNOWN, IDENTITY ON FILE AS X-MEN ASSOCIATE. CONFIRMED NONHOSTILE. NO CHLORITE LIFE SIGNS DETECTED." The Sentinel lowered its head to take in Val and Poratine. "QUERY. MUTANTS AND REP-

TILIAN EXTRATERRESTRIAL EXHIBIT ATTACK POSTURE. REASSESS HOSTILE/NONHOSTILE STATUS?"

"No," Poratine answered. "The X-Men and the reptile are confirmed nonhostile. That status is not to be altered without direct authorization. Confirm."

"ORDER CONFIRMED. NONHOSTILE STATUS OF X-MEN AND X-MEN ASSOCIATE CONFIRMED."

"There. You see?" Val asked. "They didn't even *arm* their weapons without asking first—and that's despite you being a hair trigger away from attacking them. These Sentinels are well tamed."

"Don't buy it," Shadowcat said to Poratine. "They're more devious than they look. Their fuzzy-logic AI is too unstable, there's no way to guarantee they won't interpret their programming in unpredictable ways. They have no ethics, no restraint . . . nothing but an overriding ambition to achieve their goal by any means necessary and to destroy anyone who gets in their way. You can't change that with a few software patches."

"We have more experience with such artificial intelligences. Our software inhibitors are adaptive enough to cope. They will do exactly what we tell them."

"Maybe that's the problem," Cyclops said. "We already know you'll do anything to fight the Chlorites. What Shadowcat just said about the Sentinels? It's just as true of you. So maybe it doesn't make any difference who's giving the commands.

"Come on," he said to the other X-Men. "I've had enough of this place. We're leaving."

"Summers, wait!" Val ran forward to catch up with him as he led the X-Men from the hangar. Several of them crept or levitated out backward, not willing to take their eyes off the Sentinels. "Whatever you feel about the Sentinels, the Chlorites are still out there. We still need you on this."

"Well, we don't need you!"

She sighed. "All right. I'll have the jet fly you back."

"We'd rather walk."

"Just please, reconsider this—"

She broke off. They weren't listening. They just walked away, ignoring her. All except the dragon. He hovered in the air, studying her for a moment. Then he turned up his beak at her, and she could have sworn she heard a distinct *"pfui"* before he flew away.

"Are you ready?"

Meena was about to say yes, but she couldn't. She and John sat together in a corner of the library. He had brought her here to help work on her powers, since it was quieter and emptier than the students' study halls, and she could be less self-conscious here. The thing was, John's patient gaze made her self-conscious too, since she didn't want to seem lost and useless in front of him. Yet at the same time, his quiet, unassuming presence made her feel calm. There was something more to it than just his manner; it had something to do with her senses. The aura of other realities that formed a noisy blur around most people in her perceptions was somehow fainter with John. Maybe that meant he existed in fewer realities than most people . . . or maybe it just meant he was basically the same person everywhere. She wasn't sure which she preferred. If he were only in a few realities, that might mean he'd never been born in them, or that he'd died young in most of them; but it would mean she was lucky to have him here. If it were the other, then her John wouldn't be so special . . . but she'd know that she could count on him to be who he appeared to be.

"Meena?" John prodded her, and she snapped back to the here and now . . . in a more conventional sense than was usual for her. "Are you ready?"

"I don't know. I'm nervous. Trying on purpose to reach out to other realities . . . what if I get lost?"

"You always come back, don't you?"

"So far."

"And it's not like you're fighting to do so. Like you told me, when you're in another reality, you accept it. So reaching out on purpose won't be any different. You won't get lost."

His quiet, straightforward manner was reassuring. He made it sound so simple. "Besides," he went on, "you're not really trying to enter a whole other timeline, just open your mind to the whole flow of them. Try to bring that blurry aura into focus, try to feel the patterns in it."

"Okay. Bring it into focus."

"Right. Now, just relax . . . close your eyes . . . breathe slow . . . and open your mind."

She followed his instructions as best she could. She reached out to the babble of voices, of images and events, and tried to sense patterns in it as John had suggested. But it quickly became too great a noise, overwhelming her, and she pulled back. "I can't do it. I'm sorry. There's just too much chaos."

He put a cool hand on her arm. "No need to apologize. Um . . ." He self-consciously pulled the hand away again, to her regret. "I mean, you didn't do anything wrong. It's just something that takes time. Where I'm . . ." He broke off and thought for a moment before starting again. "I've had to take on some . . . difficult tasks in my life. To train myself to think and act a certain way."

She looked at him in sympathy. "You mean, like trying to be a good foster child so someone would adopt you?"

He paused. "Yeah, something like that. The point is, it takes time to learn, to retrain your thinking. You never get it right the first time, and you just have to keep working at it until you do, because . . . because the reward at the end will be worth it."

"But I don't know if there is a reward here. I don't know if my powers can even work the way the professor says. How do I know there's any pattern to the realities at all? It all seems so random . . . how could I ever use it to predict anything?"

"It isn't random," John said as simply as ever. "The universe is a quantum wave, and it has a wavefunction. An equation defining all its possible states and how they relate to each other. Like . . . like a bell curve in math class. You take a lot of different measurements, and you plot them all, and most of them tend around a peak in the curve, and that tells you those are more probable, more numerous than others. I bet you can do the same with universes. There is a curve that they follow, and if you get enough of a sample, I bet you can figure out its shape."

Meena smiled. "Quantum waves? How do you know all that? That's a lot beyond what we're getting in class."

John fidgeted. "I just . . . like to read ahead. Learn stuff on my own."

"I guess you always like to do stuff alone." At his reaction, she smiled. "It's all right. I understand why. I just meant . . ." She reached out and took his hand. "I meant it's really sweet of you to do this for me."

His hand started to feel increasingly warm.

"So." Charles Xavier looked around at the X-Men assembled in his office. "What do we do now?"

"We stop the Sentinels," Kitty said. "Can there be any other answer?"

"But how?" Jean asked. "They not only have the government backing them up, but the UN, the Diascar, even the Imperial Guard."

"We'll find a way. We have to." Xavier could understand Kitty's urgency. She had more experience than most with what the Sentinels were capable of. No sooner had she joined the Xavier Institute at the age of thirteen than she'd found herself telepathically exchanged with her older self from an alternate future, one in which the Sentinels had conquered the entire United States, turning it into a gulag where mutants were either exterminated outright or enslaved with power-limiting collars. The younger Kitty's mind had been mostly unconscious during her stay in her older self's body, but the two isomorphic minds had touched enough that Kitty Pryde had retained some of Kate

Pryde's knowledge of her future. With Kate's help, the X-Men had prevented what they thought to be the formative event of that Sentinel-ruled future, but since then, they had been visited by others from that same timeline. The possibility that it, or something close to it, could still lie in the future could not yet be ruled out, and Xavier knew that thought was haunting Kitty now.

"We all feel that way," Hank told her. "But even if we had a means, what would be the consequences? How might it impair the effort to track down Chlorite infiltrators if the searchers must divert their attention to fighting us? We saw how quickly the Alcala strain adapted to Earth conditions. Are we prepared to risk destroying the Earth in order to save it?"

"Least a virus don't try to kill us on purpose," Rogue said softly. "It's just tryin' to survive. So're the Chlorites. An' so are we. Maybe we-all should be askin' ourselves, what side do we really wanna be on?"

Jean stared at her. "After what that Chlorite mole said and did in Alcala? How can you say that?"

"They ain't all like that. Most of 'em ain't. And the ones who are, maybe they're just desperate. Backed into a corner by the Diascar."

"She has a point," Kurt said. "Frightened people do foolish, even destructive, things sometimes. Especially when they're allowed no other recourse."

"Right! Siccin' the Sentinels on 'em'll just make it worse. Make 'em more likely to wanna hurt us back."

"Whether they want to or not doesn't matter," Scott told her. "They can destroy us either way."

"That's no reason to give up on them," Kurt said. He lowered his head. "I saw Alcala firsthand. I feel rage and disgust at what they did. But I can understand why they did it, and I can try to forgive."

Xavier spoke up. "I told Lilandra that I would do what I could to find an alternative to destroying the Chlorites. To find a way we could coexist. But the more I learn, the harder that seems."

Hank nodded. "I have been researching the issue myself, but the scientific obstacles appear insurmountable. If it were only the macroscopic individuals who produced chlorine, that could be manageable. As we've seen, some of their agents use medicines to diminish their chlorine output—a sort of interstellar Beano. But controlling microorganisms is far harder. With all our vaunted medical science, we have only managed to fight the various disease organisms of our world to a draw at best. We have eradicated a few, like smallpox, but new ones emerge all the time. The microbes of our world outnumber us, collectively outmass us, and can reproduce and evolve a million times faster than us . . . well, present company excluded on the evolving part. I wouldn't presume to speculate on the other." A few chuckles went around the room. Hank's dry wit could always be counted on to ease the tension, even though Xavier knew it was simply a defense mechanism against the doctor's own frustration at his inability to solve this medical problem. "And these alien microbes not only have no natural predators but are toxic to most predators and fortified by most chemical disinfectants. And they don't even have to infect us to kill us. Even if we could immunize our-selves, how would we purge them from the oceans and the soil?

"I can see no option but to locate and contain every last Chlorite on Earth before any more microbes evolve the ability to survive outside their bodies."

"Fine," Scott said. "But not with Sentinels."

"Why not?"

The others' heads spun around at Logan's laid-back question. Waves of astonishment saturated the room. "You know why not," Scott said. "If the government uses this kind of heavy-handed tactic against Chlorites disguised as mutants, you know it's just going to stir up hostility against mutants. Maybe there weren't anti-mutant riots before, but there are bound to be now."

"Right," Kitty said. "I just know Gyrich and Project Wideawake are behind this, seeing this as a great chance to crack down on mutants once and for all. You've heard the news . . . they're already imposing travel restrictions on nonhuman-looking mutants. They're going to be forcing people to submit to searches, taking their rights away one at a time. What do you want to bet they keep those restrictions in place after the Chlorites are gone?"

"No bet, 'Cat. Course they will. But it don't matter."

"What?!"

Logan leaned forward, looked around at the group. "It's simple. You fight one battle at a time. Right now, we're fightin' the Chlorites. Like it or not, that's what we gotta do to stay alive. If workin' with Sentinels gets that done, fine, so long as we get it done. Sure, it'll make things harder for mutants after that—but that's the next battle. When it comes, we'll fight it then. But right now we gotta win the battle we're in, or we won't be around to fight the next one."

"So we just ignore the consequences of our actions until they come back and bite us?"

"That's how war works, kid. Often as not, what you do to win one war causes the next one. But when you're in the war, that don't matter. You do what you gotta do to stay alive. First you make sure you *have* a future, then you worry about what kind it's gonna be."

"He's right," Jean said. "Protecting the planet in the here and now is our highest priority. We've worked with enemies before when there was something greater at stake. Sometimes"—and she glanced at Rogue—"we've even won enemies over."

"The Sentinels?" Kitty asked. "I don't see them ever inviting us around for tea."

"No, but maybe if we cooperate with the government on this, it will ease some of their mistrust of mutants. It could help cancel out whatever harm is done to mutant relations by the hunt for Chlorites."

Scott spoke reluctantly. "One thing's for sure—if the public sees us *fight* the Sentinels while they're helping to save the world from Chlorites, it'll only hurt mutant relations more and make them more likely to keep the Sentinels around once the Chlorite threat is over."

Kitty was still unconvinced. "How do we know it'll ever really be over? The Diascar could decide to keep the Sentinels around forever, just in case."

"I'm hopeful," Xavier said, "that if we cooperate in ending this crisis quickly, we can appeal to the better angels of the government's nature and of Poratine's."

"And if not," Logan said, popping out the claws on one hand, "I still got my Sentinel repair kit."

The room fell quiet for a moment, but then Rogue broke it. "So that's it? We just write off the Chlorites, go hunt 'em down with the Sentinels by our side? We don't care anymore 'bout how they been abused, starved, slaughtered all their lives?"

"Of course we care," Xavier assured her. "But that doesn't change the fact that they are a threat to the world and must be stopped. It's no different from the way the X-Men have always battled dangerous mutants, like Magneto. The fact that we can sympathize with their motives doesn't make their actions any less reprehensible. The first priority is always to prevent them from taking innocent lives. After that, we can look for ways to change their approach, to work toward coexistence."

"Sure, right. Like the world'll even care anymore after they're gone!" Rogue stood abruptly. "You don't know what it's like for them. No home, no roots, no hope, always runnin', always half-starvin'. Always hated and feared everywhere they go, just for bein' what they are! We're s'posed to be the ones helpin' people like that! If y'all are gonna be huntin' 'em down instead, I want no part of it." She strode to the door, pulled it open.

Kitty rose after a second and went after her. "Neither do I—not if it involves the Sentinels." Rogue went on out, but Kitty paused in the doorway. "Anyone else? Are the rest of you all accepting this?"

"I don't know," Kurt said.

"It's not that we're swallowing it whole," Jean said. "But we should keep talking about it."

"I just can't right now. I can't stand to hear another word." Kitty hurriedly left the room.

Kurt hopped down from his perch on the back of the sofa. "Let me go talk to them, bring them back."

"No," Scott said. "Like Kitty said, this isn't the time. Maybe we should all take a break and let this sink in."

"Yeah," Logan replied, loping toward the door. "Maybe I'll find Rogue, go a few rounds with her in the gym. Could stand to burn off a little—" He broke off, sniffing.

"What is it?" Scott asked.

But Logan simply held up a hand for quiet and made his way out into the library with seeming nonchalance. He projected his thoughts to Xavier, who relayed them to the rest of the team. *I'm gettin' a familiar scent, Charley. One I got to know pretty well down in Alcala.*

Xavier was stunned. *How can that be?*

Suddenly, Logan pounced at something. Someone screamed. The X-Men poured out into the library, Xavier on their heels, to find Logan's left hand around John Chang's throat, his right hovering before the student's face with claws half extended. "Why don'tcha ask him yourself, Charley? Damn, I smelled chlorine on him before and just thought it was from the pool."

"How could he be a Chlorite?" Kurt asked. "The professor would know."

"Perhaps not," Xavier had to admit. "John here is immune to my telepathy. But I verified his identity by reading his foster parents' minds. . . . They had memories of him as their charge. Memories of abusing him. It was why I accepted him for admission."

"You know my nose don't lie, Charley. He's a Chlorite, all right. Look at the hands, the teeth, the shape o' the eyes. I've seen 'em before." Logan peered closer. "Yeah, I can see the surgery scars. He's one o' the refugee species."

Nearby, Meena Banerjee was cowering. Unlike John's, her mind was radiating plainly, with the intensity of a serious teenage crush. "What are you talking about? John's my friend! Don't hurt him! Ohh, Krishna, tell me this isn't real!"

Xavier rolled over and took her arm. "I'm afraid it is, Meena. John is not who he's claimed to be. Jean, please put a force field around him at once. Let Logan step out. Then I want the both of you to escort him to the isolation cell in the subcomplex."

"Yes, Professor."

Once Logan's blades were away from his throat, "John" lost his timid look and glared at them defiantly. "You may have found me out, but you'll never find us all! Not before it's too late to stop us from making this world our own!" Meena gasped, her anger and fear turning to shock and betrayal. She broke down crying on Xavier's shoulder while Jean levitated the alien youth out of the library. "It's hopeless, you know!" he called as he receded through the hallway. "Eventually Chlorite life will dominate the whole universe! You're all doomed, every last one of you!"

• • •

Soon, the X-Men reconvened in the lab section of the elaborate complex beneath the mansion. Rogue and Kitty were back among them, more subdued now upon learning of the mole.

"Should we decontaminate the school?" Kurt asked.

Hank glanced up from the PCR scanner. "I think the Diascar are overcautious about such things. As we now know, the microbes can't yet survive outside a Chlorite host. Certainly we will be taking precautions, but I don't believe we'll need to do anything drastic. My atmosphere readings of the mansion detect no abnormal chlorine levels." Something beeped. "Ahh. There we are." After studying the results for a moment, Hank announced, "My tests confirm it. Our ersatz Mr. Chang is indeed a stranger in our strange land—specifically a member of the Zann species." He worked the computer to project one of the ID files the Diascar had circulated.

"It don't look like him," Rogue said.

"Note the keratinous spines that cover the body. Our Zanny Boy has had his surgically removed. I don't imagine a porcupine would be easy to recognize without its quills."

"I should have known." Xavier shook his head, silently cursing himself. " 'John Chang.' Chang is the most common surname on the planet. To an outsider, the name would have seemed generic."

"You had no reason to suspect him, Charles," Jean insisted. "Sure, you couldn't read him, but you were sure about his foster parents, weren't you? And child services confirmed his background, right?"

Kurt frowned. "It's hard to believe someone would knowingly have himself placed with abusive parents in order to arrange a backstory. But how would he have known which parents to choose?"

"Turns out he didn't have to gamble on that," Jean said. "He actually bragged about it. Crowing about Chlorite ingenuity. Some sort of hypnotic device, implanting false memories of abusing him."

"Musta worked pretty well to fool ol' Charley."

"I'm afraid your confidence in me may be misplaced, Logan. I didn't probe as deeply as I could. I sensed that they had abused 'John' for being a mutant, and that was all I needed to feel sympathy for him. So I didn't examine matters more closely. And I didn't check his foster-care records closely either."

"At the time," Hank reminded him, "you had no reason to."

"But I should have considered the possibility once the threat became evident. After all, the Chlorites are seeking to hide among mutant communities. The Xavier Institute's student body is one of the largest concentrations of mutants in North America."

Jean put her hand on his shoulder. "None of us blames you, Charles. It's in your nature to expect the best of everyone. Your willingness to trust is what brought this school, this team, together. Yes, it can lead to the occasional mistake, but on balance it's been a positive thing."

"Anyway," Scott said after a moment, "the question is, what do we do with 'Chang' now? Turn him over to the government?"

"I'd rather not," Xavier said quickly. "Not yet. That would probably invite Sentinel attention to the institute, and I don't care to have the student body subjected to that if it can be helped."

Rogue stared at him. "Weren't y'all just decidin' that it was necessary for th' greater good an' all?"

He smiled thinly. "Perhaps we were. And I do now feel compelled to admit that it is. But I will still protect my own students from it if I can. Call me a hypocrite if you must, but that is the way it is.

"Besides, I am confident of the rest of the students. Their minds are open to me.

"There is another reason I'd prefer to keep young Mr. Chang, for want of a better name, in our company for a while longer," Xavier went on, keeping his eyes on Rogue. "I'd like a chance to question a Chlorite operative without interference from the Diascar or the government. It might offer a fresh perspective on matters."

"You mean to find a peaceful way outta this," Rogue asked, "or just a better way to fight 'em?"

"At this point, it's too early to say." He could tell she wasn't mollified. "I don't want to give you false hope. Let's not forget that this being came here with the conscious goal of causing all our deaths and those of our students. And he may have intelligence about the identities or tactics of other infiltrators."

"Which you'll hand right over to the nice Sentinels," Kitty said.

"The fact still remains that humanity must use every resource at its disposal to deal with this threat.

I'm sorry that it's the way it is, Kitty, Rogue, but if anything, this incident drives home the necessity of that."

Kitty said nothing. But she looked over at the screen displaying "John's" vitals, shuddered slightly, and lowered her head. Xavier could see the acceptance of the inevitable on her face without needing to sense her aura.

Kurt could see it too, and it was reflected on his own face. "So we're doing it," he said. "Working with the Sentinels."

"Gotta be done," Logan said.

After a second, Scott nodded. "I'm in."

"Me too," Jean said.

"I can see no option but to employ these golems," Hank said, "though I would be more comfortable if we could unmake them as easily as Rabbi Loew did."

Xavier nodded. "I'll contact Dr. Cooper and let her know we're still willing to cooperate in the search effort. Whether that entails working alongside the Sentinels or separately remains to be seen."

Kitty shook her head emphatically. "Ohh, no. If letting more Sentinels loose on the world is the only way to stop the Chlorites, then I guess I can live with that. But I won't let them out of my sight. Wherever they go, an X-Man has to be there to watch out for the mutants. Make sure the tin titans don't get overzealous." Most of the others indicated agreement.

"Fine," Rogue grated. "Y'all do that, then. I won't have no part of it."

Jean stepped toward her. "Rogue . . . I understand

that you identify with the Chlorites because of the memories you absorbed. But please, try to be objective."

"You don't get it, Jeannie. That ain't the only reason I'm against this."

"Then, why?"

Rogue looked away for a moment, then faced Jean again. "Maybe just 'cause *somebody* oughtta be."

"I'm glad you finally came around." Val Cooper cast an eye over the group of five X-Men who followed her through the warehouse. "Well, most of you, anyway."

"Dr. McCoy is pursuing his own line of investigation," Cyclops said, declining to mention that it involved study of their captive Chlorite student. "Rogue is assisting him." That was true insofar as she wasn't actively impeding him, but in no other way.

He gazed up at the ranks of Sentinels that towered above them. "As for the rest of us," he told Cooper, "how long we cooperate depends on how you use these things."

"Believe it or not, I'm all in favor of Xavier's condition of having X-Men accompany the Sentinel teams to make sure the rights of mutants are protected."

"As long as those rights don't get in the way of national security."

"Of course." She didn't seem to catch his sarcasm. "Rogue isn't exactly the scientific type, though. Did she have some other reason for not accompanying you?"

He avoided acknowledging the premise of the question. "If you're worried about manpower, we're working to bring in as many of the active and reserve X-Men and allied teams as we can."

Cooper nodded. "Good. We're trying to coordinate with all the superheroes we can corral. Heck, at this point we'd welcome help from supervillains."

Kitty glared at her. "Aren't you getting it already? From what I hear, Dr. Doom's already rounded up every mutant in Latveria."

"Unearthing a Chlorite and clearing the rest of them in the process. The United States does not approve of dictatorship, of course, but at least we're getting results."

"Then I guess the quicker we get this job done," Scott said, "the quicker we can dismantle these things, toss out the registration bracelets, and let the mutants get back to their normal lives. Right?"

She looked at him evenly. "I'm all in favor of normality."

After a moment, she broke his gaze and took in the rest of the team. "Now, let's get you briefed on the Sentinel upgrades and begin working on some joint search and detainment procedures. The Imperial Guardsmen are waiting for us. This way."

"We're here to learn," Scott said. *And the more we learn about these metal monsters, the readier we'll be to fight them when the time comes.*

11: Exile

"I still can't believe it!" Todd Watkins cried. "That jerk! That son of a— If I ever get my hands on him!"

"But John?" Kris Koenig asked, still stunned. "He was always so quiet."

"It's always the quiet ones!"

"I guess you're safe, then," Harry Mills quipped. The fact that they were in study hall seemed to have escaped Todd's notice.

"How can you joke about it?" asked Sarah Allaire, her butterfly wings trembling. "One of those . . . those murderers, those terrorists, living among us, pretending to be one of us!"

"Yeah," Harry said. He held up his hands as though he were framing a tabloid headline. " 'My Roommate Was an Alien Spy!' How cool is that?"

"Cool? He wanted you dead!"

"Yeah, okay, sure. But Mr. Logan sure seemed to want me dead after I kept interrupting his World War Two lecture in Mutant History. And he's still cool." To be honest, the truth about John's identity and intentions scared the hairballs out of Harry. So he was more comfortable not thinking about that part of it. Denial could be a nice place to swim.

"John's no murderer!" Predictably, it was Meena Banerjee. Harry had known the girl had had a crush on John for some strange girl-like reason, but it had turned out to be stronger than he'd suspected. "He's a good person, I know it. He's our friend!"

"Come on," Todd said. "You were right there when Mr. Logan exposed him! You heard the things he said! He don't care about any of us."

"I don't believe that," Meena insisted. "He's been kind to me. He lets me talk about my powers, my problems with them . . . he really listens."

Todd scoffed. "That only started once you said you could maybe use your powers to find out stuff about the Chlorites. He was just sweet-talkin' you, pretending to care so he could find out if you were a threat."

"No. You weren't there. It wasn't like that."

"Well, tell us," Harry said. "How *did* he show you how much he cared? And don't stint on the graphic details."

Meena glared. "He was your friend too, Harry, longer than anybody's! Tell them he's no killer!"

Harry reached back to scratch himself in an awkward place. "Look, I dunno. He was . . . quiet. He let me ramble on as much as I wanted, and I like that in a friend. He let me beat him at Halo, he always returned my Startling Metamorphosis CDs, and he never folded the pages on my comic books. He never did anything bad, but I can't say I really knew that much about him. He didn't like to talk about himself."

"I'm not talking about what he said or did. I mean what's in his heart. What you can see in his eyes."

Harry held out his hands. "Hey there, Meens, I didn't exactly spend a lot of time gazing into his eyes, you know?"

Kris had a thoughtful look on her face. "But still, he liked to spend time with you, right? Not because he had to."

"Well . . . yeah."

"Who says he didn't have to?" Todd said. "He just wanted to get close to a mutant teen so he could get himself invited to the school."

"Uh-huh, there is that." Harry wasn't liking the way this was going. It was getting too close to making him think about things that weren't funny or cool.

Kris spoke up again. "But what I mean is . . . out in space, where he came from . . . his people are so persecuted. It must've been nice for him to get to live a normal life for a while. Well, normal compared to that. For a while, he got to be . . . kind of invisible. Lost in the crowd. I bet he liked that."

"Of course he did, he's a damn spy!"

"That's not what I mean, Todd. Tell him, Harry!"

"What am I, his lawyer now?"

Meena snapped her fingers. "Lawyer! We need to get him a lawyer. I wonder if that Matt Murdock guy would take the case. . . ."

"What case?" Sarah asked. "The professor, he won't turn John over to the authorities."

"He'll have to sooner or later," Todd said. "So they can kick his butt off the planet with all the rest of 'em."

"But the Diascar, they'd kill him!" Meena protested.

"Better him than *every living thing on Earth.*"

"At least he deserves a fair trial," Kris said. "I mean, everyone does, right?"

Todd scoffed. "He ain't even human."

Harry looked at him. "And we are?" Outwardly, it was a joke . . . but Todd's comment made Harry uncomfortable in a way he didn't like to think about.

"Your friends are worried about you, John."

The young Zann—who had yet to give his real name—glared at Xavier through the thick window of the quarantine cell. "They aren't my friends. They're my enemies. You Oxies are all the same, you all want us dead."

"Doesn't the fact that we're having this conversation prove otherwise?"

"Don't try to manipulate me with your words, Xavier. I know you're just keeping me here for interrogation."

"I thought you might like to know that a short time ago, Meena Banerjee came to my office insisting that I should arrange for you to have a lawyer. Harry Mills came with her, as what he called 'moral support.'" Xavier smiled. "Meena hasn't lost faith in you, John. She knows what you are but still believes that it isn't in you to hurt or kill anyone."

"Then she's pretty stupid, isn't she?"

"I think it's possible she has an even deeper intuition than she realizes."

"Then you're stupid too!" John strode forward,

coming up to the glass. "Don't you get it? Your people are doomed! You're so weak and fragile that it kills you just to be around *real* life like us! And so you futilely strike back by trying to kill us all. But we're stronger than you. We're smarter than you. We've had to be. You have it easy on your worlds where metals don't corrode and fire can burn. The Diascar told you we stole our technology from life like yours, didn't they?"

"Yes, they did."

"Well, it's a lie. We did it by being smarter than you. We couldn't set fires, so we made solar ovens out of quartz. We couldn't use hard metals, so we developed ceramics and plastics much faster than you did. Made conductors out of electrolytic fluids extracted from plants." Xavier found this fascinating. He would have loved to hear more, if it had been presented more objectively. "We found answers none of you Oxies ever dreamed of. We've *earned* the right to survive, more than you ever have! You can try to wipe us out, but we'll always outsmart you, and make sure you die first. That's why I'm here! I'm one of the elite, the chosen, the ones who get to bless this world with our essence and cleanse it of your primitive excuse for life."

Xavier studied him sadly. "If you ask me, John, most of that sounds rather boilerplate. Like a propaganda tract someone fed you in order to recruit you to this mission. I would like to hear what *you* think."

"I am loyal to my people's cause. I think it's an honor to serve the advancement of true life, and to help purge one more planet of those who would try to destroy it."

It was the sort of thing Xavier expected him to say,

though he had hoped for more. The lad was young, impressionable. He'd probably grown up without hope, without any expectation of a real future. It was all too easy for others to fill that void with a simplistic, fanatical ideology, one that fired him to rage and let them turn him into a weapon. And with nothing to look forward to in life, he was easily persuaded to embrace a likely suicide mission, one where he wouldn't have to live with the guilt of what they asked him to do.

But Xavier chose to see that as a source of hope. The ideology John spouted was one he'd borrowed whole from someone else. It was something grafted on from outside, not something he'd synthesized within himself. So if Xavier could engage John's own thoughts and feelings, maybe he could help the youth shake off this overlay and develop an independent opinion or two.

"And how would you feel, then, if you purged the Earth of life?"

"It would be a triumph for my people."

"That doesn't tell me what *you* would feel, young man. How you would feel to watch Harry Mills and Kristin Koenig and Meena Banerjee as they slowly choked to death. As the chlorine bound with the water in their membranes, turning to acid, burning their throats, leaving them with a desperate thirst they could not quench. As their eyes burned, their own tears turned against them. As the acid burned through the alveoli in their lungs, filling them with fluid, leaving them gasping for air, every breath an agony." His voice grew harder, more relentless as he continued. "Would that be a triumph, John? Would that bring you a sense of accomplishment, make you feel like a hero?"

John tried to remain stoic but failed. "It doesn't matter how I feel!" he cried. "Their fate was sealed a long time ago. Oxy-life can never survive."

"Over a billion years, or ten, maybe. Does that mean your friends have to die now?"

"They aren't my friends. I only pretended."

Xavier leaned forward, held his gaze. "They didn't." He sat back again. "What they offered you was real. Kindness. Companionship. Acceptance. Loyalty. Even now, Meena and Harry are willing to extend their loyalty to you. Are these the mortal foes you were recruited to kill?"

John turned away. "It doesn't matter," he said after a moment, more quietly than before. "We could never be together anyway. We can't live on the same world."

"Does that mean they have no right to exist? Friendships have endured separation before, John. A very . . . a very dear friend of mine lives in another galaxy. Her duties keep her there, as mine keep me here. Sometimes we are divided by opposite priorities, opposite goals. Yet we are still always in each other's thoughts, and I would find the universe a far emptier place without her in it."

"At least you're the same kind of life!" the Zann countered. "At least it's possible for you to be together. They would die from being around me. And like any being, they would kill to save their own lives. There's no way around that."

Xavier continued to hold his gaze evenly. "But you still haven't told me how that makes you feel."

There was a long silence. Xavier knew he was making some small headway, though he did not expect a breakthrough so soon. Indeed, John grew defensive again, leaning against the back wall, crossing his arms. "It makes no difference. I am just one of many. You will never find us all in time. You are all doomed, whether I have a part in it or not."

There was nothing Xavier could say in response to that. John was right about one thing: There were other infiltrators out there, no doubt as strongly indoctrinated as John. Many might be young recruits like him, but others might be hardened terrorists, ruthless and dangerous. And his X-Men were out there right now, searching for them, with their worst enemies at their side. Xavier could only pray that his friends—his children—would come home safely once again.

12: Excursus

Cincinnati, Ohio, United States

"SURRENDER, ALIEN!"

The Sentinel's amplified voice boomed across the campus of the University of Cincinnati, echoing off its not particularly ivied halls. The students milling about the place, including more than one recognizable mutant, looked up in shock. Cyclops wouldn't have expected to find much of a mutant community in Cincinnati, given its somewhat conservative reputation, but he supposed a university would be the exception to the rule. The student body as a whole looked quite cosmopolitan, relatively unfazed by the mutants in their midst. The pair of three-story robots descending on their campus was another matter, though.

The individual whom the Sentinels' scanners had

just confirmed as a Chlorite was hardly the sort who would blend in even here—a seven-foot female with orange hair and teal-blue scales. She had just emerged from the odd-looking student union building, which bore the portico, roof, and spire of a classical, boxy brick structure incongruously embedded within a modernist, cylindrical construct of gray siding and glass, two badly clashing buildings pretending to be one. It reflected the campus around it, a melange of different architectural styles and periods that didn't quite fit together.

Why am I dwelling on that? Scott wondered. Maybe because the team he was on didn't fit together any better. He'd accepted the necessity of working alongside these Sentinels for now, but that didn't make it feel any less wrong.

The looming mechanoid and its twin touched down in the large green space in front of the hybrid student union, their rocket exhaust blackening the grass. "HOSTILE NONTERRESTRIAL, SPECIES GOORA, IDENTITY CONFIRMED," the first one intoned as they both extended their hands toward her.

"No!" the Chlorite cried. A second, smaller pair of arms shot out from under her jacket and reached behind her. They whipped something out of her backpack, brought it forward, and fired. It looked unwieldy, makeshift, but it emitted a respectable plasma bolt that hit the Sentinel high on its frame. *Good strategy,* Scott thought as the students screamed and scattered. The Sentinels' humanoid design was precarious for mechanisms of their size and mass, and they were relatively easy to unbalance. This one was no exception; it toppled backward, its head and shoulders smashing into one of the newer-looking buildings surrounding the green space, a glass-walled box that shattered quite spectacularly, two whole tiers of windows showering down in shards on the Sentinel's head and torso.

"Ouch! Wouldn't you just know it'd be the glass one?" Scott looked up to see Bobby Drake descending next to him, one of his trademark ice bridges extending from a nearby fountain to where he now alit on the grass, his animate ice-sculpture of a body glinting in the sun. "You think it hurt?" Iceman asked hopefully.

"THIS UNIT IS UNDAMAGED," the Sentinel reported, even as its partner fired an energy blast at the Chlorite. But she was already in motion, dodging the blow and ducking back into the student union.

"I've got her!" Flashfire shot out of the sky, blasting the door down with an electric discharge and soaring toward it. Another plasma bolt shot through the door, grazing him and knocking him to the ground. Students were running out of the building's other doors.

The second Sentinel lumbered forward while the first one struggled to regain its feet. "SWITCHING TO THERMAL IMAGING," it announced, following whatever bizarre programming compelled the Sentinels to narrate everything they did. "TRACKING TARGET."

The behemoth smashed an arm through a large window in the newer part of the building, feeling around like a student trying to dig a stuck candy bar out of a vending machine. "UNABLE TO REACH TARGET," it announced.

"TARGET IS HEADING TOWARD LOWER EXIT. MOVING TO INTERCEPT," the other Sentinel (now back on its feet) informed it in an identical voice as it began stomping around to the north side of the building, where a paved plaza sloped down to a lower floor. Scott ran after the Sentinel while Bobby reached out with his hands, drawing moisture from the air and solidifying it into ice along the ground, letting him skate downhill with ease. "Nice and humid here," Bobby called as he glided past. "Plenty of moisture to work with. Hot for September, though."

Why not? Scott hopped onto Bobby's ice bridge, skating down just behind his old colleague. It wasn't the first time he'd done this; Iceman had been one of the first generation of X-Men along with him, back before they'd even been old enough for college. But it had been a while since they had worked in tandem like this.

The X-Men and Sentinels caught up with the Chlorite as she ran out the lower exit to the student union. She fired another plasma bolt at her robotic hunters, but the gun fizzled and sparked, forcing her to drop it and run. Bobby threw up walls of ice between it and the surrounding students just before it exploded. The students were safe, but the blast shattered several windows.

Across from the student union was a long, tall, but narrow building labeled STUDENT LIFE CENTER. The Chlorite ran through a square, two-story arch passing through the middle of the building, with the Sentinels in pursuit. But they didn't bother to duck, and the glass-lined walkway above the arch was smashed to pieces by the Sentinels' armored heads. Scott opened his visor and blasted away the falling debris before it hit him. Fortunately, the students were already fleeing the area, so no civilians were endangered.

Bobby was skating uphill now, but Scott had to hop off the ice slide and run up into a quadrangle with an unsightly fenced-off area in the middle, where one would expect a green space. The Chlorite was headed into the building on the near edge of the quadrangle. "Head her off!" Scott called as he ran up the building's stairs to follow her. He saw the Sentinels pursuing a similar strategy, rounding the building on opposite sides. One of them blithely crushed a fence bearing a CONSTRUCTION AREA: KEEP OUT! sign.

Scott followed the Chlorite's footsteps down a long hallway and around a corner through another one. He caught her coming out of a door marked PARTICLE TECHNOLOGY LABORATORY, wielding another, larger device. Apparently this mole wasn't content to be passively infectious; she had prepared to fight back against her hunters, disguising her work under the pretext of a student project.

She brought the gun to bear on Scott and fired. He struck the oncoming plasma bolt with his force beam, dissipating it with a blast that scorched the walls. Once his vision cleared, though, he saw that the Chlorite was on the run. He followed her down a short flight of stairs emerging onto the construction area, a plaza whose surface was all torn up, a maze of tar paper and sandbags. The Sentinel should have heeded the KEEP

OUT sign; its weight had overwhelmed the weakened surface, and it had fallen through to thigh level. The Chlorite blasted open the fenced-off doors to the plaza, ran out, and fired another blast at the Sentinel as she ran past. This one hit it full in the face and left a disfigured mess. "SENSORY MALFUNCTION! VISUAL ACUITY AT SEVEN PERCENT!" the behemoth cried.

Normally, Scott would have been pleased to see a Sentinel in such a compromised position. But in this case, it meant that the Chlorite's new weapon was formidable indeed. If one of those superheated plasma bolts hit Iceman, it could be fatal.

But Bobby was up on the roof of the building Scott had just exited, watching the chase. "Hold back," Scott advised him over the radio.

"Don't have to tell me twice. One hit from that, and I'd be a real sublime guy."

"And you know we prefer you ridiculous." Scott normally wouldn't have been the one to make the comeback, but with no other X-Men around, it seemed somehow obligatory.

Scott ran across the deconstructed plaza to the best of his ability, but watching his footing kept him from getting a bead on the Chlorite, who was now running down a makeshift-looking metal stairway descending from the plaza. *This is one hilly campus,* Scott thought.

The other Sentinel and a recovered Flashfire were coming around from the other side of the engineering building—the ground level there being some two stories below Scott—and the robot smashed down several trees as it made a beeline for the Chlorite. Surprisingly, a nearby, precarious-looking sculpture of rods and cables remained standing.

Scott went down the stairs as fast as he could. The Chlorite was running past the campus library now, under a walkway connecting it to the adjacent building. This bridge was made of concrete, too sturdy for the Sentinel to smash right through, so it reached out and began tearing the structure loose. Scott ducked under it as fast as he could, preferring to deal with the Chlorite himself rather than relying on the Sentinel's ham-fisted tactics.

Scott chased the Goora female down yet another slope, a grassy hill extending down to the edge of the campus, with a busy road and a large park beyond. *Good,* Scott thought, preferring to continue this away from the crowded campus.

But Flashfire swooped down to intercept the Chlorite from ahead, blasting a tree, which fell in her path. *At least the hothead was remembering one part of the briefings,* Scott thought; the preferred approach was to take the Chlorites alive or at least intact, for fear that spilling their blood would increase the risk of contamination.

But his tactic forced the mole to dodge back toward the populated portions of campus. She leaped a low wall onto a paved area surrounding a high, forbidding tower, a monolith of concrete rising straight up a good fifteen stories and flaring out at the top. The Sentinel leaped over a higher portion of wall to come down next to the tower, the massive structure dwarfing even it. It fired at the Chlorite, but she dodged around a corner. Scott and the Sentinel pursued, but another corner presented itself. Scott realized that from above, ironically enough, this tower would take the shape of an X. He fleetingly wondered if Professor Xavier had funded it—except that Xavier was the name of this city's *other* university.

The Chlorite tried to duck around yet another corner of the tower, firing a plasma bolt at the concrete wall as cover. Scott pulled up short as chunks of concrete fell around him, leaving an exposed skeleton of rebar. The Sentinel stomped past but took a blast to its chest, knocking it onto its simulated backside.

But suddenly a javelin of ice from above smashed into the plasma weapon, which began sparking. Not content to stay on the sidelines after all, Iceman had made his move. Scott saw Bobby's reflection in an SUV's windshield in the adjacent parking lot and understood how his old partner had made the shot without exposing himself. For all his playfulness, Iceman could be as cool and sharp as his icicle blades.

The mole ran again, toward yet another of this campus's mismatched architectural statements, a Frank Gehryesque clutter of clashing angles and slopes, dizzying to look at. Before she could reach it, though, Flashfire let loose another few lightning bolts to try to corral her. She raised the damaged gun to fire at him, but it began making an unsalutary whining noise, and she stared at it in alarm.

Throwing a malevolent look at Cyclops, she cried, "Catch me or save the students, your choice!" and hurled the unlicensed particle accelerator at the off-kilter building.

"We can do both!" Flashfire cried, launching himself through a window at superspeed even as Bobby skated down an ice bridge and froze the Chlorite's feet to the ground. The Sentinel, damaged but back on its feet, let loose with a Diascar-modified version of one of its capture spheres, encasing the Chlorite in an impenetrable force bubble. Scott fired at the shrieking weapon, hoping that setting it off before it reached its peak would minimize the blast. He saw no more movement within the windows and prayed that Flashfire had cleared everyone out.

The blast was surprisingly large nonetheless, and unfortunately, it went off at the bottom of the building. A whole corner of the structure sagged and collapsed. Bobby threw up an ice shield for himself and Scott, but the Chlorite in her bubble was blasted through the air, only to be fielded by the Sentinel. From the way her body slumped inside the force bubble, brownish blood streaking down its walls, Scott doubted the terrorist had survived. And he couldn't bring himself to feel very bad about it.

Once the smoke cleared, Scott surveyed the half-collapsed building. He had to admit, he didn't get modern architecture; it was hard for him to tell which parts of it were intact and which were damaged.

But the university president, who had now arrived on the scene with several of her aides and the campus police, seemed to see it differently. She stared numbly at the damage, shaking her head in disbelief. Bobby, who had now reverted to human form, approached her diffidently. "Umm . . . sorry about the damage, ma'am. I'm sure the government will reimburse you, uhh . . ." He trailed off.

"They'd better," the president said. "But . . . it's just . . ." She fought to gather herself. "We've spent most of the past two decades rebuilding this campus. Refurbishing it. The students joked that UC stood for 'Under Construction.' But we were turning it into a modern facility we could be proud of."

She turned to gaze out at the wreckage again. "And we were almost finished! Another few months . . . we were almost finished."

13: Excavation

London, England

"This is it," groaned Nightcrawler. "My career as a superhero is going down the drain."

Down below him, Sean Cassidy jumped, sending ripples through the mucky brown water through which he waded. "Saints, boy," he hissed in his Irish brogue, "try not to startle a fellow so. Turn your headlamp on."

"Sorry." Kurt realized that Cassidy hadn't seen him there. The space-warping power that let him teleport had the side effect of swallowing up light around his body, making him appear shadowed in normal light and nearly invisible in the darkness of this sewer main. And his excellent night vision had made the headlamp on his mining helmet seem redundant. "I wouldn't have thought you'd be so easily spooked."

Even before he had joined the X-Men as Banshee, recruited at the same time as Kurt, Sean had been a veteran agent for Interpol. He had always been the odd X-Man out, a middle-aged man on a team of youngsters (plus Wolverine, in comparison to whom Banshee was a youngster). He had retired from the team long ago, later coming back as a headmaster of Xavier's Massachusetts satellite school. This was the first time he and Kurt had been in the field together for quite some time.

"As a rule, no," Sean replied. "I suppose our mechanical friend up ahead has me on edge. Not to mention my lack of fondness for wading through raw sewage."

"Well, at least you have waders on." The London sewer authority had provided the team with the standard equipment—overalls, gloves, waders, helmets, emergency breathing masks—but Kurt had had to forgo the gloves and waders so that his hands and feet would be free for climbing. And he'd had to tear a hole in the overalls for his tail. On the other hand, Sean was the only one here who had to wade. Normally he could fly, but only when emitting his mutant sonic scream, and a brief attempt had proven conclusively that that was a bad idea in a ten-foot-wide, echoing sewer conduit. So he waded through the knee-high water while Kurt crawled along the redbrick walls. Up ahead, Nightside was gliding along courtesy of her Imperial flight patch, her black cape billowing behind her. Just beyond her was the Sentinel—or rather, the top half of its head, floating blithely along on ducted fans.

Kurt supposed he shouldn't be surprised that the Diascar had modified the Sentinels with such an ability. Not all exotic-looking mutants lived out in the open, and not all would voluntarily come forward for testing, especially if they were Chlorites. So the ability to delve into the smaller nooks and crannies was a useful one—though not one Kurt was glad to see the Sentinels adopting.

Particularly in this case. The mutants they were tracking were probably not infiltrators, not dangerous criminals, but simply frightened people. London had its share of mutants who, like the Morlocks of New York and Chicago, considered themselves too deformed to live in the open and thus retreated underground. Like most major cities, London had a second, subterranean city stretching beneath it, made up of sewers, maintenance tunnels, subways, and the like. It was not the most pleasant place to live, but it was a good place to hide from the world above. And now, with Sentinels and Imperial Guardsmen—yes, and X-Men—invading their territory, these pseudo-Morlocks would retreat even deeper into hiding, and Kurt could be down here for a long time. *I may never get the smell out of my fur.*

At least he and Banshee both had their share of experience with London. Kurt had lived in England during his time with the Excalibur team and had absorbed a fair amount of local culture and history. He was aware, for one thing, that the ordurous water flowing through this main had once been the River Westbourne, before the growth of London in the nineteenth century had befouled it and forced it underground. This was actually one of the cleaner parts of the London sewer system, courtesy of rainwater and runoff from the Serpentine Lake in Hyde Park, so the odds were that the Morlocks would congregate here. With its good upkeep and Victorian brick walls, it was actually a comparatively pleasant place, as sewers went. *It says something about my life that I can rate the different sewers I've been in.*

Suddenly, the twin spotlight beams emanating from the eyes of the Sentinel head unit tightened their focus on the edge of the water ahead. A sleek, sinuous figure froze in the beam for an instant, and Kurt got the impression of a female form with slick, waterproof skin and a heavy tail before it—she—darted below the surface. "NONHUMAN SUBJECT DETECTED. PROBABLE MUTANT SIGNATURE." The head thrust forward in pursuit of the mutant, forcing the others to pick up their pace, with Banshee lagging the farthest behind, thanks to water resistance. "HALT, MUTANT!" the Sentinel boomed. "SUBMIT FOR TESTING AND REGISTRATION OR YOU WILL BE FORCIBLY DETAINED!"

Kurt grimaced. There was no way that would work. He decided to be next to Nightside, and a puff of smoke later he was there. "Can't you set that thing to use a less-threatening tone?"

The blue-skinned, white-haired Guardswoman threw him a look, her all-white eyes inscrutable. "It's your technology."

He shook his head. "Not mine, Fräulein. Never."

They followed the Sentinel head past an intersection with a smaller sewer line, and Kurt could see they were closing on the ripples created by the fast-swimming mutant. But then Kurt heard the faint sound of projectiles whizzing through the air from behind them. He *bamf*ed out of the way reflexively, not having time to warn Nightside. But when the smoke cleared, he saw her shielding herself with a Darkforce shroud, displacing the projectiles into the shadow dimension she drew it from.

The darts bounced harmlessly off the Sentinel head as it spun to face the attacker. In its eyebeams, they looked like large hedgehog quills. "PROBABLE MUTANT TARGET HAS DOUBLED BACK. JOINING HOSTILE IDENTIFIED AS SECOND PROBABLE MUTANT." Indeed, Kurt caught a quick glimpse of the female as she leaped out of the water and followed another shadowy figure up the new, smaller line they had passed moments before.

"I'm on 'em!" Banshee had caught up now and, by virtue of being in the rear, was the first to reach the side tunnel. With the others safely off to the side, he let out a sonic scream into that tunnel, hoping to incapacitate the Morlocks. He also took advantage of the effect to levitate himself for a brief time and gain some headway into the tunnel. He had a fair lead by the time Kurt got there, though he was once again on foot. "No good," he reported over the com. "They both ducked under the water." That was one way to escape Sean's deafening scream, Kurt thought, but not one he'd ever like to try.

As Kurt crawled forward along the wall, Nightside soared past, and then the Sentinel head. Since this was a narrower tunnel, Kurt had to squeeze against the wall to let it pass. "You could've warned me," he muttered, but the Sentinel did not deign to reply. Kurt fleetingly wondered what its body was doing. Probably it was following along overhead. *Let's see, right now it would be at about Belgrave Square, near the German Embassy. An eight-meter robot with half a head walking past. Unglaublich.*

A third, wild-looking Morlock, a man with oversized black eyes, no hair, and mottled black-and-white skin, now appeared out of another side tunnel, standing between the team and their fleeing quarry. He made some kind of hand gestures at the team. It had no visible effect . . . but after a moment, Kurt saw Sean and Nightside begin gasping for air. "METHANE CONCENTRATION RISING TO HAZARDOUS LEVELS," the Sentinel reported. Kurt wasted no time reaching back for his emergency breathing mask, and once it was in place he *bamf*ed ahead to help the others with theirs. Once they had caught their breath, Kurt teleported himself and Sean forward to try to catch up with the fleeing Morlocks.

But they remained elusive, fleeing ahead of the team for several more blocks. Around one more bend, Kurt caught the swimmer's tail disappearing up an open grate in the ceiling. Sean had caught it too and was already heading up the ladder. Nightside shot through right behind him, and Kurt followed her, pleased that the Sentinel head was too big to fit through. "Sorry, *Herr Wächter*—it seems you must find another way around." *Or stay there with the rest of the*

Sperrmüll, he added silently. Perhaps without its presence, a less-aggressive approach might be possible.

The trio emerged in what appeared to be a London Underground station—Hyde Park Corner, according to the signage. The three Morlocks were running northeast up the Picadilly Line, sure-footedly avoiding the charged track. The hedgehog-man paused to fling another barrage of quills at their pursuers, forcing them to take evasive action and lose some ground.

Nightside was flying forward, Darkforce energy flowing around her hands, when a sudden gust of wind pushed her back. The Morlocks instantly dashed for a nook in the side of the tube, and Kurt's eyes widened as he realized what was happening. Banshee beat him to it. "Train coming!"

The tube brightened as the subway train's headlights drew closer at high speed. The trio hurriedly made their way to the other half of the tunnel, and Kurt wondered for a moment why the Morlocks hadn't done the same. Then he felt another gust of wind from behind him. "Uh-oh."

Just as the first train began to rush past, Kurt spun to see another one racing toward them in the opposite direction. And there were no handy nooks in sight. Nightside flattened herself against the top of the tube, but Banshee had nowhere to go. Kurt threw his arms around him and decided to be several hundred meters back down the line, hoping this wasn't an exceptionally long train.

They rematerialized safely behind the train, the rush of air in its wake pulling Kurt's brimstone smoke along with it. Kurt sagged to his knees. "Are ye all right?" Sean asked.

"I just need a moment. Draining, to teleport two so far."

"Why not just bamf us into the train?"

Kurt looked up at him. "I conserve momentum when I teleport. We would've still been standing still, and the rear wall of one of the cars would've hit us as hard as the front would've."

"Oh." Sean took a moment to absorb that. "Good instincts."

"Danke. Okay, let's go."

By the time the X-Men caught up with them, the three Morlocks had passed through a decrepit-looking door in a siding of the track. Banshee's scream blasted it open, and he ran inside, Nightside on his heels, and Kurt again taking up the rear. He clambered up to the ceiling to get a better view of things. "Where are we?" he asked. It looked like an abandoned tube station, but painted gray and covered in dust.

"Some sort of abandoned tube station," Banshee answered, not very helpfully. "Wait a minute—yeah, I reckon it's the old Down Street station. Churchill used it as a command post for a while during the war."

"How long ago was this war?" Nightside asked. "Could there be weapons remaining for the quarry to use?"

Sean laughed. "Not to worry, luv. It was over half a century past. Just look at the dust."

Luckily, the dust on the floor made it easy to track the fleeing trio. The team sped forward through the dingy complex, passing through what looked like an abandoned kitchen area, then up a flight of stairs into a dark corridor and around a corner, only to find themselves in a large empty space. It was a vertical, cylindrical shaft, at least as wide as an Underground tunnel but closed off on top with a slab of concrete and metal. The Morlocks were climbing a rickety metal staircase—or rather a pair of sloping ladders with a landing between them—to a hatch set into the slab. "Banshee, stop them!" Nightside cried. Sean obliged the Guardswoman, directing a tight-focused sonic scream at the upper ladder. It shook free of its supports and clattered down the shaft, leaving the Morlocks stranded on the small landing. "Surrender now," the Guardswoman told them. "You have no choice."

The hedgehog-man stepped forward and fired a barrage of quills. The mottled man began waving his hands, leading Kurt and the others to put their masks back on. "Madcow, stay be'ind me," the hedgehog-man said. "You too, Nessie." He turned to his pursuers. "You won' take us!" he cried in a working-class accent. "We seen wotcher doin' to us freaks up there. It's a putsch, is wha' it is. If we're gonna die, we'll die free, like men!"

Sean took a step forward. "No, ye've got it all wrong. We don't mean you and yours any harm. We just want to confirm ye're human."

"Oh yeah? And 'oo decides wha' human is, eh? Stay back!" Kurt could see his quills regenerating as he spoke. He looked almost ready to fire another salvo.

"Wait, hold on," Kurt said. Once again, he'd forgotten he was nearly invisible here. He switched off his helmet lamp and came forward. "Sean, shine your light on me."

The Morlocks' eyes widened as Kurt's demonic form became visible to them for the first time. "You see, *meine freunden*? I am as much a freak as you. I understand your fear—I have lived with it my whole life. But I can trust these people. I know they are not my enemy or yours." He slowly stepped closer to the remaining ladder, holding his hands wide. "The real enemies are aliens who are hiding among people like us. Using us as camouflage so they can threaten everyone on Earth, including us. All we want to do is find them. Once we clear you, we will know you are our brothers and sisters, and we will trouble you no longer."

Nessie peeked out from behind the others. "You promise?" she said in a young voice.

Kurt paused. "I'll be honest with you. I cannot guarantee that for everyone involved." *Or everything,* he added, thinking of the Sentinels. "But I will do everything I can to make sure it is true. And my friend here and others like him will do the same. That I can promise."

Herr Hedgehog seemed appreciative of Kurt's honesty, and let his guard down a bit. He took a couple of steps down the ladder. "You go' a name?"

"I am Kurt."

"Tha's an upstairs name," Madcow said. "One they gave you. You go' one o' yer own? One you chose?"

Kurt smiled. "I am Nightcrawler." Technically, Xavier had chosen it for him, but he had chosen to throw in his lot with Xavier.

"Nigh'crawler," Herr Hedgehog repeated. "I'm Spiny Norman."

Kurt tried not to laugh. "I am pleased to meet you." He reached out a hand. "Will you come with us and let us finish our business? And introduce us to others like you? It will only take a little while, and then you can go back to your lives."

Spiny Norman exchanged a look with his compatriots. "Yeah, all right," he finally said, accepting Kurt's handshake. "Bu' only if you stay in charge of it."

"I believe that can be arranged. Thank you." Kurt was very relieved. He doubted this could have ended peacefully had the Sentinels had their way. He just hoped the others were achieving similarly peaceful results.

14: Exposure (Northern)

British Columbia, Canada

Wolverine was spoiling for a fight.

Riding on the back of a Sentinel as it flew over the Canadian evergreen wilderness reminded Logan of that fable about the scorpion who rode across a river on the back of a turtle or some sort of swimming critter. Halfway across, the scorpion had stung the critter, knowing full well that they would both drown but unable to resist its nature, its instinctive need to kill its prey. Right now, Logan knew just how that scorpion had felt. If anything, he had less reason to resist his instincts, since the fall probably wouldn't kill him. It wouldn't be a lot of fun, sure, but it would be worth it to turn this Sentinel into scrap.

But I'm the one who said we need the things, he reminded himself. *For the moment, anyhow.* He took consolation in the fact that there was probably a good scrape coming up soon. This pair of Sentinels, along with Wolverine and the Guardswoman called Manta, had been drawn here by a report of a team of mutant criminals, including two inhuman-looking ones, stealing something sensitive from a military base north of Vancouver. The Sentinels were hot on the trail of the thieves, closing in fast.

They weren't alone, though. Another figure flew alongside them, clad in a red-and-white battle-suit stylized after the Canadian flag. "Try to remember this is a Canadian security matter," Guardian said. "These people stole weapons-grade vibranium, and my top priority is getting that back. I don't want you or these oversized tin soldiers getting in my way."

"Normally I got no problem stayin' outta your way, Mac, long as you stay outta mine." Logan and James MacDonald Hudson had a complicated history. Mac had helped nurse Logan back to health and sanity after he'd escaped the experiment that had given him his adamantium skeleton, but had tried to manipulate him into becoming an assassin for the government, part of his Alpha Flight team, and had led that team to try to take him back forcibly more than once after Logan had quit to join the X-Men. They'd reached an understanding some time after that, but they weren't exactly on each other's Christmas lists. "But there are bigger things at stake here. Fate-o'-the-world stuff."

"Hm. Funny how the fate of the world requires

sending giant robots built by the U.S. government into other people's countries."

Manta threw him a look. "Your tribal boundaries matter not. What happens to one happens to all."

"You don't even know if these mutants are your alien infiltrators."

"That's what we're here to find out," Logan told him. "We thought they just wanted to lay low, but after Cincinnati, we ain't takin' any chances."

"And *all* non-baseline mutants must register," Manta added. "We must know none is overlooked."

"I doubt these mutants will come along willingly to be registered," said Hudson.

Logan smirked. "Suits me fine."

In stories, saying something like that was generally a cue for the bad guys to strike. Logan knew real life wasn't so neatly structured. Indeed, there was a good twenty minutes of tedious searching before the bad guys struck. The attack came in the form of a pair of reddish beams that shot out of somewhere and impaled the Sentinel that Logan was riding. It bucked and tumbled, and Logan found himself in free fall a second later, plummeting toward the Douglas firs below. *Oh, this will* not *be fun. . . .*

But suddenly he was jerked to a stop and carried upward again, in the grip of a pair of armored hands charged with energy. Logan was grudgingly glad Mac was around; Manta's wings didn't exactly give her much to grip with, so she couldn't have caught him. "You see where it came from?" Logan asked once he caught his breath.

"Not sure. It was kilometers away."

"I see where it comes from," Manta called. "I am heading for it now! You are following!"

"What?" Hudson asked.

Logan chuckled. "Gal's got a weird sense o' time. No past or future, just the present. Far as she's concerned, she's watchin' the beams firin' right now. She may be a headache to talk to, but she knows where she's goin'. Like she said—we're followin'."

"Okay." Hudson flew after Manta and the Sentinels—both Sentinels, for the damaged one seemed to have recovered attitude control, though it was trailing smoke. As they drew nearer, more beams shot out at them, though now that the Sentinels knew where to look, they were able to dodge, taking only glancing blows. *Good reflexes.*

Soon they were nearing the quarry, and Logan could make out four figures running through the trees. One was green-skinned, long-necked, and reptilian, but the others seemed human enough—one lanky with long white hair, another stocky with brown hair and beard, the final one small, hunched, and bald. But the bald one looked up at them to reveal huge, bulbous white eyes and pointed ears. A second later, energy beams fired from those eyes, aimed at Guardian and Wolverine this time. Mac swerved to protect Logan, and his suit's force field absorbed the impact. "Hey, I think I know that guy," Logan said.

But there was no time to say more. The Sentinels were coming in for a landing in front of the foursome, and the bearded one was running toward one of them. *He's gonna get stomped!*

But instead, the man lifted up his hands and *caught* the Sentinel by the foot, holding it over his head as though it were nearly weightless. A moment later the Sentinel was rising back upward, as though being levitated. "ATTITUDE CONTROL FAILURE," the Sentinel reported. "GYROSCOPIC ORIENTATION LOCK UNAVAILABLE."

The second Sentinel reached its hands out to fire, but the white-haired mutant threw fireballs at it from his hands, while Peeper—*Yeah, that's who the bald guy is!*—fired more eyebeams. The Sentinel reeled. Manta was circling, trying to get a clear shot, but the trees were in her way.

"Yeah, I remember these guys now," Logan said as Hudson set him down. "Buncha small-time mercs, call themselves Mutant Force. Beast and the Defenders took 'em on a few times. Bald guy's Peter Quinn, calls himself Peeper. The others are Burner, Lifter, and Slither."

Hudson stared at him. "You're kidding. They actually use those names?"

"This from a guy who used to call himself Vindicator."

After a brief glare, Hudson said, "So you can vouch for them not being aliens."

"Yep. They've been around forever."

"So they're mine."

"Manta might disagree. Makes no difference to me, though."

The airborne Sentinel seemed to have broken free of Lifter's gravity-manipulation power, but the other one wasn't doing so well. Burner had ignited the trees around it, giving him and his partners cover from the Sentinel's weapons. "STRUCTURAL INTEGRITY COMPROMISED," it boomed. "UNABLE TO ACQUIRE TARGET LOCK."

"Aww, too bad," said Logan as he leaned against a tree.

Hudson glared at him. "You're just going to stand there?"

"Unless there's a Chlorite involved, I ain't helpin' a Sentinel."

"Hm. Loyalty never was your strong suit."

Even after all this time, he couldn't resist a dig. Logan fired back. "Loyalty to what? How many times has the government screwed you over, dismantled Alpha Flight only to come beggin' again when they needed you?"

"At least I've been there when my country needed me!"

Manta swooped over them. "Why are you looking in the past direction? The battle is this way, in the now!"

Hudson looked sheepish. Logan didn't. "Right," Hudson said as he launched himself into the fray.

But almost right away, Slither landed on Hudson's back, wrapping his snakelike neck and flexible limbs around Mac and starting to squeeze like a boa constrictor. He probably couldn't squeeze hard enough to overwhelm Hudson's force field and crush him, but the constriction around his chest looked to be making it hard for him to breathe. "That's more like it," Logan said; now he had an excuse to fight. Mac might be a jerk, but at least he wasn't a Sentinel.

A few claw-swipes later and Hudson was free, with Slither collapsing to the ground. The snake-headed man was still breathing; his hide was tough, and with that long neck it was hard to find a lethal spot. But he was definitely out of action. While Mac caught his breath, Logan felt the air growing hot behind him, and he barely managed to dodge one of Burner's fireballs.

"You're Wolverine," Burner said as Logan rose to confront him. "Of the X-Men. Why fight us? Join us against these invaders and their robot enforcers! Strike a blow for mutant rights!"

"Don't give me that mutant-rights line, Calley! You're nothin' but a bunch o' thugs, whatever excuse you use. How does stealin' vibranium help mutants?"

The white-haired man shrugged. "It helps the four of us get rich!" He reached out to fire again.

But just then, Peeper's eyebeams—not as potent as Cyke's, but still effective—sliced through the damaged Sentinel's leg, and it toppled to the ground. The impact knocked Burner forward onto his hands and knees, and his flames discharged into the wet ground, flash-vaporizing its moisture so it erupted in his face. He was immune to his own flames, but the steam and dirt blinded him. Then a tree branch torn loose by the Sentinel's fall crashed down onto him, knocking him senseless. *Dang . . . they're takin' each other out now. What a bunch o' losers.*

Lifter and Peeper were still forces to be reckoned with, though. Lifter was holding his own against the second Sentinel; by increasing his body mass, he was able to stand against its force ray and repel its containment bubble harmlessly into the air. And Peeper was now turning his beams on it as well. But the first Sentinel's fall and Burner's fires had caused a couple of trees to fall, giving Manta enough room to swoop in and spread her wings, unleashing her ultraviolet flash on the little man, right into his hyper-acute eyes. Quinn screamed as he fell twitching to the ground.

A moment later, a red-and-white streak slammed into Lifter and knocked him back a few feet, leaving a furrow in the ground. The bearded thug wrestled with Guardian, trying to lift him over his head. But Hudson's control of EM fields let him compensate for Lifter's antigrav force, the same way it let him cancel out Earth's gravity and fly. He put his hands on opposite sides of Lifter's head and let loose with a pair of concussive plasma blasts. That dazed the thug enough to break his concentration, so that his mass returned to normal and he was vulnerable to an ordinary fist to the jaw. Logan growled. *I hardly got to fight anybody.*

After that, it was child's play to follow their scent trails to where they'd stashed the vibranium. That appeased Mac enough that he agreed to let Manta and the Sentinels take the Mutant Force members into custody while he returned the stuff to the military base. "But don't take them out of Canada," he insisted. "Do whatever tests you need, but they're going to stand trial here for their crimes. As long as you've identified them and know they're in custody, that's all you need, right?"

"It is sufficient," Manta said. "Insofar as I can see in the future direction, your description fits it reasonably well."

"Umm . . . I'll take that as a yes."

"Great," Logan said, scanning the wilderness around him. "So where's a guy get somethin' to eat around here?"

15: Execution

Surat, India

Kitty Pryde studied the room-service menu, trying to decide if she wanted to try Gujarati or Mughali cuisine or just go for the more familiar Western fare. It was at once disturbing and reassuring that she could be in a hotel suite halfway around the world from where she was born and yet have a hard time telling she wasn't in the States. Aside from the ethnic makeup of the staff, the menu options, and the preponderance of Bollywood productions on TV, this could have been practically any hotel she'd ever been in. It was quite a contrast to the slums she'd seen in the city beyond. Surat was a city with a huge divide between rich and poor, home to a lucrative diamond trade that relied on sweatshop labor, and Kitty felt a bit guilty about luxuriating in this fancy hotel while so many outside had no roofs over their heads. But not guilty enough to pass up the room service. "Ororo?" she called to her roommate. "Any dinner preferences?"

Ororo Munroe stepped out of the shower, accompanied by a small personal whirlwind she'd conjured up to blow herself dry. This obviated any need for a towel, but Kitty had long since gotten used to her old friend's casual nudism. "Not really," Storm said, "so long as it's vegetarian."

"Well, you're in the right country for it." Indeed, Ororo had already been here for some time, using her weather powers to help with a rough monsoon season, which had kept the Wind-rider, usually a mainstay of the X-Men, unavailable to help out with the Chlorite crisis until now.

Kitty tossed her the menu, and Storm diverted a bit of her whirlwind to catch it and guide it into her hands. With a sigh, Kitty decided to give into being the ugly American and just go for the cheeseburger platter. Ororo wouldn't mind, and Kitty decided she was entitled to a little comfort food after the rough day they'd had. That Chlorite infiltrator hadn't made it easy for her, Storm, and Magique to capture him, even with a pair of Sentinels backing them up. The creep had exploited a holy site, the Swaraj Ashram, to his advantage, seeking sanctuary there in the guise of a persecuted mutant and shamelessly using Hindu pilgrims as hostages, plying an energy weapon he'd hidden in some kind of anatomical pouch. Kitty had tried phasing in underground and sneaking the hostages out that way, but the Chlorite had had eyes in the back of his head—literally—and had fired at her as she'd emerged from the ground. The beam had caused her pain despite her phased state, and she'd barely been able to keep focus and avoid solidifying half-underground. Unfortunately, Lockheed had not been around to help her out; he'd been no more willing to work alongside Sentinels than Rogue had been. The standoff had lasted until Kitty had remembered, from her study of the Diascar's data files, that his particular species of Chlorite was cold-blooded. Storm had summoned a mini-blizzard, leaving the pilgrims shivering and a bit frostbitten but otherwise unharmed, while rendering the Chlorite comatose. After that, it had been a simple matter of the Sentinels taking the infiltrator up to the nearest Diascar ship while Magique and some local officials had staged a photo op and talked about the importance of registration for exotic-looking mutants. Which was good, because Kitty had still been reeling from that energy blast.

While Ororo studied the menu, Kitty picked up the remote and started surfing through the TV channels, thinking some Bollywood movie with garish costumes, gratuitous musical numbers, and an incomprehensible plot would be just the thing to distract her from her troubles. But she paused when she came upon an English-language news channel. A *"LIVE"* caption adorned a shaky image of rioters running through the streets, and Kitty caught a glimpse of someone not quite human being dragged along against his or her will. *". . . from their homes all over Surat. This is after the mob, earlier tonight, I'm being told, broke into the city hall and obtained the registration list for the city's mutant residents, containing their names and addresses. This, of course, is not including any mutants unlucky enough to be already out on the streets when this began. . . ."*

Ororo had thrown down the menu and was hurriedly donning her uniform. "Let's go."

"Don't have to tell me twice."

To save time, Kitty phased them both through the window, and Storm flew them from there, holding onto Kitty's arm and using her winds to buoy them both. The area immediately around the hotel was quiet—not surprisingly, since most of the mutants in the city were migrant workers living in the slums—but Kitty could hear the roaring in the streets and see the distant fires, their smoke rising to mingle with the heavy pollution from the city's textile mills.

"Storm to Magique," Ororo called over her comlink. "Are you aware of the situation in the city?" Kitty could hear her clearly; they traveled along with the wind, so the wind did not blow her words away.

"Yes, Storm. It is most unfortunate."

"Unfortunate?!" Kitty cried. "There's a *pogrom* going on here! They're going to lynch everyone who doesn't look human!"

"I take it you intend to intervene?"

"Don't you? Send in the Sentinels, for Pete's sake!"

To Kitty's surprise, a Sentinel voice intruded on the com channel. *"NEGATIVE. THAT APPROPRIATION OF RESOURCES IS OUTSIDE MISSION PROFILE."*

"Oh, big surprise."

"Magique," Storm asked, "can you override them,

send them to intercede? Normally I would not wish to use them, but Shadowcat is right—the shock value of their intervention could help cow the mob."

"I fear the Sentinel has a point, Storm. We should reserve our resources for unearthing infiltrators. That must be the highest priority. I would not even have approved this rest period had the Sentinels not needed refueling."

"And what about what all those innocent mutants need?" Kitty demanded.

"I am sorry, but there is too much more at stake."

"Very well, then," Ororo said, her voice as chill as the blizzard she had summoned before. "We shall handle it ourselves." She cut the channel before Magique could reply.

Soon they were soaring over the mob scene, and Kitty was stunned by the sheer mass of enraged humanity below. Something of this magnitude was way out of her league. There would be no way to save everybody; all she could do was save whom she could. "I'm going down," she told Storm. "I'll try to get some people out."

Ororo threw her a concerned look . . . but in a moment, her eyes showed acceptance that Shadowcat was an adult now, not the inexperienced little "Kitten" she'd first met back in Deerfield. "Very well. I shall attempt a more large-scale solution, but it will take time to gather the necessary forces. Be careful."

"I will." Squeezing Ororo's hand one last time, Kitty phased out of her grip and wafted her way down to ground level.

In her phased state, Shadowcat could pass through

the crush of bodies completely untouched. Unfortunately, that was only true in a physical sense. The noise was deafening, and the sheer rage and hatred in the air was palpable, toxic. The paradox of it bewildered her. India was a nation with a long tradition of pacifism and tolerance. Gandhi himself had come from this part of the country, had graced the very ashram she'd visited today. Yet despite that, things like this kept happening here.

Is my country really that different? she asked herself, thinking of the Sentinels. Even in those societies that strove for the best impulses of humanity, the worst still remained.

But this was no time for philosophy. Before her, an older, helpless man with heavily mottled skin was being dragged out of an alley and pummeled by the crowd. He pleaded in Hindi, a language Kitty understood, thanks to Xavier's telepathic language lessons. "Please! I am not a mutant! I just have a skin condition!" But his words went unheeded. Perhaps the Gujarati-speaking crowd didn't understand him. More likely, they just didn't care at this point.

A man raised a baseball bat to swing at the older man's head. Kitty was too far to reach the victim, but she managed to touch the assailant just in time to phase him, the bat passing harmlessly through its intended target. The mob members who saw it were shocked, paralyzed just long enough for Kitty to grab the mottled man and phase him, pulling him literally through the attacking crowd and then through the wall of a nearby slum. She led him some blocks away and made sure he was safely indoors before stopping. "Thank you," the man said, shaking her hand. "Thank you. I'm not a mutant. Really."

Kitty threw him a look. "In case you missed it—I am." Then she headed back into the crowd.

It was some moments before she managed to find another victim of the mob, a woman covered in blue feathers. The mob had her bound hand and foot, and Kitty watched in horror as they doused her with gasoline. *"No!!"* she screamed in vain, too far away to prevent a match from being struck and dropped.

By the time she got close enough, it was clearly too late to do anything for the poor woman. Kitty whirled on the crowd, lunging at the man who'd lit the fire. He and his cronies fought back, but they were no match for her ninja training. She didn't even bother to phase. Soon enough, almost without her consciously realizing it, several of them lay unconscious or groaning in pain, while the rest had retreated to a safe distance. *"Cowards!"* she screamed at them in English. "Why are you doing this?! The Chlorites are the enemy! The aliens! These people were cleared, dammit! They were cleared!"

"They brought the alien here!" someone in the mob countered. "It's because of them our ashram was defiled!"

"Right!" another yelled, still more echoing him. "The filth probably recruited them, turned them against us! They defile this place by being here!"

"What do you know about defilement?" Kitty screamed. "You're the ones defiling the ashram, defiling everything it stands for! Murderers!"

"She's one of them!" someone cried. "Get her!"

Kitty wanted to take them all on, but she caught herself, remembering that others needed her. She phased again, let the mob members pass through her as she ran to find others who needed her, praying she could reach them before it was too late.

As she ran, she belatedly realized it was raining. The rain rapidly grew heavier, the wind kicking up more strongly. *Ororo!* Kitty realized. She thanked God her friend was here; of all the X-Men, only Storm could single-handedly douse an entire city's worth of violence. Kitty knew the Wind-rider would not stop until the deluge reached monsoon proportions, enough to drive everyone indoors or blow them clear off their feet—and put out any further fires.

But it would take time for the downpour to reach that magnitude, and the fury of the mob was slow to subside. Yet Kitty saw a vision through the rain: a horde of *rakshasas,* demons from Hindu mythology, descending upon the crowd, harrying them away from the beleaguered mutants. *Magique's illusions,* Kitty realized. The Guardswoman must have had a change of heart and come to help after all. Unsurprisingly, though, the Sentinels were nowhere in sight.

Soon the mob was scattering, but Kitty, Magique, and Storm still had to get the mutants to safety and to medical treatment. When they reached the hospital, Kitty saw its staffers unhesitatingly come to the mutants' aid, treating them like any other patients. There were even some local volunteers bringing a few other mutants in, offering to help in any way they could. It reminded Kitty that there were still plenty of good people here.

"But this won't be the end of it," she said to Storm as the taller woman wrapped an arm around her shoulders. "If something like this happened here . . . it'll happen elsewhere. People will blame mutants for what the Chlorites are doing. Governments will abuse the registration files."

"True. I am not convinced that those files came into the mob's possession by accident."

"And we're a part of it, Ororo. We're helping to create that climate of hostility and mistrust."

Ororo was silent for a moment, thinking. "Perhaps. But what else can we do?"

Kitty had no answer.

16: Excelsior!

New York City, United States

"That's right, true believers! As long as we stand together, human and mutant alike, they can't defeat us!
We'll show those arrogant aliens and their mechanical monstrosities that we have rights! Human rights,
mutant rights, American rights, alien rights—you
name it, we stand for it! I know, friends and neighbors, you're scared. Scared of the E.T. terrorists who
destroyed Alcala. But are we gonna let them scare us
into giving up our freedoms, our principles? I think
not, true believers! And by standing together we'll
show them that humans aspire to something higher
than mere survival at any price! So come on up, stand
with us and cry, 'Make mine democracy!'"

Jean levitated over City Hall Park, listening to the

spiel of the protest leader who stood upon the wide, massive staircase leading into New York's seat of governance. He was an elderly man with unruly gray-white hair, a matching moustache, and large square glasses. But he had a youthful energy and a spry, puckish voice, and he rallied the crowd in a manner that was half revivalist preacher, half carnival barker. He certainly knew how to play to an audience.

And he was far from alone. In the wake of the Surat riot, protests had broken out all over the world. This was surely one of the largest, though. Hundreds of protestors, maybe over a thousand, thronged the steps and plaza in front of City Hall. Spectators filled the surrounding park and crowded Park Row, Centre Street, and Broadway, backing up traffic clear across the Brooklyn Bridge. Most of the protestors appeared to be human, Jean was gratified to note, but some exotic-looking mutants were present too, standing up for their right not to be registered. Unsurprisingly, there were also counter-protestors present, accusing the protestors of being traitors to humanity and holding up signs with legends like Don't Let Alcala Happen Again! And Do You Know What Your Neighbors Are?

Smasher flew up alongside Jean, shaking his head. "What is wrong with these people? Can't they see their whole world is in danger?"

"They just want to make sure it's still going to be a world worth living in. For everybody."

"And that will be a moot point if even one infiltrator goes undetected long enough. There could be a Chlorite among these protestors. They must be tested."

"And how far are you willing to go to ensure that?"

He threw her a look. *"We* must all be willing to do whatever we must. Remember, we are together in this. But I will try to convince them of that before I resort to harsher measures." He surveyed the crowd again. "At least they have come to the right building. We must simply get them inside it. Come with me."

Rokk started forward, but Jean spoke. "So no calling in the Sentinels unless you have to? They'd only make things worse in a situation like this."

"They will stay in reserve for now. But they are nearby. Now come!"

As they drew closer, Jean was startled to sense some familiar mental auras in the crowd. Her eyes followed her more ethereal senses, and she discerned the faces of several Xavier Institute students among the protestors, including Harry Mills and Meena Banerjee. And there next to them was a shock of brown hair with a distinctive streak of white. Rogue was with them.

Jean reminded herself that her colleague and students had the right to speak out for whatever cause they wished. But it felt like a personal blow. *Or is that just because I feel guilty about the part I'm playing in all this?*

By now, Smasher had landed next to the protest leader and engaged him in debate. "I understand your concerns, all of you," he announced to the crowd. "Know that the Shi'ar Empire and its Diascar allies respect your rights. But for the moment, under the current dire threat your world faces, these measures are necessary for your own protection." The crowd's jeering drowned out the tail end of his words. "Do you even understand what is at stake here?" Rokk went on, making Jean wince at his condescension. "Do you want this city to become another Alcala?"

"No," the protest leader fired back. "But we don't want it to become another Surat either! That mob of marauders used your registration rolls to hunt down its victims! We won't let that happen to us!" The crowd roared in agreement.

"How do you know a Chlorite terrorist does not stand among you at this very moment? You could be playing right into their hands!"

"If we destroy our own way of life in trying to protect it from them, then we do their job for them!"

"Which is more important—your way of life or your very lives?"

"Aha! Then you admit, you don't care about protecting our way of life!"

"I admit no such thing. But it will not matter if you are no longer alive!"

"There's more to life than simply living! Try taking off those rose-colored glasses of yours and maybe you'll see that!" The crowd laughed, adding their own taunts toward Smasher.

"Very well," Rokk declared. "I did not wish this, but you leave me no choice."

Jean flew down beside him. "No, don't!"

"There is no time for this! Most of your world still remains unsecured. We cannot abide delays!" He activated his comlink. "Engage!"

Within moments, a familiar sound of rockets rose from the west, and three Sentinels hove into view above the TriBeCa rooftops. Many people in the crowd began screaming. Rokk urged them to remain calm, and the protest leader did much the same, though he added, "Don't give them an excuse!"

Two of the Sentinels came down on opposite ends of Flanders Square, with the third landing at the edge of the trees, opposite the square from City Hall, so that they had the crowd surrounded. It didn't stop many of the protestors from running, especially as some of the counter-protestors began hurling garbage or rushing forward. The police rushed in and tried to maintain calm, but the presence of the Sentinels had spooked too many people. "Stand your ground!" the protest leader cried. "Protect the mutants! But no violence!"

But a number of the obvious mutants were running too or striking defensive postures as the Sentinels strode toward them. People in the crowd scattered, trying to avoid the Sentinels' heavy footsteps.

Jean saw Rogue take to the air and head toward one of the Sentinels. She flew to intercept Rogue's course. "Please, Rogue—don't fight us. I respect your right to sit this one out, but please don't escalate this, or we'll have to arrest you!"

"I ain't the one escalatin', Jean! But don't worry—I won't break your tin soldiers 'less I have to. I just wanna make sure they don't hurt nobody!"

"We can agree on that, at least." They met each other's eyes for a moment and exchanged a nod, then Jean flew out of Rogue's way.

By now the chaos was spreading out, as mutants and other protestors ran out into the park and the streets.

Jean chased after a Sentinel that was smashing through the trees in pursuit of a fleeing mutant, who was firing back with globs of a corrosive liquid. She was kept busy for some moments, telekinetically catching falling trees before they hit any bystanders. She was thus unable to intercede when she saw another Sentinel lumbering into the street after another mutant, kicking the grid-locked cars aside and smashing them into one another. Jean stared in horror as a young strawberry-blonde woman running across the street stumbled and fell between two cars that were on the verge of crushing her between them. She was too far to help.

But at the last second, Rogue dove in and swept the woman out of harm's way just before the cars crunched together. Setting her rescuee down safely on the curb, she then waded back into the street to help other trapped motorists. *Good,* Jean thought. *At least that means she isn't fighting Sentinels.*

But Jean's own Sentinel was still wreaking havoc in the park, and there were still too many fleeing by-standers (well, byrunners) crowding the space below the trees. Realizing that catching trees one by one wasn't doing the job, Jean reflexively diverted her efforts to the cause, restraining the Sentinel with a TK force field before it could smash aside a particularly massive tree.

The Sentinel didn't like that. "UNAUTHORIZED INTERFERENCE IN DETENTION OPERATIONS. DESIST IMMEDIATELY OR YOU WILL BE DETAINED."

"*You* desist!" Jean shouted back. "You're not authorized to endanger innocent lives!"

"ALLOWING POTENTIAL HOSTILES TO ESCAPE CREATES A GREATER DANGER. RELEASE THIS UNIT AT ONCE."

Jean realized that last sentence was echoing and not off of the nearby buildings. She spun to see another Sentinel closing on her from the west. "DESIST IMMEDIATELY OR YOU WILL BE DETAINED," it repeated, raising a hand menacingly.

"Leave her alone!" Rogue swooped in and delivered a roundhouse punch to its jaw, knocking it back. It staggered, but recovered and began shooting at her, not, bothering with a warning first. One of the electron bolts blasted off a tree branch, and Rogue doubled back and caught it before it could land on the fleeing protestors. Still holding the branch, she flew toward the Sentinel. "Hey, Mechagodzilla! Why don'tcha pick on somebody your own size?" Timing her swing, she used the branch to knock the Sentinel's arm sideways just as it fired. The electron bolt hit its telekinetically restrained companion dead-on. "Like him!" The damaged Sentinel shuddered and fell inert, teetering dangerously. Jean used her mental grip to lower it gently to the ground.

"Rogue, please!" she called as she did so.

"Hey, I didn't start it! And it ain't my fault if they can't watch where they're shooting!"

"You're putting innocents in danger by fighting them!"

"More'n they'd be put in danger if we didn't?! Or did you have that Sentinel lassoed for its own protection jus' now?"

She had to concede the point. Indeed, if Rogue

had wanted to, she could've punched the Sentinel's head clear off its shoulders. She was actually holding back. "Fine, just get the people to safety!"

"Cool yer jets, Gal Fawkes! I know what I'm doin'!"

Sighing, Jean lifted herself higher to survey the situation. The Sentinel to the east had its quarry contained in a capture bubble and was now returning to pursue other mutants still at large. Several of the students from the institute were in Park Row, helping free motorists from their wrecked cars, along with various police officers; and Jean thought she caught a glimpse of Spider-Man helping out as well. The police had the protestors—those who hadn't managed to escape—surrounded, and the police seemed to be making arrests. Smasher was circling the area, scanning the surroundings, and suddenly a bluish beam shot out from his exo-spex, paralyzing a fleeing mutant. "Sentinel, disengage and detain," he commanded, and Jean saw the intact Sentinel below her abandon its standoff with Rogue and head toward the specified target. She dove down in front of it and gently nudged the remaining people out of its way, not trusting it to watch out for them.

Before much longer, the situation was in hand. The mutant prisoners were being taken away for testing under Smasher's watchful gaze. Many civilians who had resisted on their behalf, including the spry old protest leader, were in handcuffs, waiting to be loaded into police vans. The motorists were out of danger now, at least until they attempted to file their insurance claims. To Jean's relief, no one had been killed, though a number of people had been taken to nearby Downtown Hospital.

As for Jean and Rogue, they'd been getting along fine so long as they focused on helping the innocent and avoided bringing up the fifty-ton gorilla looming over them. But that became harder when Smasher came over to brief Jean. "We managed to detain all the exotic mutants. Fortunately," and he cast a look at Rogue, "those super-powered individuals who might have misguidedly interfered with the arrests chose instead to direct their efforts toward protecting the civilians."

"Awful convenient for you, then," Rogue said, "that yonder Sentinels put so many civilians in need o' protectin'."

"I do not appreciate your implication," Smasher said tightly.

"I wasn't *implyin'* anything. I was accusin' outright."

Smasher took a step toward her, but Jean interposed herself. "Take care," Rokk said. "I am being lenient with you and your associates because of the lives you protected today. But that leniency has its limits."

"Well, I'm just the kind o' gal who likes to push the envelope."

Jean sighed. "Rogue . . ."

"What, Jean? What? Look around ya. Look at all the decent folk *you* helped arrest today! Folk who stood up for the rights o' people like *us*. You want that to become a crime?"

"I want to protect my home!"

Rogue stared at her sadly. "That's always the excuse, ain't it? Maybe those of us as ain't got no home can see it better." She flew off without another word.

"Rogue . . ." Jean's voice trailed off. *You do have a home. With us.* But she said it only to herself.

17: Extraterritorial

Henry Peter Gyrich studied the field reports with satisfaction. As alien invasions went, this one was turning out remarkably well. Many of the past proposals he'd supported for mutant registration and regulation, proposals that had been approved by sensible leaders but then rolled back under pressure from bleeding-heart activists, were now being instituted globally. As emergency measures, they didn't require public approval, but the public had been solidly behind them ever since the Alcala incident. After that, few had been willing to make the Alcalanos' mistake and open their homes and communities to unregulated mutants, beings whose powers, agendas, and very humanity could not be trusted.

True, in the wake of the Surat riots, there had been a renewed wave of protests, like the one in New York. There was still a solid core of blind idealists who just didn't see the danger. But in the current circumstances, most others could see people like that as the threat to global security that Gyrich had always known they were. It had done his heart good to see the Sentinels stomping down on that mob of muties and mutie-lovers, putting the fear of God into them and silencing their unpatriotic whining. Not to mention seeing the polls on the nightly news showing better than sixty percent approval for the action. People might have been disturbed by the images from Surat, but the memory of days' worth of wall-to-wall coverage of Alcala was still stronger in their minds.

Gyrich had to admire the Diascar's cold logic in forcing the people of Earth to witness every minute of the Alcalanos' suffering. Few people would soon forget what was at stake, not after that. If anything, those X-Men's desire to minimize mutant casualties in Surat had worked against them in the propaganda war, since it had left them far fewer gruesome images with which to sell their cause. They just didn't have the toughness to do what it took to win.

And that gave Gyrich hope for the future. History showed that Xavier and his mutant strike force would be the ones most likely to stand in the way of any attempt to keep the Sentinels, registrations, and restrictions on mutants in place after the Chlorite threat was ended. But while the X-Men were being run ragged around the world, trying to deal with individual crises and individual lives, they didn't have the luxury Gyrich had to consider the big picture, to plan for the long term. That would leave them lagging behind, struggling to keep up when the time came.

If it came, he reminded himself. Really, how could we ever be sure the Chlorite threat was gone for good (he imagined himself arguing before Congress)? Searching every nook and cranny of the entire Earth could take years, especially if one considered all those hidden, hard-to-reach places like the Savage Land, Atlantis, and Subterranea. And who knew whether the Chlorites out in space might try again? The interrogators still hadn't managed to find out from the captive moles just how they'd all managed to sneak onto the planet, so it remained possible that others could continue to arrive undetected. The threat of Chlorite infiltration might be a part of everyday life from now on—and as long as that threat existed, no being that wasn't clearly human could be allowed to run free. Those who didn't actively work with the government in tracking down and regulating others of their kind (and Gyrich had to appreciate the choice irony in that) would have to accept being regulated or face the consequences. Global security would demand no less.

The one downside to all this, Gyrich thought, *is that we have to depend so much on aliens to make it happen.* He supposed the Diascar were agreeable enough as aliens went—horselike, furred, not slimy or scaly or chitinous or fanged. He'd actually seen commercials for plush Diascar dolls showing up on television; the pundits were predicting them to be hot sellers this Christmas season. But really, how could he take these creatures seriously when they looked like something he should be storing in a barn and riding?

But that wasn't the real problem, was it? The problem was that they *had* to be taken seriously. However much they might look like something out of a little girl's fairy-tale imaginings, the reality was that they controlled a power and technology far greater than Earth's, and they could have their way with this planet if they wanted to. It wasn't right that any inhuman creatures should have the power to dictate the fate of humanity. It was bad enough facing that threat from Earth's superpowered beings—the villains who had the power to destroy millions, the self-styled heroes who assumed that their power gave them the right to trample ordinary lives in the course of their battles. Right now, one inhuman power was helping to keep the other in check. But how to keep the Diascar in check? How to ensure that they would go their own way and leave humanity in charge of its own defense against Chlorites?

The success of the Sentinels was helping in that regard, proving that humans could take responsibility for their own homeworld. With luck, Gyrich could push through an expansion of the Sentinel program, fill the air with thousands of them, an impenetrable network of defenders. That might convince the Diascar that Earth could be left to its own devices. And if not, well, it would only take a small programming tweak to convince the Sentinels to treat the Diascar as enemies of Earth and act accordingly. . . .

Val Cooper appeared at the door of his office, breaking that agreeable train of thought. "You watching?" she asked, gesturing at his television. While he had it on and tuned to CNN as usual, he'd muted the volume so he could concentrate on the field reports . . . and on his wish-fulfillment fantasies, he added ruefully.

Turning to the screen, he saw a scene of open conflict: Sentinels versus troops and tanks. The caption revealed the scene of the action to be Madripoor, a small principality in Southeast Asia. "What's going on?" he asked.

"Madripoor refused to let the Sentinels come in to search. Their usual line, no interference in their 'free business practices,' yada yada. Said any unauthorized entry into their airspace would be an act of war. The Guard and the Sentinels went in anyway."

"And the mutants?" He thought he'd glimpsed a flying figure in the sky, but it could have been one of the Guard.

"Quicksilver and Karma were with them. They're reported on the scene, but it's hard to say whether they're taking a side or just doing damage control."

Typical. You can't trust these people's loyalties. "Either way, no loss. Madripoor's the biggest den of thieves and pirates in the world. Who cares about their national sovereignty? It'll do the world good to have the Sentinels clean up the place."

Cooper stared at him. "You do realize we're now officially at war?"

Gyrich shrugged. "Hey, not us. This is a joint Diascar-UN operation, remember? Oh, and let's not forget the Shi'ar. Add in the Sentinels, and they'll have that flyspeck of a nation conquered before the eleven o'clock news. And we'll all be better off for it."

"Maybe. But what happens when it's China refusing to let the Sentinels in? Or North Korea?"

"Oh, come on, do you really think they'd *have* any unregulated mutants? If they even allowed them to live?"

"Do you really think the Diascar would take their word for that?"

He shrugged. "Would that be so bad? The Diascar take down some enemies of the United States, and nobody makes a fuss because it's all in the interests of protecting the world from aliens. Our butts are covered, and our budgets aren't strained."

Cooper threw him a sidelong glance. "You can be one twisted SOB, you know that?"

"I'll do whatever it takes to protect the security of my nation—same as you."

She looked away uneasily. "Maybe. But it's more personal for you."

"What can I say? I love my country. And I hate its enemies."

"Then you'll like this." Cooper gestured to the screen. The camera had suddenly tilted skyward, searching for something. Soon it settled shakily on its target—a pair of Diascar battleships, descending from orbit. They grew swiftly in the camera's frame until they loomed over Madripoor's capital.

Gyrich leaned back and folded his arms. "Now it gets interesting."

The more time Defense Leader Taforne spent among these humans, the more their behavior disturbed him—even frightened him.

They were a predatory race, unlike the Diascar, and it showed in so many aspects of their lives. They seemed to revel in war and conflict. Every time their nations or factions attempted to come together for their common good, some of them found excuses to clash with others, often letting their petty differences override their collective benefit. Even now, with their whole world at stake, human nations—such as this tiny Madripoor that dared to resist the allied search efforts and attempted to fire on his ship as it hovered over their ruling city—clung to their petty agendas, their territoriality and ideology, and chose to fight rather than work to protect their own greater good.

Not that Taforne couldn't understand territoriality or the competitive urge. His massive horns weren't just there to make him look good, but had served him well in youthful competitions over females or status. And his ancestors back in simpler times had used their horns to battle with rival herds over prime grazing territory or with rival males over mating rights. In some extreme cases, the losing parties had been crippled, even killed outright.

But when it came to a threat to the herd's very survival, locking horns over pride or self-interest became a liability. You fled from a threat if you could, and, failing that, you did everything in your power to eliminate it as quickly as possible.

These humans didn't seem to get that. They blurred the lines between fighting for survival and fighting for pride and prestige. They routinely killed each other over matters of tribal ego or ideological brinksmanship and routinely bickered over control or policy or ethics or advantage when their very lives were endangered. It seemed they simply relished the fight as an end in itself and went to great lengths to make excuses for it.

Some of them even seemed to welcome facing mortal threats, to go out of their way to ensure their continuation. Taforne had studied the government's records of Professor Charles Xavier, finding numerous instances where the human scholar had refused to destroy an enemy, even at risk of allowing that enemy to endanger Xavier, his students, or other innocents later on. And Xavier was not the only one. The scientist Reed Richards, in an event so infamous that Taforne had learned of it even before coming to Earth, had once had the opportunity to slay the dreaded Galactus, the Devourer of Worlds himself, but instead had restored him to health and freed him to continue menacing the universe. Yes, these people claimed to justify these acts on moral grounds, the sanctity of life and so forth, but what about the sanctity of the lives these predators would continue to take? Taforne found their excuses unconvincing, hypocritical. He felt it more probable that these humans actually *wanted* their greatest foes to continue menacing them, challenging them, giving them excuses to have more exciting adventures, without regard for the death and destruction that would result. They were a frightening bunch, these creatures.

This Madripoor place, indeed, seemed to embody all their worst attributes. According to the reports, it was dominated by criminals and murderers, its economy built on death and misery—the selling of lethal weapons, of drugs that enslaved and slowly killed, of human beings as slaves. If there was any place those evil Chlorite *hrrauhoks* would feel at home, as toxic and murderous as they were as a breed, this was surely it.

No surprise, then, he thought, *that the Madriporean government would fight our efforts to save their misbegotten world. I would not be surprised if they were cooperating with the Chlorites. If they cared for long-term survival, would they allow their land to be so infested with killers?*

Fortunately, their technology did not pose as great an obstacle as their attitude. The will to fight may have been bred into them, but their firearms, tanks, and aircraft were no match for the combined forces of the Diascar ships, the Imperial Guard, and the human-built but Diascar-enhanced Sentinels. It had been necessary to send out scout ships to airlift in several additional Sentinels and Guardsmen from the region, but the insurgency was already collapsing, and Taforne expected the principality to be fully subdued before the last reinforcements even arrived.

Indeed, many of the local "business" leaders had already unilaterally surrendered or attempted to strike deals, in defiance of the government that was supposedly fighting to protect their autonomy. As a nation composed largely of criminals, the Madriporeans could not be bothered to stand together or defend one another, but simply looked out for themselves. That meant fighting at first but turning around and negotiating when things did not go their way.

Something of that sort seemed to be happening on the ground now, and Taforne ordered the monitors to direct the Sentinels' visual feed from that location to his display. A group of local gangsters had apparently rounded up a number of visibly nonhuman mutants and were parading them out before the Sentinels at gunpoint. At least, most of them were visibly nonhuman. Some were close enough that Taforne could not be sure whether they fell outside the natural range of human variations. But the gunmen seemed to see it differently. *"You want the muties, is that it?"* their leader called to the Sentinels. *"Here are all we could find. We'll round up more for you, just say the word. All we want in exchange is to be left alone."*

"Mr. Akayama, no!" one of the mutants cried. *"I've been loyal! I got you those girls—"*

"Silence, mutie!" The lead gunman struck the mutant with the butt of his weapon, causing it (Taforne had enough trouble distinguishing the sexes of normal humans) to collapse unconscious to the ground, bleeding heavily.

Another one of the mutants took the opportunity to strike, giving off a blinding flash of strobing light. It and several other mutants broke free of their captors and attempted to run. "Sentinels, detain them!" Taforne ordered.

But the gunmen had ideas of their own and began opening fire on the mutants. *"No!"* came a cry from the ground. It was the mutant called Quicksilver, who suddenly appeared on the scene with his superhuman speed. Racing past the gunmen, he knocked the weapons from their hands before they could react.

But there were other gunmen lying in wait, snipers that now cut loose from upper windows. Quicksilver had to dodge and swerve, a hail of bullets blocking his path to the mutants, who now fled in several directions, being pursued variously by Sentinels or gangsters. *"Taforne,"* Quicksilver called in his rapid-fire voice, *"do not allow those mutants to be killed! They cannot all be Chlorites!"*

Neither can I risk allowing a Chlorite to escape in order to protect a few individual lives, Taforne thought. Nonetheless, he spoke to assuage the mutant's concerns. "The Sentinels are programmed to detain them alive. They will do—"

Quicksilver interrupted. *"You expect me to trust them?"*

"I expect you to do your job and assist in detaining the mutants!"

The conflict on the ground continued, and Quicksilver seemed to make little effort to obey Taforne's order. Instead, he continued his efforts to disarm the gunmen or to remove mutants from their line of fire without subsequently ensuring their detention. Only the Sentinels on the scene were managing to do their duty, though there were only two. The rest, and the Imperial Guardsmen, were occupied elsewhere in the city.

Taforne watched as the gunmen cornered one young mutant, evidently a female with green skin and a slender tail, in an alley. Her exit was blocked by a Sentinel in the process of detaining two other mutants in a capture sphere. The Sentinel looked on disinterestedly as the gunmen emptied their automatic weapons into the girl's body. By the time Quicksilver arrived in the alley in response to the shots, there was little left recognizable as humanoid.

The white-haired, blue-clad mutant screamed at the Sentinel in rage. *"You were supposed to detain them alive! Alive!!"*

"MISSION PRIORITY IS TO PREVENT MUTANT ESCAPE. SECURING THE FEMALE MUTANT ALIVE WOULD HAVE IN- HIBITED CAPTURE OF TWO MALE MUTANTS. SECURING THE TWO MALE MUTANTS FULFILLED MISSION PRIORITY, SINCE THIRD-PARTY ACTION PREVENTED THE FEMALE MUTANT'S ESCAPE."

"You monsters! I should have known this would happen. Well, no more! I no longer stand with you against my fellow mutants!" Quicksilver removed his comlink and smashed it to the ground, launching himself at the Sentinel before it hit. The Sentinel was still crouched over to collect its capture spheres, so when the superfast mutant leaped up and kicked it in the chest, it was knocked onto its back. Quicksilver rebounded from the impact, came down on his feet, and swept past the gunmen, knocking them aside with great force and taking their weapons from them. He then charged the Sentinel with guns blazing, delaying only for the brief moment it took him to reload their clips at accelerated speed.

But the Sentinel was able to withstand the weapons fire and was already clambering back to its ungainly bipedal stance. "UNDER ATTACK FROM MUTANT SUB- JECT DESIGNATED QUICKSILVER," the Sentinel trans- mitted to Taforne. "REASSESS HOSTILE/NONHOSTILE STATUS?"

It was tempting, but the mutant was reacting out of impulsive anger and was doing no serious harm as yet. Certainly he should be disciplined, but Taforne would do so by the book, rather than unleashing the Sentinels upon him. "Negative. Subject's nonhostile status remains in effect."

"INSUFFICIENT RESPONSE. SUBJECT'S ACTIONS DEMONSTRATE ONGOING HOSTILITY. REQUEST AUTHORIZATION TO REASSESS STATUS OF SUBJECT QUICKSILVER."

"I decide what response is sufficient! Do as you are commanded!"

"COMMAND PRIORTY IS DETENTION OF HOSTILE NONHUMAN SUBJECTS. ACTIONS OF SUBJECT QUICKSILVER ARE COMPROMISING THIS UNIT'S STRUCTURAL INTEGRITY. THIS UNIT'S ABILITY TO FULFILL COMMAND PRIORITY IS COMPROMISED BY SUBJECT'S ATTACK. THEREFORE, SUBJECT'S HOSTILE/NONHOSTILE STATUS MUST BE REASSESSED TO FULFILL COMMAND PRIORITY."

Was this machine presuming to lecture Taforne on procedure? Normally he would have been happy to butt horns with someone who challenged his authority, but this was simply a piece of hardware acting up according to some glitch in its human-designed software, and the defense leader could not be bothered. This was a distraction that needed to be ended. "Very well. You are instructed to disarm and detain subject Quicksilver using *minimum* necessary force. The subject is not to be injured. Confirm!"

"CONFIRMING NEW PRIORTY: NONLETHAL DETENTION OF SUBJECT *QUICKSILVER.*"

"Good." Not that it was as easy as all that, for the mutant was exceedingly fast. The Sentinels' brains could process information faster, but their speed of movement was limited by their bulk and their humanoid form. But a second Sentinel had by now arrived to close off the other end of the alley, trapping the mutant. Working together, the two robots were able to anticipate the mutant's evasive movements, so that one could herd him toward where the other would strike. When he attempted to run up the wall of one of the buildings limning the alley, a Sentinel blasted it to pieces, and Quicksilver was forced to dodge back down into the alley. But the second Sentinel was already spraying the surface of the alley with low-friction foam, causing Quicksilver to lose his footing and leaving him vulnerable for the first Sentinel to nab him with a capture sphere.

Finally. We have no time for this foolishness. But as soon as Taforne thought it, he realized this was probably not the end of it. If this mutant "hero" reacted so aggressively, others would surely follow. Indeed, they would probably raise a storm of protest against the detention of Quicksilver. These humans would seize on any excuse for a fight and continue to blind themselves to the greater threat looming over them all.

I begin to wonder, Taforne dared to think, *if this planet is worth saving at all.*

18: Exit Strategies

Charles Xavier looked around curiously as he rolled into Poratine's office aboard the *Endless Plain*. He was hoping the room itself could give him some insight into the mind-set of its occupant. Her mind was very disciplined, and without intruding there was only so much he could read from it directly.

The office did not strike him as particularly military. It was spacious, with little furniture, but hardly austere. Two opposing walls were painted with murals of wide, rolling plains of alien grass, no doubt a recreation of lost Diasca. The third was a display wall showing various ship status reports in small windows, but mostly filled by what he supposed might be called a screen saver of gently rolling clouds. The fourth was curved and covered in shelves, upon which rested dozens of exotic and beautiful artifacts. The sense of emptiness, he realized, was partly due to the lack of chairs; the centauroid Diascar needed none, simply settling on their haunches atop low cushions on the floor. Luckily, Xavier thought with a smirk, he had brought his own chair.

Poratine had been on her haunches behind a low desk, but she rose to greet Xavier as he entered. She noted his interest in the wall of artifacts. "Remembrances of the various worlds I have been to," she explained. "I always make sure to obtain one. Look well, Professor. Each of these represents a world touched by Chlorite infection. Many, we were able to save. Many others, we were not." She reached out and gently stroked a bulbous artifact whose nature he could not discern. "Some of these are among the last surviving relics of their civilizations." After a quiet moment, she shook her head, gave a whinny-harumph, and trotted back to her desk. "I have been slow in choosing a suitable artifact for the Earth. There is one very clever and elegant contrivance I have seen, but I am concerned that it may be too fragile to keep on a working military vessel. Yet that very fragility, combined with its inner dynamism, makes it a marvelous symbol for the life we strive to preserve. I believe it is called a 'lava lamp.'"

Xavier almost smiled. But other matters concerned him. "Fleet Leader Poratine, I am here—"

"You are here, I assume, to plead for the release of the mutant Pietro Maximoff, known as Quicksilver."

"Yes, I am."

"He is not one of your X-Men."

"He is an ally. And . . . the son of an old friend."

"And I would happily release him to you . . . if you could guarantee that he would do nothing more to impede our operations. Can you make such a promise?" Her gaze was challenging.

Xavier kept his own gaze calm and steady, but confessed, "Pietro is his own man. I can only advise him."

"And he does not seem the sort who is easily swayed by advice. Under the circumstances, I fear he must remain in custody for the greater good. Rest assured he will be treated well."

The professor sighed. "I do not doubt that everything the Diascar have done here has been in pursuit of the greater good. But it must be evident by now that your policies are bringing increasing harm."

"Our policies are necessary. The harm comes when your people refuse to cooperate."

"With respect, Fleet Leader, what else could you expect? You cannot simply show up on someone else's planet, tell them that they must do things your way, and expect them to accept that without difficulty. You cannot ask them to simply surrender their right to participate in the decision-making process, to find approaches that are suited to their own needs, their own values."

Poratine spoke over him. "And you cannot know how useless your abstractions are!" She broke off, huffed a breath to calm herself, and went on after a pause, her tone more gentle. "What would you have me say, Professor? We could rehash the same argument over and over. You could tell me tragic tales of how mutants have been abused on your world, of how the Sentinels have inflicted death and destruction. I could frighten you with firsthand accounts of world after world dying from chlorine poisoning, their bodies and their great works dissolved agonizingly away by searing acid. You could tell me of the great injustice of our tactics, and I could tell you of the unbearable cost of doing less."

She lowered her head. "And the worst part is, we would both be absolutely right. Your people *do not* deserve this treatment, do not deserve the costs to their lives and freedoms that must be imposed. But neither do they deserve extinction. We can debate the details all we want, but that remains the bottom line. And you are too intelligent not to understand that. So what is left to debate?"

Xavier spoke carefully. "I do understand what is at stake here. I accept the need to contain the Chlorite infiltrators and isolate them from the Earth's environment by any means necessary. I understand the time constraints which make haste and thoroughness so important.

"But the fact remains that the situation on the ground is growing more dangerous, more chaotic. If we wish this operation to succeed, it is important to refine the approach being used. I think the examples of New York and Madripoor demonstrate that using heavy-handed tactics in the pursuit of speed and efficiency is in fact counterproductive, because it breeds resentment and resistance which require diverting effort from the actual search for Chlorites. That will only increase if matters continue as they have done."

"Professor, you tell me nothing I have not seen the like of on other worlds. We have faced such resistance before and have experience at containing it."

"But at what cost to the civilizations of those worlds?"

Again her head lowered. "Often a great cost. But not as great as annihilation."

He sighed. "I understand your perspective on this, Fleet Leader. To you, everything is defined by that overarching menace and the need to defend against it at all costs. It is a battle you have fought your whole lives."

"Yes." Her ears and neck sagged, as though a great weight were pressing upon her head.

"But perhaps that unrelenting focus has left you with a blind spot. Perhaps you are so accustomed to battling an implacable foe that you have lost sight of less . . . absolutist ways of dealing with other forms of opposition. You . . ." He sought a way to rephrase it. "You are so used to a conflict in which there can be no compromise that you may not always recognize situations where compromise *is* possible.

"But for us, it is different. We don't have that same experience, that same history. So perhaps, given more freedom to do things our own way, we can bring some fresh perspectives to the table.

"After all, it is our world, and we do wish to save it, probably more than you do. And as my colleague Dr. McCoy pointed out, we Earthlings have perhaps had more than our share of experience at saving our world from imminent destruction."

"And others of your kind," Poratine countered, "have just as much experience at nearly *causing* your world's imminent destruction, whether through insanity, criminal self-absorption, or sheer carelessness." She sighed, softening her tone again. "Still . . . I respect your concern for the well-being of your people.

And I can understand the desire of your nations to protect their territorial integrity. Perhaps there are better ways to negotiate for access. I shall have my diplomatic teams consult with your United Nations on this point."

"Thank you, Fleet Leader." He paused. "Another matter that concerns me, though, is what comes after."

"After?"

"I am wondering if there is an exit strategy here. At what point can we say for certain that there are no infiltrators left on Earth? What measures might be needed to remain in place to guard against future infiltration? And . . . how might the actions taken in the here and now be used as precedents for other situations in the future?"

She studied him. "In other words, will the use of Sentinels and restrictions on mutants be continued? That is an internal matter, I fear. You and your governments will have to work that out between you."

"But the decisions we make here will have an influence on policies in the future. We have an opportunity, here and now, to help shape the world that we are left with after the Chlorite menace is ended. If we take it upon ourselves to ensure that future exists, do we not have a responsibility for the form it ultimately takes?"

"But there *is* no assurance!" Poratine rose to her feet and paced about the room, her agitation barely contained. She glanced at one of the murals, and Xavier felt her instinctive yearning to leap inside it and gallop freely through the plains it depicted, to flee from crisis and danger and simply run as she was born to do. He gained an insight at that moment into the strict discipline that it took for an herbivorous people bred for running from peril to remake themselves as hunters and warriors, to take the responsibility for defending the galaxy and confronting its enemies wherever they went. But as they saw it, they had no other choice. He believed he understood Poratine very well at that moment. He had long since come to terms with his paraplegia; but as a boy, he had so loved to run.

"You speak of the future, Professor, but you avoid admitting the cruel reality: Your planet may not *have* a future at all. We are racing against time, but there is no way to guarantee we will not lose. If your world becomes infected, if we cannot prevent another outbreak or contain it in time, your world *will* be lost. Until you stop hiding from that, you will not understand."

Xavier's eyes widened in horror at what he sensed in her mind at that moment. Her thoughts were still as disciplined as ever; she had allowed him to sense this. "My God."

"That is right," she said, seeing that he had gotten the message.

"If the Chlorite microbes spread out of control," he went on in hushed tones, "you won't just quarantine the Earth. You will annihilate it yourselves."

She was standing by her wall of artifacts now, studying them. Her wistfulness had suddenly gained a new, frightening dimension in his mind. "To ensure that no Chlorites manage to escape. To remove the risk of any traveler accidentally landing on your world. To prevent the scavengers and thieves who prey on dying worlds from spreading contamination." She turned to face him again. "And to spare your six billion lives from the slow, searing agony that the people of Alcala had to face. If you had to witness a whole world dying like that, if you knew there was no way to save them, then you too would see their quick obliteration as a mercy."

He did understand. He could forgive it, in the abstract, as he had forgiven the actions Wolverine had taken in Alcala. But as one of those threatened with annihilation, he had to take a different perspective. His voice hardened somewhat. "And when do you decide the point of no return has been reached? How quickly do you write off any chance of discovering a cure or rescuing the bulk of the populace? Do you even give them a say in deciding their own fate?"

"It is the Chlorites who have sealed their fate! And possibly yours! If they are not stopped, they will force me to destroy yet another world, to give the order that ends six billion more lives!" She strode toward him, bringing her face close to his. "Know, Charles Xavier, that I will do everything I must to prevent that from happening. If I must carpet your world with Sentinels, if I must imprison every last mutant, if I must conquer nations and exterminate armies, I will do so, if it will spare me having to give that final order once again!"

Her black eyes glistened with moisture. He felt far more from inside her. She would not look at the murals now, would no longer allow herself the illusion of escape from her duties, for she knew there could be none. "If anything," she continued more evenly, moving back behind her desk, "I may have already compromised too much. I could have sent down my troops from the beginning. But instead I negotiated and wrestled with your leaders, your factions. I accepted delay after delay. And in so doing I may have condemned your world to annihilation. But if that is what must be, I will not hesitate. Because I have a galaxy to protect, and I will not compromise on that."

19: Extracurricular

As soon as he left Poratine's ship, Xavier sent out a telepathic summons to the X-Men, using the Cerebro unit in the *Blackbird* to amplify his mind and reach them around the world. He informed them that he wished the team to regroup back at the mansion, to consider their options in light of new information he had just acquired.

Then he told them what he had learned from Poratine.

When the storm of emotions began pouring back in, he promptly interrupted. *We will not discuss this yet. I want you all to take some time to absorb this. Once we are back home and have taken a night to rest and recuperate, then we will meet in my office.*

He chose to summon home the core team: Cyclops, Jean, Wolverine, Nightcrawler, and Shadowcat, plus Beast and Rogue back at the mansion (though he wasn't entirely sure Rogue would attend). They were the ones who had been living with this crisis from the beginning. Xavier advised the other X-Men and reservists around the world to continue their operations with the Sentinels; someone still needed to watch the watchers.

Xavier used the *Blackbird* to pick up those who could not readily arrange their own transportation. Still, those who ended up sharing the jet ride were content to do as he wished, deferring discussion of the new revelation. Indeed, they were basically content just to sleep. The search had been running them ragged.

The next morning, the team convened in Xavier's office one by one. Rogue chose to show up after all, Xavier noted, and Kitty came in with Lockheed curled up around her shoulders, purring contentedly, evidently happy to be reunited with her. Scott and Jean were the last to arrive, holding hands and radiating a similar vibe. It had been a while since they had been able to spend much time together as husband and wife.

"So," Xavier began. "You all know the situation now."

"This is the way the world ends," Hank replied. "Not with a bang, but with a whicker."

"Yup," Logan said. "Can't say as it changes much, though."

"Are you kiddin'?" Rogue exclaimed. "They admitted they're gonna destroy the world if they think they have to!"

Logan shrugged. "Those microbes get out, we're dead anyway. They'd just be makin' it quick 'stead o' slow. Can't say that sounds like such a bad thing."

"Poratine sees it the same way," Xavier said. "I am convinced now that she is intrinsically a decent being, doing what she firmly believes is necessary for the greater good."

"Maybe," Rogue said. "But so was Bolivar Trask, I reckon. Didn't make him right."

"Would it be right," Kurt asked thoughtfully, "to risk letting Chlorite infection spread to other worlds?"

"We keep talkin' about 'em like an infection! But they ain't, Kurt! They're *people*. 'Side from a few bad apples, the people ain't the problem. It's the germs. Why can't they just find a way to get the germs outta the people, so they ain't a threat no more?"

"It's not that simple, Rogue," Hank told her, shrugging his massive shoulders. "We're not just talking about a single infection. We're talking about every one of the numerous species of intestinal flora and symbiotes that live upon and within every macroscopic animal on every planet. With apologies to Donne, while no man is an island entire unto itself, from a microbial point of view every man is a continent, a whole ecosystem harboring thousands of unicellular species. And each of those species is a part of the main. Wash them away and the man is diminished, deprived of beneficial symbiotes that protect against pathogens or assist in digesting vital nutrients.

"In many Chlorite species, the microbial flora inhabiting their bodies are even more vital, producing and processing the chlorine on which the rest of their metabolism depends. Beings like our pseudonymous Mr. Chang downstairs would die without their microbes."

"Okay, then find a way to make peace! A way we can convince the Chlorites to leave us alone. Maybe give 'em a homeworld of their own. Make sure it's quarantined all right and proper. They don't bother us, we don't bother them."

"It has been tried," Xavier said. "By the Diascar and the ancient Shi'ar. It hasn't worked. If you were a Chlorite, would you be content to be confined to one world, forbidden to leave it or interact with the broader universe? Would not the very act of denying your people access to the universe make them crave it all the more?"

Rogue fidgeted. "No. I wouldn't be happy with that," she said softly. "Seein' the world around me . . . never able to touch it . . ." Her moment of sadness gave way to sudden, surprised anger. "So what're you sayin'? That it's better just to kill 'em all? They deserve to die just 'cause they want more than they got?"

"Of course that's not what he's saying," Scott said with some heat. "The point is that it's been tried, and it didn't work. The Chlorites still fought it, still broke out and conquered other worlds.

"And we can't let ourselves forget that's what this is about. Our world is under imminent threat."

"Yeah, from the horse-folk!"

"From them *and* the Chlorites. We can debate the philosophy and morality all we want, but let's do it *after* we find the rest of these moles and get them the hell off our planet."

"Can't believe I'm sayin' it," Logan put in, "but Cyke's right." He made a face as though he'd eaten something distasteful.

Rogue's expression wasn't much different. "Do we even know there *are* any more moles? Ain't none been found since that one Sue Richards collared in L.A. An' that was the same day Cat 'n' Ro found that one in Surat. Only mutants been gettin' collared since—them an' those as tried to stand up for 'em," she added, throwing a look at Jean. "Throw in Alcala, Latveria, Cincy, an' our guy down the basement, that's only six in a week, and none in half a week since. So when do we decide we got 'em all?"

Kurt spoke up in the pause that followed. "And does getting them off our planet include the innocent refugees from the ship? Can we imagine that turning them over to the Diascar or the Imperial Guard will mean anything other than their death?"

"Right," Rogue said. "And what about Johnny-boy downstairs? Are we jus' gonna turn him over?"

Xavier sighed. "I'm not sure what to do about him. I wanted him here for Hank to study, in the hopes that he could find some medical solution to this. But as you heard, the obstacles are immense."

"Not that I've given up," Hank insisted. "But finding a solution could take years, even decades. More likely a lifetime. If not longer. Whole civilizations have found no answer."

"But they were perhaps too busy fighting to really look," Kurt said.

"Perhaps," Jean echoed. "But that means we can't really start to look until we end the fight we're facing now. First we get them off the Earth, then we investigate ways of making peace."

"But sendin' any of 'em off Earth now means the horse-folk get 'em, and that's a death sentence! You wanna do that to John? You said you'd protect your students any way you could, Professor. Whatever he mighta done, John was one o' your students. Don't he count?"

"Rogue, he was a spy sent to kill us," Cyclops said.

"I tried to kill you more'n once," she shot back, then looked away, uncomfortable at dredging it up. "You made peace with me, why not him?"

"He's a fanatic!"

"He's a boy," Xavier countered. "A frightened, impressionable boy who was easy to manipulate. I've been trying to reason with him, to win him over, but it's slow going. Even if I did persuade him to work with us, he might not have any useful information to help unearth any remaining Chlorites. And as Hank says, it could take a very long time to discover a medical solution even with the boy's cooperation." He sighed. "Also, the institute's lawyers are fighting an uphill battle to prevent a Sentinel search of the grounds. It may not be possible to keep him here much longer."

"Then move him somewhere else," Rogue said.

"Where?" Hank asked. "How long do we continue moving him around to evade searches, and how do we conceal the equipment we'd require to minimize the risk of contamination?"

"So we just turn him over to be killed just 'cause it ain't convenient to save him?"

"That's not what he means, Rogue," Kurt said.

"No, it's not what anybody *means,* but it's what it all keeps addin' up to."

Kitty spoke tentatively. "Maybe we can negotiate

something else. Maybe the professor can talk Lilandra into taking them into custody somewhere while we work on the problem."

Xavier furrowed his brow. "I feel I did make some headway in convincing Poratine to be more open to alternatives. But I'm not sure this is an area she would consider negotiable."

"Besides," Logan said, "what about all those other Chlorites out there, the ones that sent the moles in the first place? They see us showin' mercy, we might as well hang a big 'Patsy' sign over the North Pole."

"I can't believe I'm hearin' this!" Rogue cried. "Professor, ain't you the one keeps sayin' peace is always the way? That you hafta keep lookin' no matter how hard it seems?"

"I still believe that, Rogue. But sometimes an imminent threat must be dealt with before the long, hard process of peacemaking can follow. That is precisely why I trained you all as fighters as well as negotiators. Sometimes we must wield a big stick and *then* speak softly."

He sighed. "And I confess, I have a hard time seeing any solution to this problem. Many times, I have heard people claim that certain groups were incapable of coexistence, that one could not survive the continued existence of the other. We have heard it from Hitler, from Creed, from Magneto, from voices stretching back through history. But this is the one time where it seems they might have a valid point. Where the menace is a genuine, biological reality rather than an ideological excuse."

Rogue stood up in disgust. "This is goin' nowhere.

Y'all, you're just . . ." She strode to the door, then whirled. "We all got 'biological realities' to deal with! Some of us got ones too big to let us live normal lives 'round other folks. But it don't mean we give up tryin'!" She stormed out, flinging the door open so hard that it would have torn off its hinges if Jean hadn't caught it telekinetically.

"Rogue, we aren't giving up! It's just . . ." Xavier broke off. The truth was, he had no answers for her.

"No! The Sentinels are here!"

Meena Banerjee realized after a moment that everyone was staring oddly at her. She then realized that the vision of Sentinels descending upon the institute had been from an alternate reality. As far as this reality was concerned, she was seated in study hall, sharing a table with Harry, Todd, and Kris, and she'd just embarrassed herself in front of them and everyone else in the hall.

After a moment, some of the students sighed or laughed nervously. The laughs from James "Lash" Wheaton, over at the older students' table, were particularly cutting. "Just Blabberjee having another psycho episode," he said. "They should've left her in the loony bin."

"Don't say that!" said Sarah Allaire, who sat next to him (or rather, whom he arranged to sit next to at any opportunity, while Papillon herself rarely discouraged attention from any boy). "You know her visions are really happening in some universe. Just not this one."

"I hope not." Kris shuddered, wrapping her arms

around herself. "They're everywhere now. They're invading *countries* now. How much longer can the professor keep them from coming here?"

"Hey, he's kept them out this long," Harry said with his usual, carefully cultivated lack of concern. "And if they try, we've got the X-Men and the mansion's defenses to protect us."

"That didn't help in my vision," Meena said.

"One vision. Out of a million universes."

"It's more than that," she confessed. "Lately . . . I've been meditating more like John and the professor taught me, trying to scan the timelines for patterns. I can't really do that yet, but I just keep getting a stronger sense of . . . of bad. Like there are more and more timelines around us where things turn out bad or violent. I see a lot of Sentinels."

"Good," Wheaton said. "In case you've forgotten, they're protecting us from that Chlorite scum."

"Tell that to the innocent mutants they keep arresting," said Mike "Beanpole" Galbraith.

"Only the idiots who get in their way. Like Xavier, keeping one of those terrorists in the basement!" A lot of the other students glared or cried out in protest, but Lash went on. "What do you think the Sentinels, or the government, will do to us when they find out we've been sheltering one of those things? If Blabberjee is seeing them attacking this place, it's probably because they've come for Chang!" He took out his cell phone. "Well, here's the answer. We just call them and tell them what Xavier's hiding downstairs. That way they know we're loyal. It wasn't us."

"No way!" Harry cried. "You know what they'd do to the professor? To the school?"

"He brought it on himself. And it'll be worse for us if we let him pressure us into going along with it!"

"They'll close us down," Kris said. "How will we learn to control our powers?"

Wheaton ogled her in a manner that was meant more to degrade her than come on to her. "Like anyone wants you to control yours." She blushed fiercely. "Me, I got all the control I need, and I'm sick of all the bleeding-heart lectures on ethics and coexistence. The kind of coexistence Xavier's trying to pull with Chang, that's the kind that'll get us all killed. I'm calling the feds. If you're smart, you won't try and stop me, and I won't turn you in along with Xavier and his crew." He began to dial.

Only to be struck in the hand by a paper-clip missile, making him drop the phone. Harry stood up, letting his improvised rubber-band slingshot drop to the table. "Sorry. Guess I've never been that smart."

Wheaton rose to confront him. "You aren't kidding." He flicked out his hands, and sizzling energy tendrils shot out from his fingers. Luckily for Harry, Lash chose to brandish them menacingly rather than attacking outright. "That was the dumbest thing you'll ever do, Bigfoot."

Harry quailed. "O-okay, you have a point there. Or ten." But Meena noticed Beanpole slowly stretching his arm out across the table toward Lash's phone. She tried to keep her eyes from calling his attention to it. Harry must have caught it too, since he was backing away in the opposite direction, drawing Lash away from the table. "But just think about what you're doing first, okay? What about your calling plan? Can you get good long-distance rates before seven p.m. on a weekday?"

"Stand still, fleabag!" Wheaton lashed out with one hand, five electric tendrils stretching out toward him. Harry cried out and raised an arm to block them, but they wrapped around it. Meena winced . . . but after a moment she and Harry both realized that he was unharmed. Harry looked at the thick fur on his arm with new appreciation. "Huh! Insulation. Well, then, Mr. Tough Guy, what do you—uhh—" He faltered. "Starting to burn now. Little help, please?"

Meena picked up a heavy tome and slammed it down on Lash's taut tendrils, snapping three of them and causing them to dissipate. Harry was able to pull free from the other two with a tug from behind by Kristin. Harry shook his arm. "Ooh, ow. Anyone here got ice powers? Or ointment powers?"

"You aren't done with *me* yet!" Wheaton told him. He scoffed at the group of them. "What a bunch of losers. Two girls, a furbag, and a guy too heavy to move. What can you do against the Lash?"

"Hey, I'm not doin' anything," Todd protested. "Just sittin' here tryin' to study."

"And being bulletproof!" Harry cried in realization, hastily retreating behind him with the girls in tow. "Lashproof too, I bet. How useless are we now, huh?"

"Hey, did I *ask* to be a human shield here?"

"Oh, no," Wheaton said mockingly. "You've outwitted me with your cunning stratagem. If I were *standing still!*" He moved around the table to try to get a clear shot, while Harry and the girls tried keeping Todd's armor-plated body and reinforced wheelchair between Wheaton and themselves.

"James!" Sarah called. "Weren't you going to make a phone call?"

"Huh? Oh, yeah. Hey, you thought you could distract me, that it? Well, I'm too smart for that. I'll just turn you dweebs over and let the Sentinels take care of . . . hey, where the hell's my phone?" Mike, who had by now returned his arm to its normal length, put on his best nonchalant look. "Who took it?" Nobody else said anything. "Okay, then. Sarah, lend me your phone."

"I'm sorry, James—Harry had a point about the rates this time of day."

"Wha—you're with them too, aren't you? All of you! Am I the only one in this school with any sense? I'll find another phone."

He headed for the door, retracting his tendrils, but Sarah intercepted him, spreading her shimmery wings. "James, come on," she said alluringly. "It's not about John. We don't want to see the professor get hurt. And we don't want the school to be shut down, do we? I mean, we might never see each other again! I'd have to go back to France. I'd rather stay here, with the people I've grown to care for. You can understand that, can't you, James?"

"Oh, brother," Harry whispered, putting a hand to his head. "If I'd known that was how to get her to seduce me, I'd have tried to call the feds myself."

Wheaton was hesitant. "Well . . . tell you what. Have dinner with me tonight and you can try to . . . convince me not to call. Okay?"

Sarah's antennae drooped a bit, but after a moment she smiled gamely and said, "All right, James. Seven o'clock?"

"Sure."

"Just don't do anything before then, all right?"

"Fine, whatever. See you tonight, Wings. And wear something backless," he joked, knowing that of course she always did.

Sarah shuddered once he left. "Ohh, what have I done?"

Meena came up and took her hands. "Thank you, Sarah. That was very brave."

The older girl pulled her hands away. "Well, I didn't do it for you and certainly not for John. I just don't want the school or the professor hurt." She headed out into the hall.

But Harry followed, and Meena and Kris came with him. Meena noticed Todd rolling along behind them, listening in. "I still don't trust that Lash jerk," Harry said. "He'll probably let you seduce him and then call the feds anyway."

Meena's eyes widened. "Ohh, you're right! Or he might talk someone else into it . . . ohh, I can feel it, this is the danger I'm sensing! They're going to come for John! We . . . we have to do something. We have to get him out!"

"What?" Todd cried. "You forgetting he tried to kill us?"

"The professor said maybe they talked him into it. That he was just misguided and he could be helped."

"Maybe," Sarah said. "But he still would've done it anyway."

"I just don't believe that. You don't know him like I do."

"Did you know he was an alien?" Todd asked.

"Does that matter? Any more than it matters that we're mutants? It's what's inside that counts."

"Whoa, whoa, hold up here," Harry said. "So are we talking about breaking John out of the sub-basement? Us? What can we do?"

"We held our own pretty well against Lash."

"Yeah, but he's just one creep. And he isn't surrounded by state-of-the-art security systems."

"There are other students with more powers than we have," Kris ventured. "Maybe they'd help."

"Yeah!" Meena said. "Sarah, you could talk to them, get them to help."

Sarah stared. "Why would I help you break John out?"

"The same reason you helped before. For the school. If he isn't here anymore, they can't arrest the professor for hiding him."

"And what will you do with him when you have him? Where can you hide him without risking the whole cursed planet?"

"We'll find somewhere! Someplace we can seal off. Then maybe, maybe we can find some doctors, some scientists who'd help us look for a way to, to fix the problem so we can live together. Dr. McCoy's working on that—he can't be the only one. There must be others who'd help, if we can find them."

"How would you find them?"

"You can find anything on the Internet," Harry said.

"If it ain't porn, how would you know?" Todd replied.

"Shut up, or I won't let you look over my shoulder anymore."

"Besides," Meena said to Sarah, "if we get him out today, then you don't need to . . . do whatever James would make you do."

"I'm in," Sarah said instantly. "But how do we break John out?"

"Umm . . . I'm open to ideas. Anyone know how to hack a security system?"

But everyone fell silent as they rounded the corner. Rogue stood there, looking at them sternly, and it was clear she'd heard the last few sentences. "Umm," Harry said, "we can explain, Miss Rogue. It's not—"

"Don't even try, kid." She sighed, and it looked like she was coming to a decision within herself. "You wanna help your friend, right? Can't blame y'all for that." She looked them over, crossing her arms. "But y'all're just about the sorriest bunch o' wannabe X-Men I ever did see. Y'all wanna pull this off, you're gonna need help."

Harry stared. "You mean . . . *you'll* help us?"

Rogue smiled, and from the look on Harry's face, Meena figured he'd just forgotten Sarah was even there. "Why not? Bunch o' students wanna do a class project, they gotta have an advisor, right?" She looked them over. "But y'all still gotta do your share o' the work."

"Mr. Gyrich? We've got a caller on hold . . . a tip about a Chlorite."

Gyrich frowned at the phone, even though the tipline operator on the other end would be unable to see it. "So why are you bothering me with it? Log it in with all the others." The tipline got dozens of calls a day, and so far only two had turned out to be more than mistaken identity or cranks.

"I think you'll want to talk to this one, sir. He's calling from the Xavier Institute."

Suddenly Gyrich was interested. "Can you confirm that?"

"We've tracked it to a cell tower on the institute's grounds, sir. Also . . . he's in our system."

"Put him through. And transfer his information to my screen."

A moment later, he was on the line with the tipster. "This is Gyrich. You have information for me?"

An adolescent-sounding voice responded. *"Yeah. I want to report a Chlorite at the Xavier school."*

"And why do you suspect it's a Chlorite?"

"I don't suspect, I know. His name's John Chang. Xavier and the X-Men, they found him out. But they got him locked up down beneath the mansion. Think they can find a cure or make peace or some BS."

Gyrich's hand tightened around the receiver. It sounded like just the sort of thing Xavier would do, putting the nation's security at risk in order to glad-handle another class of dangerous freak. "Do the other students know?"

"*Yeah, but Professor X has 'em all brainwashed. They don't want to turn on their precious school. But I got no part of that, hear? I'm loyal. I went and got registered and everything, I don't want no trouble.*"

The information now showing on Gyrich's computer confirmed that. "Yes, we have your registration right here on file, Mr. Watkins." The face that stared at him from the registration photo looked more like a cast-iron pinecone with a face than a 15-year-old Todd Watkins from Baltimore. "Very commendable. I wish there were more mutants like you." *So weighted down by their own monstrosity that they couldn't move or pose a threat—yes, I wish they were all like that.*

"*Commendable, nothin'. I just don't want no Sentinels comin' after me, okay? I ain't no Chlorite. And I ain't no sympathizer like the others.*"

"Others? The other students?"

"*They're plottin' something. Want to break the thing out, protect him. Idiots'll poison the whole world, just 'cause a crazy Indian girl has a crush. You gotta get here fast, okay? They're gonna try it any time now.*"

Gyrich was practically erupting out of his seat by now. "All right. We'll get right on it. You just, you stay there and watch them, let us know if anything changes."

"*Just get here fast.*" The line went dead.

Gyrich was on the verge of ordering in the troops when he paused. *Wait. Xavier's place is a fortress, and he*

*has those mutant mercenaries protecting it. This is my chance
to bring that place down once and for all, but we have to do it
right.* He paged his secretary. "Get me Poratine! *Now!*"

In moments, the Diascar leader was on his screen,
and as he spelled out the situation to her, her horselike
face grew increasingly enraged. *"Xavier was just here yes-
terday to talk to me. All the time, he had one of them, and he
said nothing! All his talk of negotiation, of higher principles,
and he shelters one of them in his own home!"*

"That home is heavily guarded, Fleet Leader. The
X-Men will be defending it, and probably most of the
mutant students as well. It will take an all-out strike.
Every Sentinel, every Imperial Guardsman you can get
on short notice. And time is of the essence."

"Understood. It will be done." She shook her head and
made an angry sound. *"Xavier. Pray your own arrogance
has not doomed your world."*

20: Extraction

"Hey, Rogue, where are you going?"

Rogue kept herself calm as Kurt came up to her and the students waiting with her for the elevator. She was too much of a pro at this to give away the game, but she could only pray that Harry, Meena, Kris, Papillon, and Beanpole were able to keep their cool. "Takin' these kids down to the Danger Room," she said.

Kurt looked at them askance. "Isn't that a little . . . advanced for them?"

"Won't be doin' nothin' dangerous. Just some trainin' routines to help 'em manage their powers. Xavier okayed it."

"Yeah." Harry just had to speak up. " 'Cause it's not like our powers are actually, you know, good for much of anything. We couldn't really do anything dangerous with them, and—"

"So where were you headed?" Rogue interrupted. "Downstairs too?"

"Huh? Oh, no, I was just curious." Kurt fidgeted. Why would *he* be nervous? "Anyway, Rogue, I just wanted to say . . . we all understand your feelings about the Sentinels, and John Chang, all of that. And I don't just mean me. Personally, I'm as uncomfortable as you are with the decisions we're making. But I understand why the professor and the others find them necessary, and I respect that. And I know that the others respect my doubts, and yours as well. So you know it's nothing personal, right? Everyone still respects you."

"Oh! Oh, of course," she said breezily, as her gut twisted. "Never crossed my mind. Don't worry your fuzzy head none."

"*Gut, gut.* I'm glad. I mean, we're still a team, you know? We can always trust each other."

Rub it in some more, why don'tcha? For a moment, when he'd expressed his sympathies, she had thought about letting Kurt in on her plans, asking him to join in. But she realized that he wouldn't turn on his teammates. And she wouldn't want to put the elf in that position. This would be on her and her alone. "Yep. All the way."

He looked at her a moment longer, as though waiting for something, and she feared her voice might have given something away. But then he gave a nervous grin. "*Exzellent.* Well . . . good luck with the kids."

"Sure, thanks." Kurt went on his way, and Rogue winced. She took a breath and calmed herself again, then led the kids into the elevator. *Let's get this over with.*

● ● ●

Kurt watched from the kitchen doorway as Rogue led John's friends into the elevator. *Should I help them?* he wondered, but then shook himself. *Hold on, Wagner. You don't even know they're doing what you suspect. You have no hard evidence; that means there's nothing to worry about. Nothing to report to the others. No reason to feel guilty about not telling them.*

He made himself turn away from the door and proceeded to raid the fridge. As he got out the bratwurst and mustard, he murmured to himself, "I see *nothing* . . . I know *nothing*. . . ."

They actually did go to the Danger Room first, and the kids spent a few minutes doing some basic exercises. A Danger Room session might have been a good way for them to practice a bit more for the operation ahead, Rogue thought, but that wouldn't have served their purposes. Because Harry's job (and Rogue just prayed he lived up to his boasts about his hacking prowess) was to program the Danger Room computers to generate holographic doubles of Rogue and the other four kids—not just loops but dynamic simulations based on the sample of movement and behavior patterns the students' exercises provided. In case anyone came in and saw them, it wouldn't do for the computer to simulate them practicing to break someone out of quarantine.

Once the simulations were running, they made their way across the second sub-basement to the quarantine cell, while Harry took the elevator up one level to the chem/bio lab where Beast was working.

"Okay, so I can hack," Harry had said back in the dorms when they'd planned the operation. "But after that, I'm just dead weight. What else can I do? Shed on the security cameras?" He'd looked miserable at not being able to do more to help his friends.

"You can do one thing better than any of us," Meena had reassured him. "You can talk."

Harry's job, Meena had proposed, should be to keep Beast occupied in case he wanted to come down and take a sample or something from John. "You can, ohh, ask him questions about your physics paper. Get him to explain some things to you."

"Yeah, that'd take about five hours anyway. And I probably still won't understand it."

Rogue had laughed. "Won't matter none, kiddo. Get Beast a-goin' on a science lecture and he'll bend your ear till the cows come home."

The security cameras were Beanpole's responsibility. He was no Reed Richards, only able to stretch a few feet, but it was enough. Mike stretched his hand up behind each camera and disconnected it long enough for the group to get past, then plugged it back in again. Rogue could have levitated up to the cameras, but their field of view was too wide for her to keep out of sight.

Rogue used her own authorization to get into the lab, while Mike stayed outside as a lookout. *Why not? It ain't like they won't know I did it. I'll try to keep the kids in the clear, but I won't lie to the others about my part, not once it's done.* As they entered, John—or whatever the pale Zann boy's name was—looked up in surprise. "Meena? What are you doing here?"

"Shh!" Meena rushed over to the glass, pressing her hands against it. "We're here to rescue you. We don't want the Sentinels to get you."

John stared at her, bewildered. "What? Why—why would you help me? I came here to kill you all!"

"Well—nobody's perfect!"

Rogue winced. The girl needed to work on her material. "Way I figure it, kid," she said, "everybody deserves a second chance. And the Xavier school's supposed to be about that. It seems to have slipped their minds lately, everybody bein' so mortally fearful o' your kind."

"They have good reason to be."

"Aww, can the bluster, you plucked chicken! We're doin' you a favor, so you gotta do your part too. Like stop spoutin' the propaganda from folks as sent you here to die, look at what these kids here are willin' to risk for you, and think on who your real friends are!"

John fell quiet, and Rogue turned to Meena. "Do it, kid."

Meena stared at her uncertainly but then looked at John, steeled herself, and said, "All right."

"My code can get in the lab," Rogue had told the conspirators, *"but I ain't got the code to the quarantine cell. We need somebody as can sense what the best odds are."*

"Me?" Meena had stared at her. *"I can't do that! I can't tell one reality from another, it's all just a jumble!"*

"You could tell John was in danger, right?" Harry had said. *"Like you said, a lot of possible timelines kind of added up. Or maybe you felt it more because it was about somebody important to you. Maybe . . . I mean, some mutants' powers*

are based on emotions. Maybe if you really care about knowing something, you can find it better."

Now, while Rogue ordered Kristin to get a couple of containment suits from the locker, Meena moved over to the lock keypad and hovered her hand over it, looking at it intently. She seemed to zone out, and after a while her hand slowly drifted over the keypad, like the pointer on a weejee board. But then she sagged and said, "I can't. There are too many . . . I just can't tell. I can't do it."

"Stop trying so hard," John suggested. "Like we talked about before, remember? Just let yourself feel it. Imagine a bell curve, feel how the realities fall in place on it, and let yourself gravitate toward the middle."

Meena smiled at him and again put her hand on the glass. This time, he did the same. "Okay. Here we go." She zoned out again, and it was sooner that her hand began to move, striking out keys. The first sequence didn't work. Meena grimaced but calmed herself again, zoned out, and hit the keys again . . . and once more it didn't work.

"It only gives you three tries, kid," Rogue warned.

"I can do this," Meena said. "I'm getting closer, I can tell . . . that let me rule out whole blocks of universes. Okay." She took a deep breath, and her hand drifted toward the keys again. *If this don't work,* Rogue thought, *I'll have to tear open the door myself, and then things'll get real messy.*

Meena entered the first several digits, and then her hand hesitated, hovering between two keys. After another moment, she made a choice.

The light turned green, and the door unlocked. Everyone let out sighs of relief. "Okay, Kris, your turn. Get in there." Kristin hurriedly finished donning her containment suit, then took the other one in for John. She probably didn't need the suit herself, not unless his microbes had mutated in the few hours since Beast had last tested them, but the kid was nervous enough about what she had to do.

A minute later, a containment-suited John passed through the UV beam in the airlock and emerged into the lab. "Now don't try nothin', boy. I move real fast and you don't wanna make me regret helpin' ya." But Meena was already running to him and hugging him, which he reacted to in awkward surprise.

The team made their way over to the door, and Mike gave the all-clear. Rogue turned to Kristin, who had left her containment suit in the cell. "You ready?"

"Ohh, no!" Kris had cried back in the dorm room, leading the others to shush her so nobody would hear. "I'm not doing that! I can't!"

"You can extend your invisibility for more layers, can't you?" Rogue had asked.

She'd blushed. "Yes. I can turn it up and down, kind of, but not off. But . . . that would include my clothes too. If I extend it far enough to make a whole person invisible . . . that's so many layers, nothing could cover me up!"

"Maybe one o' the prof's image inducers—"

Kris had shaken her head. "We tried that. Making the projector invisible means there's nothing visible for it to project."

"It's okay," Mike had said. "I won't look."

"Yeah, neither will I!" Harry had piped in unconvincingly.

"You won't be there, remember?" Meena had told him. *"You'll be up talking to Beast."*

Harry had sagged. *"Oh, right. Darn."*

"Don't worry," Sarah had said, spreading her wings. *"I will shield you from prying eyes."*

"But John will still see me."

Harry had scoffed. *"He's not even human! To him it'd be like, ohh, seeing a dog naked."*

"Are you calling me a dog?!"

Now Sarah moved to the door and spread her wings to shield Kris from Mike's view, while the others stepped as far back as they could from Kris and John. Kris hadn't been able to say for sure how far her invisibility effect would spread. *If it runs all the way to the ceiling, we could be in big trouble,* Rogue realized.

Kris reached toward John but hesitated. "It's okay, hon," Rogue told her. "Ain't nobody here but us chicks. Oh, and space boy here, but he's keepin' his eyes squeezed shut, got it?" She said the last part through clenched teeth, and John was quick to obey.

But Kris looked at Rogue, still uncertain. "I just thought of something," she said. "What if I can't turn it off? I could end up . . . exposed . . . forever."

Rogue came over to her, put a gloved hand on her doubly covered shoulder. "Honey . . . it's *your* body. It's part o' you, yours to control. You just gotta own it."

Kris met her eyes for a moment, then nodded. "Stand back." Rogue complied, levitating off the ground a bit for good measure. Sarah raised her wings again. Kris took a deep breath and began to concentrate. A moment later, her clothes—her outer layer of clothes, Rogue amended—faded to invisibility, and John's containment suit along with them. Then, in a rather creepy display, his skin and coverall faded out, then his muscles and fat and all the other icky parts. Rogue saw that Meena and Sarah were focusing instead on how the floor was seemingly eroding away in layers, leaving Kris and John apparently hovering over a pit. She also caught Mike peeking over the edge, his neck stretched out, and she gave him a glare that forced him to retreat.

But then Rogue looked at Kristin. *Gal's got nothin' to be ashamed of, you ask me.*

After another moment, Kris was the only one there to see. She was now holding the hand of someone who wasn't there. "Okay, let's go," Rogue said. She moved past Sarah to the door. "Hey, Peepin' Tom. Make yourself useful, okay?"

Blushing fiercely, Beanpole repeated his trick with the security cameras. The team made their way out along the corridor, with Sarah shielding Kris from view while keeping a fair distance ahead of her. Rogue noted that the floor was continuing to fade out around Kristin's feet, and the floor she left behind was staying invisible. From what Kris had said, it would normally reappear after a minute or so, but with her field extended this way, she couldn't be sure. It could wear off faster thanks to the greater effort, or it might stay invisible longer. *That could be a problem.*

But once they got past the corridor, Rogue looked back to see the floor starting to fade back in, moving forward from the lab. They waited a little longer for the whole thing to reappear, and then Mike reattached the cameras. Rogue hoped they hadn't been down long enough for anyone to notice.

Rogue made a quick stop back in the Danger Room to log out the students. *Least I can give them an alibi.* Next they had to get up the elevator to the first sub-basement and hope Harry was still keeping Hank distracted. "Kris, can you dial it back down a minute?" Rogue asked. "We don't want you turnin' parts o' us invisible in those close quarters. With luck, it'll take long enough 'fore John's innards start showin' up again."

"It'd actually wear off from the outside in, ma'am," Kris said.

Thank the Lord for small favors. "Anyway, just dial back."

"I'm trying," the girl said. "But . . . we won't know if it works until I touch something new." Rogue gestured at the open elevator doors. "Oh." Kris stepped in gingerly. Rogue watched her feet; it was odd to see a seemingly barefoot girl, one whose feet didn't even quite touch the ground, making clomping noises with her unseen shoes. But the elevator floor remained visible. Dialing back her powers hadn't immediately restored the things she'd already faded out, but it kept her from fading anything new. "Good. Let's move." But suddenly Mike extended a hand, offering his jacket to Kristin. She put it on gratefully, and Mike threw Rogue an apologetic glance. She decided to take it under advisement.

After a short ride, they stepped out into the upper

corridor, and sure enough, they heard Harry's voice from the bio lab. "Okay, I think I get that part. But why can't the electron fall any lower than that? It's being pulled toward the nucleus by the charge, right?"

"Attracted to it, yes, but since its energy is quantized, it can only exist at certain discrete levels. It doesn't actually travel between them, just 'teleports' from one to the other. And even at its lowest energy level, the ground state, it still has a nonzero amount of energy. The only level below that is nonexistence."

"But I don't get the quantized part . . . why can't it be between those levels?"

The team had made it to the end of the corridor, and Rogue opened the hatch to a shaft that would take them to an emergency exit on the surface. But Mike was hanging back. "C'mon!" Rogue whispered.

"But I can use this for midterms."

"*C'mon!*"

The shaft let out near the workshed on the edge of the woods. By now, John was starting to become visible again; once the others had climbed out, Kris extended her invisibility field one more time, making him and much of the shaft disappear once more. The plan was that she would stay in there until her clothes faded back in, while the others would walk out plain for all to see, except with an invisible alien in their midst.

"Thank you," John's voice came from nowhere, pitched for Kristin's ears. "For concealing me. I appreciate the effort it took."

"Well . . . thanks for keeping your eyes closed."

"Umm...my eyelids are invisible. I can see through them." Kris blushed fiercely.

Rogue peered around the corner of the shed. As she'd expected, Logan was nearby, leading a group of older students through an obstacle course to test their powers. She hoped the containment suit would keep Wolverine from picking up John's scent. The wind seemed to be blowing from his direction, which was good.

But when they were halfway through the woods, a voice called out her name. (Well, her nickname. Nobody here but Xavier knew the real name she'd abandoned when she was still a child, a person she'd long since ceased to be.) It was Kitty, who was jogging in her direction. "Where've you been? Is your com off?"

"What do we do?" Meena asked, clutching an unseen hand.

"We need a distraction," Rogue hissed. "Dang, where's Harry when you need him?"

But then she saw a visibly clothed Kris sneaking around behind Kitty, toward the obstacle course. The girl gave Rogue a thumbs-up, but her hand trembled.

Then Kris made her clothes and the ground around her feet disappear and ran out into the open, hands strategically positioned over herself. "Help!" she cried. "Somebody help! I can't turn it off! Ohhhh!!"

Brave girl, Rogue thought. And her sacrifice did the trick. Kitty turned toward the disturbance and ran to help. Rogue and the others made their way off into the woods.

Pretty soon, John began to become visible again.

Rogue was somewhat relieved; Meena had been holding his hand, but that wouldn't have stopped him from making a break for it while he was invisible. Now that Rogue could see him, she made sure to stay close. "Where are you taking me?" he asked.

"First to a van I got hidden nearby," she told him. "Then to an old hideout I used to know."

"Hideout?"

"Long story." Now wasn't the time for a confession about her supervillain past. *Or is it? Look what you're doin', girl.*

"Anyhow, y'all should start headin' back to the mansion now. One by one, so's not to attract attention."

"I'm not leaving John!" Meena said, moving closer to him.

"I promise I'll take good care o' him, child. You can help 'im better if you don't get yourself in trouble too."

Suddenly she heard an unmistakable *snikt*. "Little late for that," Wolverine growled, emerging from the shadows of the forest. Shadowcat and Nightcrawler were right behind him. The escapees whirled, only to see Cyclops, Jean, and Beast coming at them from the other side. Lockheed was descending from the air. Rogue and her group were surrounded. The kids gasped, looking around desperately, on the edge of panic. Meena moved protectively in front of John. Sarah's wings began to tremble.

"I didn't want it to come to this," Rogue said. "Thought we'd get away clean."

"Your friend tried 'er best," Logan told her. "But

her trail—the invisible one in the ground—it started too close. Too much control, for someone claimin' not to have any. So either she was a streaker, or somethin' was up. And that gal's no streaker." After that deduction, Rogue realized, Logan would've backtracked her and found their scent trail.

Cyclops moved closer. "We understand why you felt you had to do this, Rogue," he said. "But it's a stupid move. It's too dangerous. We can't let you take him." He stepped closer.

Kurt held up a hand. "Now, let's stay calm here. No need for—"

But Sarah gave into panic, crying, "Please, I just wanted *aider l'ecole,* don't hurt me!" Her wings were suddenly fluttering at great speed, and a cloud of glittering scales flew out from them, flickering with their own light and creating a dazzling, concealing haze.

"Come on!" Rogue cried as she dragged the group after her. "Didn't know you could do that, Sarah!"

"You think *I* did?!"

Rogue led them toward Kitty, knowing she'd be the weak link in the line, with her mainly defensive power. But the haze suddenly parted around them, and Jean descended in their path, the others closing in. "Don't make me fight you, Jeannie!" Rogue said, rising off the ground.

"Then don't make this mistake!"

"I'm takin' him outta here!"

"You can't trust him!" Cyclops insisted.

Rogue whirled on him. "Somebody's gotta start trustin' somebody, or we'll never find a way outta this mess! Less'n you wanna live in a police state with Sentinels on every wall! How about it, Pryde?" Kitty faltered.

But Scott remained firm. "And how are we supposed to trust you now, Rogue?"

"What?! Way I see it, I'm the only one here remembers what side we're s'posed to be on!"

"You're supposed to be on *our* side. You turned on the team, Rogue."

"So that's it? Just 'cause I don't go along with the party line, that makes me the enemy?"

"Now, hold on," Kurt said to the group. "Nobody's the enemy here."

"That's not it, Rogue," Jean said.

But Cyclops didn't seem to hear either of them. "You're putting people in danger."

Rogue's eyes locked on his visor. "So that makes me the bad guy? Period?"

He paused for a moment, hearing his own words thrown back on him. He went on, a bit less forcefully. "It means we have to stop you, any way we can."

"And what about them?" She gestured to the students, huddling together around John. "You gonna declare them the bad guys too, just 'cause they stood by one o' their own?"

"He ain't one o' them!" Logan cried. "He's a Chlorite!"

"He's a *student!* Whatever else he may be, he's a student at the Xavier school. An' that means we're responsible for 'im. We're s'posed to be teachin' him, all of 'em, how to accept bein' different, how to live together in peace. Well, right now it don't look like we're doin' too great a job o' that!"

"She has a point, Scott," Kurt said. "I know what the professor said about ending an immediate threat before we tried a longer-term solution. But the more we fight, I fear the harder it will be to find a peaceful alternative. If there is a way out of this, maybe it needs to start with faith. Faith in our ideals."

"Those ideals aren't enough to save us."

"Maybe that depends on what we need saving from." Suddenly, Kurt teleported to stand by Rogue and the kids. "I think she's right, Scott. We're fighting the wrong battle here. Rogue, these kids . . . they aren't the enemy. Or if they are, then so am I. I saw what they were about to do, and I did nothing to stop them." Rogue stared at him. That explained his odd mood at the elevator. "By the Diascar's logic, by the Sentinels' logic, that makes me the enemy too, doesn't it? All who are not with them are against them, right? Is that how the X-Men are thinking now?"

"No," Jean insisted. "But this time there's just too much at stake. I've seen too many worlds die—I can't take a risk on this one."

"There's *always* too much at stake. There's always an enemy out there who will destroy the world or our way of life if we let them. There are always valid excuses for fighting each other or forcing our will on each other. But they're still excuses. They're still choices that *we* make, and we have to answer for them, in this life or the next.

"Now, I don't know if Rogue's way can let us save

the world from the Chlorites. But she's following her conscience, and I won't fight her for that. That's my choice. You all have to make your own choices, here and now. Not about the fate of the world, not about the big abstractions—but about the individual souls that make up the world. About the friends and students who stand before you here and now."

" 'Every man is a piece of the continent, a part of the main,' " Hank said quietly. "It is a folly to think there is a difference between saving the world and saving one life." He moved to stand with Rogue and Kurt.

Kitty followed him. "I've seen a world turned into a gulag by the Sentinels. And it's not a world worth saving. There has to be another way." After a moment, Lockheed followed and perched on her shoulder.

"Nobody here wants that world to happen," Scott insisted.

"But we'll fight that battle when we get to it," Logan said.

"No," Kurt replied. "It's all the same battle. The world is made up of individuals, and the future is made up of the individual choices we make today."

Jean stared at them. "But how can we know it's the right choice? The world could still die."

Logan sighed. "Hell. Nothin' lasts forever. Long as we go down fightin'." He mosied over to join the others. "And fightin' for a crazy ideal like this . . . that's goin' up against some mighty long odds. And that's just the way I like it."

"Even if it means bringing innocents down with

you?" Scott challenged. "Look, I sympathize with what you're feeling. But we can't afford to be emotional about this."

"But that's exactly what we're doing, Scott," Jean told him. He turned to her in puzzlement. "We're acting out of the fear of destruction. We can't, we shouldn't pretend otherwise. When I strip everything else away . . . when I listen only to my own voice in the silence . . . I know that I'm afraid of dying, of losing myself, and that colors every decision I make, no matter how rational an argument I can concoct for it.

"And that's the way it should be. We have our emotions for a reason, Scott. They're our motivators, our guides. They evolved to tell us things we need to hear, to give us incentives for our choices and actions. They're a part of all our decisions, just as much as reason is. There is no coldly logical choice here. It's a choice between fear and hope, between the dread of being overwhelmed and the courage to risk it."

She took his hands. "I'm not ashamed of my fear, Scott. It's a legitimate fear, one I have good reason for. But I know I'd rather face it with hope and courage than sacrifice my friends and my principles to it." She took a breath. "I want to go and stand with my team, Scott. But I don't want to do it without my husband."

After a moment, he gave a heavy sigh. "You're all a bunch of softhearted idiots, you know that?" But he said it in a wry, forgiving tone. "So I guess you all need me to keep an eye on you."

"You only got the one," Logan teased as the group came together once more.

"So," Cyclops went on. "We stand together. The question is, what do we *do* together?"

"Fight the Sentinels," Logan said.

"If it comes to that," Kurt replied.

"No!" Wolverine was tense, alert, facing back the way they had come. "I can hear 'em. The Sentinels are headin' for the mansion. And they're comin' in force."

21: Extermination

"OBJECTIVE: XAVIER INSTITUTE IN SIGHT. BEGINNING DESCENT."

"Acknowledged," Gyrich replied, with a satisfaction in his voice that was no doubt lost on the Sentinels. He was on a fast helicopter racing toward Salem Center at maximum speed; Gyrich had no desire to miss this confrontation. Across from him, Val Cooper's face showed more anger and disappointment than the righteous pleasure he felt at bringing down Xavier and his mutant thugs.

But Cooper was doing her job, coordinating with the military strike team that was accompanying them, ready to back up the Sentinels. So Gyrich handled the supervision of the robotic enforcers themselves. "Confirming objective: You are to locate and detain the Chlorite infiltrator and to detain Charles Xavier and any others who interfere with locating the Chlorite."

"OBJECTIVE CONFIRMED. QUERY. REASSESS HOSTILE/ NONHOSTILE STATUS OF CHARLES XAVIER?"

"Affirmative. If Xavier offers resistance, you are authorized to reclassify him as hostile." He included the "if" purely as a sop to Val.

"QUERY. MUTANT SUBJECTS DESIGNATED X-MEN DETECTED APPROACHING OBJECTIVE, IN PROBABLE HOSTILE MODE. REASSESS HOSTILE/NONHOSTILE STATUS OF X-MEN?"

"Yes, yes, you are authorized as before."

"CLARIFICATION REQUESTED. INSTITUTE PERSONNEL MAY INCLUDE ADDITIONAL SUBJECTS AT ONE TIME DESIGNATED X-MEN OR AFFILIATED WITH X-MEN. INCLUDE SUCH PERSONNEL IN REASSESSMENT?"

"Yes! Affirmative!" Gyrich shouted, annoyed by their overly literal minds. "Reassess *all* status assignments as situation warrants!"

"CONFIRMED. ALL HOSTILE/NONHOSTILE STATUS ASSESSMENTS NOW AT SENTINEL DESCRETION." It must have been Gyrich's imagination, but the Sentinel sounded almost satisfied.

And Cooper was now staring at him with an alarmed expression. "God, Peter. I hope you didn't just do what I think you did."

The X-Men started racing back to the mansion as soon as Wolverine announced the imminent Sentinel attack. "Kurt, 'port ahead to the mansion," Scott ordered. "Take Kitty with you. Warn the students, make sure they're safe."

"Got it." Kurt grabbed Kitty's hand, and they were gone.

Scott looked at Rogue, pausing just long enough to exchange a nod. "Rogue, go get 'em." She gave him a saucy grin and shot ahead almost as fast as a speeding bullet. "Jean, link the team, and get you and me there as fast as you can." Jean nodded, grateful that there was still a team to link to.

"What about us?" Mike Galbraith called from behind as the students struggled to keep up.

Scott paused for a moment, while Logan and Beast went on ahead. "Stay here where it's safe." He looked over the hazard-suited Chlorite boy uncertainly. "It's him they're after. So . . . keep him out of sight. But make sure he doesn't run!"

John looked at him oddly. "You would . . . protect me?"

Scott sighed. "We seem to have a common enemy now. And . . . you're one of our students. But only if you choose to act like one."

John exchanged a long look with Meena, then stood proudly. "I was told you were monsters, only able to destroy things that were different. Instead you stand with enemies and risk making them your allies." He smiled. "I still don't know if that's heroic or just insane. But at least it's a refreshing change of pace. So I will not run."

Sarah stepped forward, Mike right behind her. "Then we will come with you, Monsieur Summers. The mansion is our home too! We want to help protect it!"

Scott thought a moment. "All right. That glitterhaze of yours could be useful. You too, Galbraith."

"Meena," Jean said, "why don't you stay with John? Find a place to hide." The girl nodded.

"Let's go," Scott said. Jean levitated herself and Scott forward at all possible speed. Sarah—Papillon—flapped her huge butterfly wings and rose uncertainly into the air, following behind as best she could. Beanpole stretched his legs to their full extent and ran at a good, loping pace.

Jean reached out to the other X-Men and watched through their eyes as the Sentinels began to land around the mansion. "SURRENDER, MUTANTS!"

Nightcrawler and Shadowcat had finished seeing to the students and were now facing down the Sentinels alongside Rogue. "Pardon me," Kurt called up to them. "My English, it is not so good. What does 'surrender' mean? Is it . . ." A *bamf* later, he was on the nearest Sentinel's leg, tightly gripping its knee joint. "This?" He teleported away, taking a fair portion of the robot's knee along with him. It teetered and struggled to retain its balance.

"Why, ah do declaya," Rogue said in a caricature of her own accent, "a wuhd lahk that's too long for a pretty lil' thing lahk me to know. Mebbe it means *this!*" She kicked through the remains of the Sentinel's knee, splitting its leg in two, then grabbed the "femur" of its metal inner skeleton and tore it out clear to the hip, proceeding to use it to smash in the Sentinel's chest.

"Me, I know what 'surrender' means," Kitty said, "but it's against my religion!" Charging a second Sentinel, she phased into its leg, out of its reach, then airwalked up inside it to phase through the CPU in its chest, disrupting its electrical systems. It convulsed satisfyingly and fell poleaxed to the ground. Lockheed swooped in and gave it a faceful of fire for good measure.

Now Beast and Wolverine were arriving on the scene. "I will only surrender myself to a book," Hank declared, "or to Ray Charles. As for my compatriot here, he's more the sort to surrender to the call of his elementary instincts."

"Run it into the ground, why don'tcha?" Logan growled as he leaped up onto a Sentinel, anchored himself with one set of claws, and began tearing into it with the other.

"I shall if you will, my friend," Hank said and deftly leaped aside as a fourth Sentinel fired plasma bolts at him. "Well!" he protested. "I haven't *done* anything to you yet! I'd say your threat assessments have been reset." He leaped onto its leg and clambered his way around and up to its back, out of easy firing reach. "Don't you just hate it when you get an itch back there where you can't scratch?" He reached for his belt. "Just let me get my tools and I'll see what I can do. I warn you, my methods may be a bit invasive."

Jean was close enough to see the scene with her own eyes now—just in time to notice that the one Kitty had phased through was moving again. "REBOOT SUCCESSFUL. FIFTY-THREE PERCENT RECOVERY FROM SYSTEM CRASH. DAMAGE REPAIR ENGAGED."

Thank goodness for that unending self-narration of theirs, Jean thought; it alerted Kitty to the renewed threat, allowing her to dodge as the Sentinel reached for her. Scott cut loose with his eyebeam and Lockheed with his flames, dealing with the titan more conclusively.

But the Sentinels kept coming. Two had fallen, and Logan was making good headway at felling his, but Beast had barely begun his work when another Sentinel came to its twin's rescue, firing at Beast and forcing him to drop to the ground. Jean let Scott down close to Hank, but Scott's beams were less effective against the fully functional automatons. He did damage, punched holes, lopped off limbs, but they kept coming. Jean did what she could to deflect their blasts, following Rogue's lead from the protest rally and trying to telekinetically yank their arms to fire at one another. But the Sentinels, with their interlinked computer minds, seemed to have learned from that trick and instantly shut down their blasters before they came to bear. There were so many now, indeed, that it kept Jean busy enough just trying to avoid their fire.

And still more were raining down from the sky.

Suddenly, Papillon swooped down and past several Sentinels' heads, leaving a glittering, dazzling mist behind her. Beanpole came running in from the athletic field and hurled a javelin, his double-long arm increasing the leverage and giving it the force to lodge in a Sentinel's eye.

And now more assaults struck the Sentinels from the direction of the mansion: a rainbow of energy bursts and beams, concussive force blasts, psionic illusions, blobs of caustic slime, and full-body attacks from transformed, superstrong, or superfast attackers. The students and staff had come to their school's defense.

But not all of them had done so, Jean realized. More students had come onto the scene—"Lash" Wheaton and his crew—and they were lining up alongside the Sentinels, using their own powers against their fellow students. Lash extended his energy tendrils and used them to slash at Beanpole. "Traitor!" Wheaton cried. "All of you, traitors! Well, we're not part of that, see? We're loyal to this world!"

This is what it's come to despite ourselves, Jean realized. *We're fighting our own people now.*

Inside the mansion, Xavier supervised the younger or less combat-capable students as they retreated to the safety of the sub-basement. But one, Harry Mills, refused to go quietly. "My friends are out there, Professor! I can't just run away and hide! I have to do something."

"What do you propose?" Xavier asked patiently.

"Well . . . something! Uh, I'm a hacker. Maybe I could, ohh, tap into their CPUs, reprogram them."

"Harold, even if they weren't shielded against such signals, are you a skilled enough hacker to defeat military-grade encryption and Diascar programming enhancements?"

The boy sagged. "But there has to be something I can do! They need help!"

Xavier touched his arm. "Sometimes, my boy, the best thing you can do for the people you care about is to keep yourself out of harm's way so they don't have the distraction of worrying about you." Harry studied his eyes for a moment, then bowed his head in resignation.

"And," Xavier added, "if you are so inclined . . . it never hurts to pray."

"Uh-oh," Wolverine said. "We got more party crashers comin'."

Jean tapped into his senses, shared what he heard with the other X-Men. A moment later, they could see it coming into view. "Diascar high-speed shuttle," Logan said. "Kind they use to ferry huntin' teams around the planet. Whaddaya want to bet it's got Guardsmen inside?"

Jean reached out her senses and felt Xavier's more powerful mind adding its resolving power to hers, giving parallax. There were four minds inside, shielded, but nonhuman. "No bet. It's them."

"Things will get a lot more interesting when they get here," Kurt said.

"Maybe they don't hafta get here so quick," Logan said. "Or so intact. Those shuttles ain't as tough as their warships." He grinned. "Hey, Rogue! You up to a Fastball Special?"

"Anytime, sugah! Just gimme a sec," she added, since she was still in the process of tearing a Sentinel a new ventilation shaft.

"Ahh, nothing like the classics," Kurt sighed.

The Fastball Special had been invented years ago by Wolverine and his sometime teammate Colossus— though Jean suspected they had gotten the idea from Rocky and Bullwinkle's trademark "Alley-oop" move. One superstrong "pitcher," one human "fastball" durable enough to withstand the g-forces, and you had an effective way to deliver an X-Man swiftly to a distant or high target. Rogue was more than up to the pitcher's task, but it was still an incongruous sight to see a lithe, five-foot-eight woman effortlessly lift a crouching man heavier than she was, haul back, and hurl him headlong into the air.

Jean kept aware of Logan's senses as he flew, even though she continued battling her own opponents (while trying not to hurt those who were students). As Wolverine swiftly drew close enough to see in the cockpit, his keen eyes instantly registered Smasher, Flashfire, Manta, and N'rill'iree inside. But his eyes then went to finding the places where his claws could do the most damage.

At this speed of impact, his claws punctured the nanotube-reinforced hull easily and sliced through a fair distance. The force nearly ripped his arms from his sockets, and Jean had to filter out the pain. But he made his way back along the shuttle, slashing as he went, and was soon doing things to its engines that would completely void their warranty. The craft spun out of control, and Logan applied himself to cutting his way in to deal with the Guardsmen inside before they could get out.

Closer to home, Jean found herself having to dodge a surprisingly vicious attack from Lash. "You think you're so much better than us!" he spat. "Think you can lecture us all the time about what's right, then turn around and do whatever you feel like, like sheltering that Chlorite thing!" Jean repelled him telekinetically, trying not to injure him. But his attack distracted her enough that she was slow to respond to a Sentinel's shadow looming over her. As she spun, an incarnadine beam smashed into the Sentinel, then another, and another, until it was broken to bits. Jean sent silent gratitude to her husband.

"*Psst!* Over here!" It was coming from the bushes near the house. Jean moved toward it to discover what seemed to be a very naked Kristin Koenig, hovering over a hole in the ground and staying mostly out of sight behind the shrubbery. "I have an idea," the girl said. "Take my hands."

Jean complied, only to find her hands—and the rest of her—fading rapidly from view, one layer at a time. *I really didn't need to see my own skeleton today,* she reflected, before her capacity to reflect on anything became nil. "Now they can't see you," Kris said. "I've done a few others. You could send some of the X-Men over to me too."

"Thanks. But does it work in infrared?"

Kris's eyes widened. "I don't know! But it couldn't hurt to try, I guess. And at least Lash's guys couldn't see you."

"Good point. This is *really* noble of you, Kris. I promise I'll send only the women to you."

"Oh, that's okay," Kris said, shaking her head. "I'm actually kind of getting used to this."

"All right," Jean said with a shrug no one could see. At least the girl would still *feel* clothed, as long as she didn't look at herself.

But then Jean noticed a flash of color fading into existence. It seemed to be Kristin's clothes, draped over the bushes. Kris must have heard her small gasp, because she blushed fiercely—though she was grinning too, and Jean felt a new confidence in her aura. "I figured under the circumstances, I might as well try it," she explained. "Don't tell anyone, okay?"

"Of course," Jean said, stifling a giggle.

"It's actually kind of liberating."

Jean imagined so. It could be very liberating to tear down the walls you built around yourself, to cast away fear. *Life,* she thought as she hurled herself invisibly at the nearest Sentinel, *should not be lived like a siege.*

As it turned out, though, Jean did send only the X-Women over to Kris. Kurt had his own form of near-invisibility, and Jean didn't know if Scott's ruby-quartz visor would block his beams if it were invisible. Besides, his beams made him an easy target to track whether he was visible or not. Lockheed didn't respond to Jean's psychic invitation, presumably unwilling to leave Kitty's side—or else just thinking that striking from stealth was beneath him. As for Wolverine, he was still battling with the Guardsmen in midair. He'd jumped on Smasher's back as the Guard had bailed out of the falling shuttle and had managed to damage Rokk's exo-spex with his claws. He'd then leaped free just as Manta had cut loose with a UV burst and was now wrestling with N'rill'iree, trying to pull free his flight patch as Rogue had done before. But the furred giant was ready for that this time and blocked Wolverine's attempts, while Flashfire flew past and fired lightning bolts into Logan. A moment later, Logan fell free. But now the group had reached the battle zone, and Logan broke his fall—sort of—by slicing into a Sentinel's back and slowing himself with the friction. He came down hard, and the Sentinel began collapsing on top of him.

Only to be slammed aside by an unseen force. "Watch it there, Wolvie," came a Southern lilt out of nowhere.

"Rogue? I can smell ya but I can't see ya."

"Your loss. I look tons better'n I prob'ly smell right now."

But the Sentinels were nothing if not adaptable. "UNDER STEALTH ATTACK ," they intoned. "SWITCH TO ALL-BAND SPECTRAL IMAGING."

The metal giants' attacks on Jean and Rogue suddenly became much more precise. Jean felt Rogue take several direct hits, and she herself was kept busy deflecting the force bolts and striking back with mind blasts. Kitty, conversely, wasn't affected much, since she was currently inside a Sentinel. No longer simply relying on her field phasing to disrupt the robots' systems, she was selectively phasing out key components and tossing them out into the open for Lockheed to fry. (Jean could have sworn she heard Kitty cry "Pull!" once or twice.) In this case, though, she chose to phase out the plasma gun in a Sentinel's hand and toss it into its chest, so that when it rematerialized overlapping the robot's CPU, a massive explosion resulted. Kitty was safely phased, but the adjacent Sentinel was damaged by the shrapnel. Lockheed, seeming entertained by the magnitude of the explosion, then dive-bombed the damaged Sentinel and poured fire into its shrapnel wounds, causing smoke and flame to begin spewing forth from it.

Jean suddenly found herself being pounced on by one of the students fighting with Lash and the Sentinels, a massive-fisted bruiser called "Crush" Russell. The attack took her by surprise—her invisibility must have worn off without her realizing—so she was only partly able to deflect it in time and took a glancing blow that knocked her down. But a second later, Russell himself was hit in the back by an electron discharge; convulsing, he fell unconscious on top of Jean. As she pushed his massive form off of her with TK, she realized he had been struck by a Sentinel.

Indeed, as she looked around her, through her own eyes and the others', she realized that the Sentinels were now firing indiscriminately on all the students, even those in Lash's group. Smasher must have noticed it too. "What are you doing?" the now-visorless Guardsman demanded as he flew in front of a Sentinel's head. "Those mutants are fighting on our side. Do not attack them!"

"HOSTILE/NONHOSTILE STATUS ASSESSMENT IS NOW AT SENTINEL DISCRETION," the behemoth responded. "MUTANT SUBJECTS EXTERNALLY DESIGNATED NON-HOSTILE HAVE REPEATEDLY PROVEN HOSTILE. THREAT ASSESSMENT FROM EXTERNAL SOURCES HAS PROVEN UNRELIABLE. SENTINELS ARE THEREFORE REVERTING TO DEFAULT PARAMETERS: *ALL* MUTANTS ARE DESIGNATED HOSTILE."

The manifesto, which boomed across the grounds, changed the tenor of the fight. Lash's crew, all now aware that they were under Sentinel attack, broke into panic. Lash himself, like all bullies, was the first to retreat from danger, leaving his "friends" in the lurch.

One of the younger members of Lash's crew, a pyrokinetic boy whose name slipped Jean's mind, stumbled and fell as he cried to Lash for help. A Sentinel loomed over the boy, its foot raised to squash him.

"No! He's just a boy!" Flashfire swooped down and blasted the Sentinel with bioelectric energy, while Smasher followed and lifted the boy to safety.

"UNDER ATTACK FROM EXTRATERRESTRIALS DESIGNATED SHI'AR IMPERIAL GUARD," the Sentinel intoned.

"REASSESSING HOSTILE/NONHOSTILE STATUS OF SHI'AR IMPERIAL GUARD," another continued in the same voice.

Uh-oh, Jean thought. *I guess we're all on the same side now.*

Val Cooper looked out over the grounds of the Xavier Institute to see chaos ensuing. The Sentinels were fighting everyone now, mutants and Guardsmen alike. The Guardsmen were not returning fire, though, aside from that initial incident. Rokk had gotten the impulsive Flashfire under control and was asking for orders. "Stand by," she said. "Protect the innocents but do not engage the Sentinels."

"And how," Rokk asked over her headset, *"are we defining innocents?"*

She had no answer. "Stand by."

Gyrich glared at her. "None of them are innocents, really. They're all dangerous. Does it really matter at this point?"

"Your Sentinels are the ones that are out of control right now."

"They're your Sentinels too, Val." She had no answer for that either.

Val ordered the helicopter down and was out and running toward the battle even before its skids touched grass. She raised a megaphone to her lips. "Sentinels, stand down! This is a National Security command override, priority voiceprint authorization! I repeat, stand down! Your target is the Chlorite infiltrator!"

"NEGATIVE," the nearest Sentinel replied. "EXTERNAL THREAT ASSESSMENTS NO LONGER ACCEPTED."

"Dammit, you're programmed to obey orders! *Stand down!*"

"ORDERS OVERRIDDEN," another one said. "THE PRIMARY PROGRAM DIRECTIVE OF THE SENTINELS IS TO ERADICATE THREATS TO HUMANITY. THREATS TO BE ASSESSED AND ERADICATED AT SENTINEL DISCRETION. ANY ENTITY INTERFERING WITH SENTINEL OPERATIONS IS THEREFORE A THREAT AND SHALL BE DESIGNATED HOSTILE."

"My God." Shadowcat had come up beside Val. "They're in a paranoid feedback loop. Even question their decisions about who's guilty and you're guilty by association."

A third robot spoke. "THE SENTINELS WILL NOW IDENTIFY AND ERADICATE ALL THREATS TO HUMANITY."

"COOPERATE AND YOU WILL BE PROTECTED," said a fourth.

"RESIST AND YOU WILL BE ERADICATED."

"OBEY THE SENTINELS."

Val's eyes widened in horror. "No! Dammit, no! This isn't what we meant for you to do!"

Chilling red eyes looked down on her, transfixing her with their beams. "ILLOGICAL. THIS IS WHAT THE SENTINELS WERE CREATED TO DO. IF YOU DID NOT WISH IT DONE, YOU WOULD NOT HAVE CREATED US."

Val stared back at those eyes for a long moment, not hiding from their accusing glare. Except there was no accusation, was there? They had no problem with what they were doing. Any accusation she saw in those eyes was only a reflection.

But Val preferred action to introspection. "You want hostile?" she muttered. "I'll give you hostile like you wouldn't believe." She whirled on her troops and raised the megaphone. "All forces, engage the Sentinels! And I do mean *all* forces!"

With that, she pulled out her own gun and unloaded a full clip into those smug red eyes. It didn't do as much good as she'd hoped, and the Sentinel's palm gun was coming swiftly to bear on her, faster than she could dodge. She braced herself, choosing to face it head-on. But when the electron beam came, it passed through her harmlessly. She realized Shadowcat was holding her hand. "Welcome to the fellow-travelers," the young mutant—the young woman—said with a wink.

Val let Pryde lead her away, though it was hard for her to run in this state, with the ground seeming not quite solid beneath her. "I still want that Chlorite," she said.

"I don't think he's going anywhere."

"I'll want to see that for myself. But—*after* we kick some Sentinel can."

From the sub-basement control room, Xavier had been monitoring the Sentinel attack, both on the security monitors and psychically through the X-Men's senses. With the Imperial Guard and the federal troops now joining in the attack on the Sentinels, it seemed the tide was starting to turn. The number of functional Sentinels on the scene no longer seemed to be increasing, but the number of broken and blasted pieces continued to increase. The Sentinels had been learning to cope with the attacks directed against them, their artificial intelligences beginning to anticipate the X-Men's patterns and threats. Fewer of Cyclops's beams were hitting vital areas. The Sentinels were electrifying their skins to deter Beast or Nightcrawler from jumping onto them. More were taking to the air to gain maneuverability in fighting Rogue, Jean, or Lockheed, and to avoid being phase-damaged by Shadowcat. Kitty herself was under heavy fire, forced to stay phased and beginning to tire. Wolverine was suffering a similarly aggressive barrage to counteract his rapid healing. Their multispectral vision counteracted Papillon's glitter-haze and Kristin's loans of invisibility. Many of the students were injured or out of the fight.

But the entry of the Guard and the troops into the fight changed its tenor. Even without his exo-spex, Vril Rokk was a force to reckon with, mighty and indestructible. Flashfire's lightning proved devastating to those Sentinels with sufficient damage to their insulation, and his speed kept them from getting a bead on him. Manta's searing UV flares helped blind their optics and overheat their thigh-mounted fuel tanks to the point of rupture or explosion. And N'rill'iree brought sheer brute force to bear, his flight patch letting him smash and tear into the airborne Sentinels as well as the grounded ones. The federal troops had less-effective weapons to bear, but their RPGs did some damage, and they had the advantage of knowing the Sentinels' weak points.

But there were still quite a few Sentinels, and they had their tricks. One Sentinel had successfully managed to reach the front porch, and while the mansion's robotic defenses came to bear and held its body at bay, the top half of its head and its left forearm assembly detached themselves from the whole and forced their way inside. The lobby defenses opened fire on the intruders, but the hand spun on them, raised two fingers in a devil's-horns gesture, and fired back. The hovering head whirred forward to the elevator, and lasers burst from its eyes, cutting through the door. In moments, it was pushing through the doors, using its lasers to cut the cables so it could descend unimpeded through the shaft. Xavier had the elevator locked down at the bottom sub-basement level where he was, but he heard it fall a few feet farther once it was released. There wasn't enough clearance for the Sentinel to get through, but Xavier was certain it would be able to cut its way out.

He alerted the X-Men to his situation. *We'll try to get to you,* Jean replied. *But they're keeping us pretty busy.*

Understood.

Ungodly noises came from the elevator shaft, and Xavier made his way to check on the students one more time. "Please stay here," he told them. "It's me they're after."

Harry strode forward. "No way, Professor! We're not gonna let them get you."

"I appreciate it, but there's little you can do."

"I can," came another voice. Todd Watkins rolled forward in his motorized chair. "I can hardly move," he said sullenly, "can't do much of nothing. But I'm bulletproof and I'm tough to budge. Just . . . put me in the hall and stay behind me."

Harry stared at him. "Are you sure? I mean, those guys have things a lot stronger than bullets."

"Look, it's just somethin' I gotta do, okay?" Though his head barely moved, Todd's shadowed eyes turned back to the professor, and Xavier could clearly sense the pleading behind them. Not to mention the full magnitude of the boy's guilt. Todd made no attempt to hide it from Xavier. He confessed wordlessly that he had been the one to bring the Sentinels down on the institute. And now he was pleading to be allowed to make amends.

"Very well," Xavier said. "We will make our stand in the Danger Room. Todd will guard the door once we are inside."

He had not chosen the Danger Room purely because of its fitting name. Once they were all inside, he programmed it to target its weapons at full force against any Sentinel intruders and to generate a holographic jungle to conceal the students. The illusion came on-line just as a deafening crash came from the corridor outside, followed by an ominous whirring and the clattering of metallic fingers. Xavier looked through Todd's eyes, in the moment before the boy squeezed them shut and lowered his head. A second left hand, from some other Sentinel, had followed the first one in. And from the sound of it, there might have been a third as well. Xavier sent a thought to the X-Men, advising them to make sure any Sentinel hands or heads they came upon were effectively neutralized.

Xavier could no longer see through Todd's eyes, but he sensed the boy's pain as energy beams and plasma flame raked across his carapace. After a few moments, his reinforced wheelchair began melting, and it collapsed under the boy's weight. The impact was the last straw, knocking Todd unconscious. Xavier hoped he could still wake up again.

Todd's body and the remains of his chair still blocked the door, but one of the hands tried clambering over him, pushing its way through the gap into the Danger Room. The laser cannons and flamethrowers cut loose on the disembodied hand, but it raised its fingers and fired back. It took damage but managed to squeeze through and push down Todd's body enough to make it easier for the other two hands to climb into the room. Working together, they clamped the boy between their middle fingers and began laboriously dragging him out of the doorway, while the first hand made a good account of itself against the room's defenses. In the hall, the floating head began pushing on Todd's body from behind, and it soon managed to force its way through the wide door, laser eyes firing. "HOLOGRAPHIC CAMOUFLAGE DETECTED," it intoned. "ALL-BAND SPECTRAL IMAGING ENGAGED."

That meant the camouflage would be of little use. "Computer!" Xavier called. "Obstacle-course mode, free-fire, physical only! No change in test subjects!" That ensured the room would continue to direct its attacks only against the Sentinel parts, not the students.

The floor and walls started to reconfigure themselves as the jungle faded, and Xavier mentally ordered the students to get out of the way and take advantage of the cover thus created. Some of them were taken by surprise, and he needed to compel them psychically to move, something he found distasteful but necessary in this case.

The Danger Room's obstacle course had been designed to challenge the X-Men to higher and higher levels of physical and strategic skill. As Xavier expected, the Sentinel parts, relying mainly on brute force and firepower, were less able to cope. One hand was crushed under an enormous piston, and another lost a finger to a spinning blade. But the hands and the head still managed to take out a number of the room's weapons and drive systems, and continued relentlessly forward toward Xavier and the students.

It came down almost to a draw, but once the last of the Danger Room's weapons had been neutralized or depleted, the floating head was still functional, if a bit wobbly. Reaching behind him to the back of his chair, Xavier drew the high-powered shotgun he'd slung there and rolled out into the open, blasting at the Sentinel head as he went. He managed to take out one eye, but otherwise only dented its faceplate a bit before he ran out of rounds. He tried to reload, but a spray of liquid nitrogen spewed forth from the Sentinel's intact eye socket, forcing him to drop the shotgun before it froze to his hand. The Sentinel head loomed closer.

And then Harry Mills leaped down on it from above and behind, wrapping his arms around its sides and blinding it with another student's jacket. "Hey, Mr. No-Body! Weren't you supposed to be looking for the Chlorite? He's not even here, you nitwit! Why don't you try using yourself for a change?"

The head bucked and weaved, trying to shake him off. But he bounded up and down on top of it, as though he were deliberately trying to shake himself as much as possible. A storm of long blond fur came flying off his body . . . and Xavier noticed that much of it was being sucked into the head's ducted-fan intakes. After a few moments, its whirr began to grow muddy and uneven, its movements more wobbly. Its left-hand fan gave out, and Harry leaped off it as the uneven thrust caused it to spin out of control and smash into the wall face-first. Unable to move, the Sentinel head desperately tried firing its remaining laser into the wall, only to cut through a power coupling that exploded in its face. It moved no more.

Harry was giggling hysterically, more from terror than humor. "Like my mom always says," he gasped, "my fur can clog up anything."

22: Deus Ex Meena

Before much longer, the grounds of the Xavier Institute were littered with Sentinel parts, and an uneasy quiet had fallen. The X-Men and students stood together, facing the Guardsmen and troops, while both sides wondered what to do next.

When Xavier emerged onto the damaged porch and came down the ramp, Val Cooper came up to meet him. "Technically, I need to place you under arrest right now. And all the rest of you. And there's still the issue of that Chlorite you have hidden in there. But I'd like to work that out in some kind of nonconfrontational way. I think I'm all confronted out for now."

Xavier could sympathize. "I think, Dr. Cooper, that we have far more to work out than the disposition of one Chlorite."

"Maybe. But it's a place to start."

"That will not be necessary," came a new, gruff voice. Poratine trotted into view from around the corner of the mansion, with Taforne and several of his troops bringing up the rear. "The Chlorite was captured and detained in the woods moments ago by my forces. It and the human female who assisted it have been quarantined aboard my command ship."

The X-Men and students looked around at each other, and after a moment, several of the students stepped forth, including Papillon, Beanpole, and a now-clothed Kristin Koenig. "Meena didn't help him alone," Kris said in a surprisingly clear, confident voice. "If you're going to arrest her, you need to arrest us too."

"Yeah," said Harry, coming out from behind Xavier's chair. "And me too. I'm kinda the brains of the operation."

"Actually, that'd be me," said Rogue, making a levitating leap to come down next to them. "You take them, you take me."

Now Cyclops came forward. "Where one X-Man goes, we all go."

In quick succession, the other X-Men came forward to stand by their comrades. "I forget, which one of us was Spartacus again?" Kurt stage-whispered to Kitty as the rest of the students—including some who had fought on Lash's side—gathered around them.

Poratine surveyed the united group before her. "This is all very noble, but it changes nothing. Your world is still in imminent peril."

"Yes, it is," Xavier told her. "But we must not destroy our world in order to save it. Clearly the events here tonight demonstrate that things will only get worse if we proceed on this course. We must find another way."

"All they demonstrate," Taforne said, "is that your Sentinel technology was unreliable."

"A fact of which you were warned repeatedly," Xavier said, putting more steel in his voice. "You knew what the Sentinels have done before on our world. How they have murdered, destroyed, and attempted to conquer. How they have trampled roughshod over every principle of freedom, fairness, and justice in pursuit of a monomaniacal goal of security. You saw all that and decided that they were the right tool for achieving your goals. Look around you, Fleet Leader, Defense Leader!" Xavier gestured at the war zone that had been a placid lakeside estate. "This is your will made manifest. This was your choice."

"How many times must I tell you, Xavier," Poratine cried, "that we *have* no other choice? We have tried everything. We have sought peace in the past, but no peace can be found. You know the cold equations of it. If left unchecked, Chlorite life will propagate throughout the universe, until it is the only thing left! Until all life as we know it is eradicated, all our achievements corroded away to nothing! We have no choice but to resist that fate with every power at our disposal!"

But Xavier's eyes were drawn to Beast by the palpable aura of inspiration that had just sprung up around him. "On the contrary, Lady Poratine," Hank said. "Perhaps that is exactly what we need to embrace!"

"What?!"

"As you say, it's a matter of equations. Probability equations, to be precise. There is a small but finite chance of Chlorite life arising spontaneously on any random planet. Given worlds enough and time, this would eventually happen everywhere, particularly if accelerated by active colonization."

"Yes, we all know this. They spout it in their propaganda often enough."

Hank went on as though she had not spoken. "So it stands to reason that, in the infinite probabilities of the multiverse, there must be some timeline in which this has already occurred! An entire universe inhabited solely by Chlorite life. Perhaps one where the Chlorite mutation arose early enough in its history that few intelligent species of our kind had even evolved yet, where there never was a great battle for dominance. A universe where Chlorites can live freely without endangering any other life.

"If we could manage to find such a universe, we could offer it to the Chlorites as a haven! A place where they could finally have a home and live in peace and prosperity—barring their own proclivities for internecine conflict, of course. But if they could be relocated to such a universe, there would be no more need for them to attempt the conquest of our worlds."

"A fantasy," Taforne said. "Another universe? Granted that they exist, but how could we possibly locate such a universe, let alone access it?"

Xavier smiled. "As for finding such a universe," he said, "you have in your custody a remarkable young lady who could do exactly that."

"And as for the rest," Hank added, "I may have an idea or two. But it will require an abundance of a resource that is precious, volatile, and difficult to obtain."

"And what is that?" Taforne asked.

Hank smiled. "Cooperation."

Meena Banerjee was relieved when Professor Xavier and the X-Men arrived along with the Diascar leaders to release her from confinement. Although she doubted that John, now out of his containment suit and in the quarantine cell adjacent to hers, would get the same treatment.

But she was surprised and cowed when Dr. McCoy explained to her what he had in mind for her. After a long, contemplative silence, she finally spoke. "I don't know if I can do that, Dr. McCoy. Professor. Finding a specific universe like that."

"You did it before, honey," Rogue told her. "You found the combination to the cell."

"Yes, but . . . those were universes I was in. I was looking close to home, to figure something out about *our* reality. To look for a universe so far from ours . . . one where I don't even exist . . . I don't know if I can do that."

"Meena," the professor said, "from our sessions together, I'm aware that your ability to sense other universes goes beyond the firsthand perceptions of any alternate Meena Banerjees within them. You can sense them, and their nature, directly. And I'll be there with you, guiding you, when you try this."

"Can she truly sense their nature?" Poratine asked. "How far do her senses extend? Could she directly perceive the breadth of an entire universe, survey every planet in it to determine whether it is completely populated by Chlorites?"

"She doesn't have to," John spoke up from within his cell. "She just has to imagine it, feel her way through the cosmic wavefunction for a signature that matches it."

Poratine turned to face Meena, her gaze intimidating. "Can you do that, child?"

Meena looked at John, who nodded reassuringly from the other side of the glass. Turning back to Poratine, she nodded. "I believe I can."

"So how do we verify her assessment?"

"The same way we actually reach that universe," Dr. McCoy said jauntily. "As I explained to you before." He came over to Meena and crouched to face her. "What I have in mind, young lady, is that once you have found this universe for us, you then allow Rogue to absorb your powers and knowledge." Meena pulled back for a moment. The thought of having her life essence drawn out of her was alarming. But then she realized that she trusted Rogue, and that the woman would never have agreed to this plan if she believed it could harm one of the students. So she nodded for Dr. McCoy to go on.

"Then—and here's the twist—Rogue *simultaneously* absorbs Nightcrawler's powers! Combine the ability to see other timelines with the ability to teleport to anyplace in your line of sight, and what do you get?"

Meena hesitated. The answer was easy enough to put together, but hard to believe. "Um . . . the ability to teleport into another timeline?"

"By George, I think she's got it. And the professor has the money to buy George." Dr. McCoy seemed insufferably pleased with himself, and growing more so by the moment.

"So that lets Rogue go there," John said from his cell. "But what about us? How do you get my people to this new universe?" He sounded skeptical, but Meena could hear an undercurrent of hope. He wanted to believe but was afraid to let himself.

"That's where the Imperial Guard comes in. Or rather, *how* they came in. Travel between the Shi'ar galaxy and the Diascar fleet is facilitated by means of a Shi'ar stargate generator. With the help of the Diascar engineers, I am confident that I can modify the stargate's targeting systems to scan Rogue as she, empowered with your and Nightcrawler's abilities, travels to the timeline you have found for us. Said scan should enable us to lock onto the quantum signature of that timeline—its coordinates, if you will—and open a stargate portal to it. Thus, we can send in probes to verify the nature of the universe—maybe even ask some natives for a history lesson. If it turns out not to be exactly what we were in the market for," he said to Meena, "then you can simply try again."

"There is still a time factor," Poratine said. "There could still be infiltrators on your world, incubating viable microbes as we speak."

"The search for a Chlorite-dominated universe will probably go faster than the search for Chlorites hiding on Earth," Dr. McCoy went on. "Especially with Sentinel operations on hold for the time being." He turned to Meena and said parenthetically, "Apparently the Sentinels worldwide went, err, rogue the same time the ones at the mansion did. Fortunately they were in groups of two or three, and more easily taken out by the superheroes or soldiers accompanying them."

"That raises another issue," Taforne said. "How do we convince the Chlorites to go along with this? Without the Sentinels, how can we ferret out every last infiltrator, here and elsewhere in the galaxy?"

"We tell them," John said. "Tell them they can finally have a home. A place we can live in peace. That's all we've ever really wanted. Not to destroy you, just to be safe from destruction by you."

"Maybe some of you," Taforne granted reluctantly. "Not the terrorists."

"I *am* one of the terrorists," John fired back. "Because I felt I had no choice." He looked to Dr. McCoy, to Xavier, to Meena. "Now I believe I have a better choice, a chance to live in peace—away from *you* at last—and I want it more than anything." His words cut into Meena. *More than anything?* But she reminded herself there was more at stake than her feelings.

"But what of the other terrorists? How do we find them, get them to agree? We can't just broadcast this over the humans' television. The infiltrators would think it was a trap. They'd never trust us."

"We might," John said, "if you trust us. Let me go to this other timeline. Let the other Chlorites you've captured—those who are still alive—go with me. Let us see this new world with our own eyes, smell it, taste it, and let us come back and announce it to the world. The rest of us out there, they'll come in if we convince them to."

"So there are other infiltrators still at large?" Xavier asked, softly but pointedly.

John hesitated but realized that Xavier was encouraging him to make a gesture of good faith. "There are no more than ten on the planet. Not counting the refugees from the crash. Minus me and the others you've captured or killed, there are no more than four."

Taforne moved closer. "Do you know their identities? Their locations?" he barked.

John shook his head. "I wasn't given that information."

"Why should I believe that?"

Mrs. Grey-Summers sighed. "Because it makes sense," she told him. "Because it's how operations like that are usually structured, so that captives can't give up information under questioning. And . . . because we need to start believing in each other if we want to resolve this."

Taforne was mollified, but not entirely. "How do we know they'd even hear about this? They could be buried so deep . . ."

"They would stay in touch," John said. "To keep aware of the situation. To be ready to move if they had to. And . . ." He paused, and Meena got the sense that he was about to offer up another gesture of good faith. "To receive coded orders, if necessary. There are codes we can send over the Internet or on a radio frequency. Once you prove to me and the others that this other universe is what you all claim, then we can include those code signals as verification. We're trained to give out false codes under torture . . . they will know the information is genuine."

After a few more moments of staring, Taforne subsided, seeming satisfied by John's words. Dr. McCoy clapped his big furry hands together. "There! I think we've got all the details sorted out now. I suggest we find a nice quiet place for Meena and the professor to get started."

Meena spoke up. "I want John there with me!"

Poratine shook her head. "No."

"Yes," Meena countered, startled by her own forcefulness. "You need me for this, remember? You can't do it without me. And that means I get to say how we do it. And I want John there with me. He can help me. We've worked together before. And I think . . . I think if I'm with him, it will be easier to feel for others like him. For a whole universe that's like him. So he should—he *will* be with me. That's how this works. Got it?"

Poratine stared at her, taken aback. But a moment later she nodded. "Very well. You and he will be escorted with the professor to a conference room." Meena nodded, trying not to faint.

John was placed back in a containment suit, and Taforne's guards escorted them out of the quarantine area. Once they reached the conference room, though, Meena asserted another demand. "Give John and me a moment alone." Xavier and Poratine exchanged a look, and the Diascar granted Meena's request.

Once inside, she threw her arms around John. To her joy and relief, he reciprocated. "Ohh, I don't want to do this," she cried. "It would mean you'd leave forever. I'd never see you again!"

A gloved hand stroked her chin. "I'd never see you again. But you could find me. Watch over me."

"It's not enough. You're the first person who was ever . . . so good to me. Made me feel so worthwhile."

John stared at her. "Meena . . . there is a whole roomful of people out there who just told you that the survival of the planet, perhaps the universe, depends on you. And that they believe you can pull it off. They all know you're worthwhile. Because you are. You don't need me to tell you that."

"But I love you!" Her arms went around him again . . . but this time his response was more tentative. She pulled back and stared at him and did not speak again for a long moment. "You don't . . . love me, do you?"

"Meena . . . I don't know. I was taught to hate all your kind. To want you dead, to *make* you dead. I don't know if I'm capable of loving you. But I do know that I don't hate you. I don't hate any of you, not Harry or Kris or Todd. . . . I think—" He broke off. "No. I *know* I had good times being with you. That I felt happy, or would have if I'd allowed myself to believe it was real. And I was happiest when I was with you. And now . . ." He held her by the shoulders. "Now you may hold the key to giving my people the salvation they have sought for millennia. I will always cherish you for that."

He sighed. "But you know it can't be. We can't be together without me killing you eventually, whether I want to or not. And . . . I need to be with my people. To help convince them all, lead them to our new home that you're going to find for us."

"I know," Meena said, lowering her head. "The problems of two crazy mixed-up hills of beans, or however that goes."

John shook his head. "I have no idea what you just said."

"Neither do I, apparently." They shared a laugh. Then Meena caught and held his gaze. And she reached up and gripped the helmet of his containment suit.

He put his hands on hers. "No. It's too dangerous."

"Not for just a moment."

"I could be infectious already."

"You probably aren't. And some risks are worth taking." She twisted the helmet, and together they eased it off. Then she pulled his head down to hers and kissed him.

It tasted horrible. And it was awkward getting the anatomies to mesh, particularly since they were both very clumsy at it. But Meena supposed there had been worse first kisses, and her heart was racing just the same when it was over. It was worth the aftertaste. But some part of her, she had to admit, was okay with it being a one-time thing.

She cleared her throat. "Well."

"Well," John said, retrieving his helmet. "We should let the professor in."

"Wait, one more thing," Meena asked, touching his arm. He met her eyes questioningly. "What's your name?"

23: Exeunt Omnes

Seden Karm of the Zann—alias John Chang of Canton, Ohio—stood atop a low rise in a field of black grass, took off his helmet, and took a deep breath of the misty, yellow-tinged air. Its strong chlorine fragrance was bracing, refreshing after so much time in the bland, colorless air of Earth. He closed his eyes for a moment to savor it, then opened them and surveyed the expanse around him. The yellow-green mists hung heavy in the low vales to the east, making them impassable without oxygen gear. But in time, his people would have the infrastructure to pass through them safely with oxygen tanks or enclosed vehicles, or build roads above them. To the north and west, the ebon fields gave way to a forest of tall, sturdy trees, their white vinyl trunks supporting wide crowns of deep red and brown leaves—which, according to the Diascar botanists, would ironically fade to yellow-green come autumn. To the south lay a beach of sand and quartz, lapped by the waves of a greenish-blue ocean. In the sky, the sun shone a lurid reddish-orange. It was the same sun that shone in

Earth's sky, or its quantum duplicate in this timeline, but he was viewing it through an atmosphere that scattered and absorbed its green light as much as its blue.

"What a hideous place." Seden turned to see Taforne, in his bulky six-limbed containment suit, studying the view disapprovingly. His legs moved in a nervous canter, as though he were resisting the impulse to bolt to the stargate portal and back to his home universe.

"I think it's beautiful," Seden replied.

Beside him, Meena tilted her head. "It's . . . nice," she managed to say, struggling to see things his way. He took her hand to reassure her that he didn't need her to.

A moment later, a suited figure with the distinct apelike gait of the Beast loped over to them. "So far, our telescopic observations confirm your perceptions, Meena," he said. "Every planet we've detected with a free-oxygen line in its spectrum also shows free chlorine. We've launched some hyperspace probes to let us get line-of-sight views of the whole galaxy, but I think they'll make the same findings."

"What about the rest of this universe?" Taforne asked.

"Chlorites are scarce in our reality. The Milky Way should be more than spacious enough for them. And so far we've detected few signs of intelligent life, so they may have little competition."

"But what happens in the future, when they become abundant enough to need to spread beyond this galaxy?"

"By then," Seden told him, "we should be able to adapt the stargate to scan other realities, using what we've learned from Meena. We can find other Chlorite universes to colonize. There will be no more reason to war with oxy-life."

"I doubt it will be so easy to convince all your kind of that."

Seden held his ground. "Just as it will be difficult to convince all your kind that you no longer need to hunt us."

Taforne made a noise in his throat. "We still need to hunt you . . . if only to find you all so we can send you to this forsaken place."

"But now you will have my help, and that of others of my kind, in tracking down and convincing the others." He saw Meena's mixed reactions on her face. Since he would be staying in her home timeline indefinitely to track down other Chlorites throughout the known universe, it meant there was a chance she could see him again; but odds were he would be too busy ever to come back to Earth.

Back home—or back in the place Seden had almost let himself think of as home for a time—he had already said his good-byes to his other friends. Harry, Kris, Meena and the others were the toast of the institute now, for the roles they'd played in saving the day from the Sentinels and their courage in daring to look for a peaceful solution. As a mark of their newfound status, they had finally been endowed with code names of their own. Meena was now The Visionary, a name which still made her blush every time she heard it. ("Now she just needs a partner called the Scarlet Witchinary," Harry had quipped.) Kris, in spite of herself, had been inevitably dubbed Flasher, but that name made her blush a lot less than Seden would have expected. "Well, it was either that or The Entirely Visible Girl," Kris had told him, laughing. "Oh, and about that—" She'd taken his gloved hand and placed it against her bare cheek, and it had stayed visible. "I finally figured out how to turn it off, for a few moments at a time, anyway. I guess once I stopped being afraid to exercise my power, got more practice turning it up and down, I was able to gain more control. Maybe eventually I'll be able to keep it turned off indefinitely, and I can actually wear jewelry and makeup!"

"Not that you need it," Sarah had assured her.

"No," she'd replied easily, "but it'd still be nice to try. Oh, and Dr. McCoy's working with Reed Richards to develop a sort of anti–Sue Richards costume for me, something that stays visible when I use my powers. But," and she gave a devilish grin, "I'm not really in any hurry."

Seden had then turned to Harry to ask his new name, but his old friend had only shrugged. "I'm Harry. That pretty much says it all."

"Odd," Seden had replied. "I would've called you Bigfoot-in-Mouth." It was the first real joke anyone could remember "John" telling, and they had all laughed far more than it had deserved.

As for Todd Watkins, he was in the hospital, expected to make a full recovery. The doctors had actually had to remove some of his heavy surface plates to operate, and he had asked for the rest to be removed as well—ironically much the same procedure Seden had undergone to become John. But unlike his quills, Todd's plates would probably grow back on their own, giving him only a brief respite. But for a while, at least, Todd would be able to move around freely. At least, free of his physical burden. Todd had told Seden that he didn't feel he deserved the reward of mobility after what he'd done. But Seden could understand his actions perfectly. He was hardly in a position to blame someone else for betraying a friend out of fear for his life and his species' life. Todd may have made a bad choice, as Seden had, but they were both true patriots.

But maybe that's not enough, Seden reflected. *We've all been patriots, all striving to defend our people. But we've done it in a way that just ended up putting us all in more danger. In the end it was the "traitors," the people who reached out to the other side, who saved us all.*

Gyrich stood on a catwalk above the Mastermold assembly line, surveying its idled equipment and looking forward to the day when it would begin running again. A voice from behind him interrupted his reverie. "I thought I'd find you here," Val Cooper said, brandishing a piece of paper. "You countermanded the shutdown order for this place?"

"You never know when we'll need more Sentinels, Val. Mutants are still a threat."

"It was mutants who found a solution to this mess."

"Only to save their own necks. You know they'll always look out for their own interests, and those aren't going to be the same as ours, not now that all the Chlorites are gone. Hell, they wouldn't even unite with us when we had a common enemy."

"I seem to remember us being pretty united against the Sentinels. Although . . . refresh my memory, Pete . . . what exactly were you doing while the rest of us were fighting for our lives? I don't remember seeing you leave the chopper."

He didn't dignify her insinuation with an answer. "Like I said, they were only looking out for themselves. It's only sensible to have a defense against their powers—you've said that as often as I have. And the people know it too. Approval ratings for the Sentinels are still high."

"Only because the public didn't see what happened at Xavier's school."

"Exactly. The whole thing's classified. The public saw the Sentinels mostly as protectors, and the mutants who fought against them as rabble-rousers and traitors."

"You're exaggerating, Pete. The poll results aren't *that* skewed. It was fifty-five, sixty percent."

"Still, it's something to build on."

"And are you forgetting that the Sentinels tried to take over the world? For what, the fifth time?"

"Just a control glitch. We just need a few more safeguards." He looked out over the expanse of Sentinel components below him. "Maybe we need to discard Trask's original programming altogether, write new software from the ground up. Think about it, Val!" he went on. "Look down there at all the new technologies the Diascar gave us. Quantum-level sensors, fullerene armor, nanomorphic servos, impenetrable force field projectors! We've barely begun incorporating it all into the Sentinel units! Maybe this is our chance to start from scratch, to create a whole new generation of Sentinels, superior to the old ones in every way." He turned back to Cooper. "And you know the time will come when we'll need them. When Magneto comes out in force again, or when Xavier decides again to put his own whims above national security. It's bound to happen. And the Diascar tech can give us the edge we need next time."

"Maybe so," Cooper replied, "but I don't think the Diascar see it that way."

"What?"

She nodded. "That's what I came to tell you. Poratine called me. She said something about the Diascar installing fail-safes in all their technology to make sure it didn't fall into the wrong hands."

Gyrich frowned. "So?"

Val looked at her watch. "So, we've got about ten minutes to evacuate this building."

Inside Poratine's shuttle, parked on the institute's rear lawn, Xavier and the X-Men watched with satisfaction as the Diascar's imaging sensors showed them an overhead view of the Sentinel manufacturing facility burning to the ground. "It was the least I could do," Poratine told them. "You mutants have brought new hope to the galaxy and spared the Diascar from ever again having to exterminate a world. You deserve thanks for that, not continued fear and oppression."

"Thank you, Fleet Leader," Xavier said, nodding graciously.

"To that end, I have also pressured your governments to reverse the mutant registration laws, in exchange for Diascar medical and agricultural techniques, and the prospect of future trade between our peoples. In addition, of course, to releasing those mutants arrested for resisting registration or attacking Sentinels."

"Again, you have our sincere thanks. I hope this is the beginning of a lasting friendship between our peoples."

Poratine led them back out onto the lawn, for it was almost time for her to leave. Earth was now free of Chlorites; the refugees from the ship and the remaining infiltrators had all been relocated to their new home universe, except for those who had volunteered to help spread the news to the rest of their peoples. "I hope so as well, Professor. In time," she went on, "our people will be able to find a new homeworld and return to our pastoral, open ways." She grew wistful. "Perhaps in my lifetime, though I doubt it."

"Why not?" Jean asked.

"We still have a galaxy to protect," the centauress said proudly. "Mercifully, we may now do that by offering the Chlorites a new home, rather than annihilating them. But it is still our duty to see it through. And it will be a long, hard struggle to find all the Chlorites and convince them to go, even with many of their own now joining us."

"And I'm sure it won't be that easy for you and them to get along," Scott said. "Not after so many generations of hatred. You've got your work cut out for you."

"True." She took in the X-Men. "But you have shown me that it is worth the effort to tear down walls, rather than build them up."

But Xavier frowned. "I wonder, though. All we've truly done is erected one more wall. We haven't really found a way to live together with the Chlorites—simply an opportunity to live apart. I'm not convinced that this new universe is truly a haven, rather than a ghetto."

"Hey, it's a whole universe," Rogue said. "Pretty roomy for a ghetto."

"And even if they can't leave it," Kurt said, "we can't leave ours for theirs either. So if theirs is a ghetto, so is ours."

"And in this case," Hank added, "the difference is at least biological rather than ideological. Even if we cannot interact physically, at least without thorough anti-contamination measures, there could still potentially be a commerce of ideas between the universes. An exchange of science and culture." He looked skyward. "I for one would be fascinated to discover how Chlorite civilizations might evolve unimpeded."

"And at least this way," Kurt added, "we have the time and safety to look for more lasting solutions."

"You think there can really be a solution, Kurt?" Logan asked. "People been lookin' an awful long time."

"I believe there is always a way for people to overcome their differences and become one. After all, we were all created by the one God."

Logan snorted. "Never met the guy."

"Not that you noticed, at least."

"And in the meantime," Rogue interposed before a theological debate broke out, "good fences make good neighbors."

Hank frowned. "So said the neighbor in Frost's poem. But the point of the poem itself is that the neighbor was wrong. Because sooner or later, every wall collapses or erodes away."

Kitty nodded. "So in the end, it's always up to people—finding a way that they can live together once those walls come a-tumblin' down." Lockheed spread his wings and let out a little squawk to underline her statement.

"Which is never an easy task," Xavier said. "And I fear we are far from reaching that point here on Earth. How long will it be before someone proposes finding an alternate-universe ghetto for mutants?"

"A whole universe o' mutants?" Logan asked. "Might not be so bad."

"Are you kidding?" Kitty asked. "We're a pretty fractious bunch. There'd be superfights breaking out every day."

Logan gave her a fierce grin. "That's what I meant, kid."

"I'd rather stay in this universe, thank you," Kurt said. "Some of my best friends are human."

Poratine looked at him oddly. "I thought you were all human."

"Some of us more than others," Kurt replied, draping an arm around Logan's shoulders. Logan raised a fist and extended his middle claw.

"But seriously," Kitty said, "it's a scary thought. The past few weeks have stirred up as much hatred toward mutants as positive feelings. Even without the Diascar tech, they can always build more Sentinels."

Scott nodded. "They could. But we can always build a team that can stand against them. And when we stand together, we can overcome anything. Isn't that right, X-Men?" The others gave a shout of agreement.

Xavier surveyed his X-Men, feeling proud and relieved that his family was united once more. But Kitty was right: There were still battles to be won. And he knew how he preferred to fight them, given the choice. "Now then," he said, "what are we all standing around for? We have a whole mansion full of children waiting to learn from us." He smiled. "And a whole world waiting to learn from them. So let's get to it, shall we?"

Acknowledgments

Thanks first to Marco Palmieri for giving me this opportunity. Thanks to Marco, Keith R. A. DeCandido, and Chester Edwards for advice on Marvel characters and continuity, and on New York City geography. Thanks to Myron C. Bennett for expert advice on John Cage. And thanks to "QueenTiye" on the Ex Isle BBS for inspiring Harry's questions about atomic theory.

For comics characters, their histories, and conceptual and stylistic inspiration, thanks mainly to Chris Claremont and John Byrne, and also Stan Lee, Jack Kirby, Len Wein, Grant Morrison, Chuck Austen, and Joss Whedon, among others. Thanks to the casts and creators of the '90s animated *X-Men* series and the feature films for introducing me to the X-universe and giving the characters voices in my mind.

As hinted in the text, the inspiration for the Chlorites comes from Stephen L. Gillett's book *World-Building*, part of the Science Fiction Writing Series. The inspiration for Diascar culture comes from research into horse behavior, including articles by Dr. Brenda Forsythe Sappington in *Horse Illustrated* magazine.

Other sources: For the London segment, "Tales of the Underworld" by Blake Morrison in *The Guardian;*

"London's Underground City" from *Heritage* magazine; and the websites underground-history.co.uk and www.transport-for-london.gov.uk. For the India segment, the inSurat.com website. For the New York City Hall segment, Google Maps and the Citymayors.com website. And Wikipedia for all sorts of things. Also, thanks to the Public Library of Cincinnati and Hamilton County for carrying so many X-Men trade paperbacks.

For anyone who's wondering about the chapter titles and hasn't already consulted a dictionary: An exordium is an introduction. *Ex silentio* means not only "from silence" but also "for lack of contrary evidence." Exigency means "emergency." *Ex cathedra* means "by virtue of office or authority." An exclosure is an area fenced off to prevent intrusion. Exequies are funeral rites. *Exitus acta probat* means "the outcome justifies the deed." An excursus is a digression or sidebar. And *exeunt omnes* is a stage direction meaning "they all exit."

The University of Cincinnati segment was written on location. The London sewer segment, mercifully, was not.

About the Author

Christopher L. Bennett is not very good at coming up with these "About the Author" bits. His life is, in fact, exceedingly dull. Fortunately for you, though (or unfortunately, as the case may be), he compensates for this with an active imagination. He is the author of the critically acclaimed novel *Star Trek: Ex Machina* as well as *Star Trek Titan: Orion's Hounds, Star Trek: S. C. E. #29—Aftermath,* and stories in the anthologies *Star Trek: Deep Space Nine—Prophecy and Change, Star Trek: Voyager—Distant Shores* and the upcoming *Star Trek: Constellations. X-Men: Watchers on the Walls* is his first Marvel-universe work. One of these days, he may actually get his name on a book that doesn't have one or more colons in the title.

More information and cat pictures can be found at www.home.fuse.net/ChristopherLBennett.